IF MINDS HAD TOES

Lucy Eyre

CHIVERS

British Library Cataloguing in Publication Data available

This Large Print edition published by BBC Audiobooks Ltd, Bath, 2007.
Published by arrangement with Bloomsbury Publishing PLC

U.K. Hardcover ISBN 978 1 405 64098 5
U.K. Softcover ISBN 978 1 405 64099 2

Printed and bound in Great Britain by
Antony Rowe Ltd., Chippenham, Wiltshire

To Ben and Jim

CHAPTER ONE

Lila opened the door of the study. The room was dark; it was midday but the shutters hadn't yet been opened. She went to the window to let light and air into the musty room. The study appeared to be empty, but Lila checked under the desk and in the large cupboard, just to be sure. Socrates must be lurking somewhere else. On the table was some orange peel, a bit of cheese rind and a glass with some stale dregs of liquid. Lila threw away the food and picked up the glass. On second thoughts, let him do his own washing up.

Where was he? Lila had already looked in his bedroom and, given the freak rainstorm, she was unlikely to find him in the citrus grove. Socrates was meant to be chairing a meeting of the Management Committee, but he was rarely where he was supposed to be. Especially when being in the right place meant taking part in a discussion of 'Points for Action'. Lila had been sent to search for Socrates out of courtesy, even though the other Committee members preferred it when he couldn't be found. His persistent interrogation irritated them. Last week he'd caused a forty-five-minute delay in the debate on whether it would be a good idea to grant Epicurus a licence for a new restaurant, by demonstrating that none of the Committee had a firm grasp of the meaning of 'good'. And how could they possibly decide whether it was a good idea or not, if they couldn't properly define a 'good' idea?

Despite his bureaucratic ineptitude, Socrates was President of the World of Ideas, having held the post for a record 2,109 years. He'd arrived a few hundred years earlier and it had taken him a while to work his way up to the top, albeit the competition was less fierce in those days. Once in charge, Socrates had clung on firmly. He'd been allocated the post until such time as he chose to resign it—primarily to avoid the hassle of elections. Socrates' age hadn't stopped him campaigning enthusiastically, which tired everyone else out far sooner than him. Thomas Hobbes had been his ruthless campaign manager: all political messages, he said, should be distinct, nasty, brutish and short. Friendships were regularly ruined at election time by vicious disagreements over the ideal model of democracy, the social contract and suchlike.

Lila Frost was much younger than Socrates. She'd been in her early twenties when she'd arrived in the World of Ideas. Her philosophy PhD remained incomplete, or so her inconsolable parents had assumed. Lila was Socrates' secretary. Being special assistant to the President was a good way for ambitious recent arrivals to get somewhere. She was very good at her job, although not as good as she would have been if she had believed that anyone noticed. She was attractive—slim with glossy dark hair, big brown eyes and a nose that was only just too small. More importantly for her present position, she had a razor-sharp philosophical mind. She chewed the skin around a perfectly manicured nail and wondered whether it would be appropriate to tell off Socrates for not being at the meeting.

The World of Ideas was full of philosophers, of sorts, who didn't see why being dead should get in the way of a good debate. It is fairly obvious that no one with an interest in philosophy would miss out on discovering the truth behind the great mystery of what happens after death. At last! Frustratingly, the World of Ideas, although a pleasant surprise for those who were convinced there was nothing more (and for those who were secretly terrified of hell), didn't provide the whole answer. It turned out there was also death (or possibly life) after the World of Ideas. Certainly it wasn't the end and, equally certainly, no one had ever reported back from the beyond. Sometimes thinkers were simply not heard of any more and people assumed they'd 'gone to the other side'. Occasionally, people got fed up with the World of Ideas and committed an implausible post-mortem suicide in order to be rid of the place. Life here was always comfortable—the weather excellent, the company exclusive—but some grew to feel that, whatever it was, it wasn't exactly living and they'd rather try some proper dying.

Lila suddenly guessed where Socrates might be, and set off up the grand wooden stairs. As she approached the library, she heard his voice. Bingo.

CHAPTER TWO

'Ben, isn't it? Take a seat.' Tony Swan pushed aside a stack of *What Car?* magazines to create a small gap. Ben sank down on to the uneven foam sofa; Tony placed himself opposite on an old office chair with one arm missing.

'Let's begin,' said Tony, holding a pad with *Barclays Business Banking: taking your business to new heights* printed across the top. 'Name?' he demanded.

'You already know.'

'Just answer, please. I'm filling in the form.'

'Ben Warner.'

'Relevant experience?'

'I've bought chips here.' Ben had been buying chips here for years—with his pocket money—so it seemed the obvious place for his first proper summer job.

'Anything else?'

4

'I had a weekend paper-round last year.'
'Good. Steal any papers? My little joke. Can you drive?'
'Yes,' Ben said proudly.
'Excellent. The last guy used to pick me up from the pub after a few pints.'
'Actually, I'm too young to drive properly.'
'Bloody minicabs.' Tony put his instant coffee down on a mug-stained SupaSun holiday brochure from the previous year. 'How old are you anyway?'
'Fifteen and a half.'
'Let's say sixteen. Remember that, if the man in the shiny suit from the council comes round. When's your birthday?'
'21st January 1991.'
'What year?'
'1990.'
'1990. Correct.' Tony wrote it down. 'Now, shall we discuss your duties?'
Ben nodded.
'So, shop floor. First and foremost: service. Keep smiling. A happy server means a happy customer. That's almost a mission statement here at Cod Almighty.'
'Mushy peas on earth and friendchips between men.'
'Never forget: an unhappy customer is like a straight boomerang. It never comes back! Get the order right, give the correct change, keep wiping the counter top, and *above all* smile.' Tony demonstrated his instant grin. 'Let's

5

keep those boomerangs curvy and the chips flying out of the shop.'

'As long as the *chips* are straight. Wouldn't want them to boomerang back.'

'As for behind the scenes—or "back office"—you need to unload the deliveries and help me with the stocktake. Our policy is FIFO on fish.'

'What does that mean?'

'It means, my son, First In, First Out. When you go to the cool room to get more fish for the fryer, you take the bits that have been there longest and save the new stuff for later. Leave the management initiatives to me and you'll fit in well with the team.'

Ben looked around the tiny office. 'Who's the team?'

'Me.'

'How many others are you interviewing?'

Tony consulted his pad. 'None. I am, however, impressed by your go-getting attitude. An entrepreneur like you understands that only losers who need state protection believe in the minimum wage.' Tony stood up and re-tucked his red polo shirt into his trousers. 'You start tomorrow lunchtime.'

'I've still got another week of school.'

'The self-made man appreciates the value of on-the-job learning. Can you start at the weekend, then?'

6

CHAPTER THREE

Lila had no trouble spotting Socrates as soon as she entered the library. He was holding court as usual. 'Picture the scene,' he was saying—not for the first time. 'I am alone in the witness box. I stand in front of the whole courtroom and the five hundred jurymen.' He paused for effect.

He stood with his back to a roaring fire, his audience small but rapt.

'And I told the jury, humble as ever'— Socrates bowed gently—' "if the Oracle at Delphi says I am the wisest, it cannot be a lie! It must be because I have the wit to know what I do not know." '

This triggered a murmur of approval. All wisdom starts with an acceptance of ignorance. There was hope for everyone!

'After the verdict I told them,' Socrates said, thrusting his stubby chin upwards, ' "I may leave this court condemned to death. But you, my accusers, will go forth convicted by *Truth herself* of the greatest wickedness and injustice." '

People clapped.

Socrates acknowledged it with a little wave. 'I saw myself as a stinging fly, the city of Athens as a self-satisfied thoroughbred horse. It was my duty to provoke them out of complacency, make them think properly. All day long I never settled, buzzing everywhere, rousing, reproaching, reproving.'

'One might hope,' a man interrupted, suitably provoked out of complacency, 'that you would be bored of telling this story after two and a half thousand years.' Ludwig Wittgenstein was lying across a padded armchair with his head on a cushion and legs over the side, making notes in the margin of his book with a short pencil. He found the philosophising-fly business unbearably annoying; all the more so since one of Socrates' fans had taken his favourite chair by the fire.

'I was put to death for teaching philosophy,' said Socrates. 'It's hardly trivial to be executed. They swatted me away without compassion. Our colleagues need to realise how lucky they are to be in this place where philosophy is encouraged.'

The group nodded vigorously.

'I'd go as far as to say adored.'

Wittgenstein choked and struggled to sit up. 'I've suffered for philosophy. It almost drove me mad.'

'*Almost*,' said Socrates, suppressing a smile.

Ludwig Wittgenstein suffered still. Those admirers gathered round Socrates. Wittgenstein remembered his own followers. He'd persuaded them that studying philosophy would ruin their lives. His natural magnetism

8

had ensured that they'd obeyed every word. On his suggestion his greatest student had gone to work in a canning factory. Wittgenstein didn't regret it exactly, but he did miss them.

'Don't be so hard on yourself, Ludwig.' Socrates crossed the room, trailing acolytes.

'Don't be so soft on yourself,' Ludwig Wittgenstein said. 'Your philosophy is old-fashioned and pointless. Accosting people on the street to ask what is "justice" or "goodness", pretending to be ignorant yourself so that you can expose their foolish views through your inane questions . . . what a waste of time.'

'Do you refer to the process of critical thinking *universally known* as the Socratic method?'

Wittgenstein scowled.

'Fact is, eating three cream crackers in a minute is easier than reading your philosophy.'

'Grown-ups prefer food with texture to sloppy semolina. Admit it, you don't understand a single word I've written.'

Socrates wouldn't admit anything of the sort, especially if it might be true. 'Whose fault is that?'

'I have produced a work of genius,' Wittgenstein said. 'Am I also required to produce sufficient intelligence for you to understand it?'

Socrates snorted.

'Revealing my ideas to you is like casting pearls before swine.'

'Well, really! Anyway'—Socrates was aware of the danger of losing the crowd—'my philosophy is not old-fashioned. Nor new-fashioned. These are questions for the past and the future, central to people's lives. Not only can they still be considered, they cannot not be considered.'

'Everyone thinks about them,' said a voice.

'Do they?' Wittgenstein asked. 'Certainly not properly. But do you really think people need this kind of philosophy in their lives? Do you think *normal people* worry about the metaphysical problem of free will? No, they worry about how to pay off their debt. How to live the good life? No, they care about their sex life. The true nature of reality? No, they just want a promotion. How does the mind work? Absolutely not! At most, they ponder what car to buy. It's all they're good for.'

'Then the world needs another Socrates to shake them up,' said a pert young fan gushingly.

Socrates gave her one of his special smiles. The effect was ambiguous: he was, it must be admitted, spectacularly ugly.

Wittgenstein scowled. 'That's the last thing the world needs. An analysis of the logic of language, for example, that's philosophy. A woolly discussion about the *meaning of life*, by contrast, is simply not a valid subject for

10

discussion. That's why philosophy—proper philosophy—is a pursuit for specialists. Only maybe three people have ever been any good at it.'

Socrates raised his eyebrows. Wittgenstein wasn't usually that generous about the other two.

'True philosophy isn't supposed to be popular,' Wittgenstein said.

Philosophy could never be popular enough for Socrates. 'I bet I could take any "normal person", as you say, and get them to think about these questions. Not only that, but they'd love it.'

'You're on.'

'Eh?'

'You bet? You're on. Take any one of them and make him love philosophy.'

'Easy peasy,' said Socrates, feeling quite the philosophical hero. Hadn't he inspired generations of students? I can make anyone love philosophy, he thought, except for you.

'If you can do it,' said Wittgenstein, 'I'll . . .' He paused, wondering how far to go.

'You'll what?'

'Yes! A bet, a bet.' Maggie, a woman of a certain age, jumped up from her chair, shivering with excitement. 'I do love a gamble. If Socrates wins, then you have to admit he's right. That philosophy does play a part in ordinary people's lives.'

Wittgenstein nodded gravely. It might seem

11

like low stakes but, as everyone knew, admitting he was wrong was as bad as it got for him. 'Wait, though,' he said, deconstructing the matter. 'There are two parts to this bet. I say that proper philosophy is too difficult for your Joseph Blogg.'

'Which I deny,' said Socrates. 'Anyone can be taught to think.'

'That part is trivial, since you won't be showing him the difficult bits anyway. I do not include your fluffy ideas in "proper philosophy". My central claim is that your non-analytic, taxi-driver philosophy is no good to anyone. "Make him love philosophy," you said.'

'Yes,' said Socrates, wondering where this was going.

'So, teach him your philosophy and see if it makes his life better.'

'No problem.' If the unexamined life was not worth living, which was obviously true, then a life with philosophy was unambiguously better than one without it. But how to make someone realise this?

'If I lose the bet,' said Wittgenstein, 'then I'll admit I'm wrong.' His voice caught on the words. 'That your philosophy indeed is as valuable as my work.'

'*More* valuable.'

'And if you lose? Socrates has not yet indicated his price of defeat.'

The whole group turned to look at Socrates.

12

He took a deep breath. 'If I lose then I shall step down gracefully. I'll resign my post as President and you, Ludwig Wittgenstein, can run this place from now on.'

People gasped. None of them had ever known another President in the World of Ideas. Passing on the reins was shocking enough, but—to Wittgenstein! It didn't bear thinking about.

'It's a deal,' said Wittgenstein, prematurely savouring the taste of power. He stuck a marshmallow on a long-handled fork and toasted it over the fire.

The group was excited. At last there was some political action—the first in hundreds of years. Maggie was already organising side bets. No one knew exactly when she'd arrived in the World of Ideas, nor whether she was actually interested in philosophy, but she was fun to have around so no one ever bothered to ask. There was a rumour that she used to write romantic novels.

Lila watched the progress of the betting. Socrates was the odds-on favourite. She guessed that this was more out of hope than conviction. Philosophy making your life better—who ever heard of such a thing? Wittgenstein had certainly set up the bet cleverly. Perhaps he was as gifted as he claimed after all.

'Lila! Come here a minute.'

She broke away from the group. 'Yes, Mr

13

S?'

'We—that is, you—need to find a suitable person from Over There. I assume, Ludwig, that you will grant me the privilege of selecting the best possible candidate.'

'I have equally little faith in any of them. You are free to choose your victim. But play by the rules—you have to get one who doesn't know anything about philosophy.'

'Quite so. One thing we don't need is another "expert". A blank slate, you might say.'

'Actually,' said a mole-like man with bushy hair, 'there's no such thing as a blank slate. Not really. Everyone is born with innate—'

'Indeed,' said Socrates. 'It should be someone young. Catch them at the curious stage, before life batters all original thought out of them.'

'Not too young,' Wittgenstein said. 'We're not running a crèche.'

'No indeed. OK, Lila, I hope that's clear. Someone about fifteen is probably best. Strong enough to cope with the experience, but open to the unexpected. You know the type.'

'Someone whose life will be made better by philosophy,' said Lila.

'Quite,' said Socrates.

CHAPTER FOUR

Clare Wilson's tongue poked out of the side of her mouth. 'Valley fold . . .' She checked the instructions in her book. 'Now double mountain fold . . .' She looked over at Ben. 'Inside rabbit-ear fold . . .'

Ben pretended not to notice.

'On both sides . . . Need three hands for this one . . . followed by crimp.' Clare squished and twisted the green paper into shape. 'Finished!'

She triumphantly presented her creation to Ben. 'I've made an origami dinosaur for you. It's supposed to be a brontosaurus.'

Ben was horrified. He looked around the classroom to check that no one had seen. Clare was a bit intense. He'd probably like her if she didn't have such a crush on him. In fact he might not even mind the crush if she was a bit less obvious about it.

'Looks more like a slug than a dinosaur.'

Clare's face fell.

'Funnily enough, brontosaurus was always my favourite kind of dinosaur,' Ben added, by way of compensation.

She still looked miserable.

'Maybe show me how to do that sometime.'

'Really?' The clouds parted. 'When?'

It was all his fault, Ben decided, for being nice to her in January when she'd been new.

15

Her parents had split up and she'd moved here with her mum halfway through the school year. Since their surnames were next to each other in the register, Clare sat at the desk beside Ben. He'd shown her round school on the first day. Only a tour of the school, and now an origami brontosaurus. The price of a good deed.

'Are you doing anything after school today?' Clare asked.

'Sorry, I've got a job interview,' Ben lied. He looked desperately around the room. It was the last day of term. Phil and John were playing cricket with Trevor's ruler and rubber. The honour of providing the equipment was enough for Trevor—he wasn't allowed to play.

'What's the job?'

The rubber landed on Ben's desk. He bowled it neatly back, hitting Phil on the nose. Amy and Jenny were smearing banana on the board rubber and giggling. Helen was filling up the board with maths equations so that Mr Miller would have to use the banana wipe.

Lacking a better strategy, Ben told the truth. 'Working in the fish-and-chip shop.'

Two people sitting in the back row were texting each other.

'Cod Almighty? On Wells Street? I could come and visit you one day, in the shop, in the holidays.'

No thanks. 'You could.'

The classroom was hot. Ben looked past

16

Clare out of the window at the science block. Clare was all right really; it's just that Ben didn't—wouldn't—want to go out with her. He would have found it difficult to say why, exactly. She was quite pretty; maybe a bit large, but nice skin, no spots. It basically came down to the fact that no one else wanted to go out with her. Fit Susie was flirting with Steve again. Ben's hands balled into fists. He wanted to ask her why someone so amazing was interested in such a thug. Actually, he didn't want to ask. The logic of relationships was as fixed as it was incomprehensible.

'You can keep that.'

'What? Oh.' Ben uncurled his hand and spread out the crumpled green paper: the extinct dinosaur. 'Thanks.'

Ben shut the slugosaurus in his textbook.

'Why do we believe in dinosaurs?' whispered Clare conspiratorially.

'It's history,' said Ben, watching as Susie chewed the ends of her hair and assessed Steve's new trainers.

'But what if it's all made up? Everything they tell us, all our lessons and books. How would you know? You're not ever going to check if those dinosaur bones in the museum are real.' Clare grinned.

'I suppose . . . I don't know.'

The history teacher arrived late, though no one minded.

'OK. Final lesson on the Russian

17

Revolution.' Mr Miller reached for the board rubber. The girls were giggling uncontrollably. 'Calm down, class.'

CHAPTER FIVE

' "We—that is, you—need to find a suitable person . . ." ' Lila repeated Socrates' words to herself as she walked to the monitor room. She pulled hard on the door—the handle was stiff—and yanked it open. Lila turned on the machine and the screens slowly lit up.

Socrates had no clue. 'You know the type.' Ha! These legendary 'normal people' were hardly queuing up to come here. Lila pulled a chair up to the console and adjusted the volume. Not that any of them actually knew about this place.

This was definitely Lila's trickiest assignment so far. If Socrates lost the bet, she would be back where she'd started. Lila still had a lot to prove: she'd only been in the World of Ideas just over thirty years. It would probably take another hundred to graduate from 'clueless upstart' to 'arriviste'. Her weak point, however, was also an asset: she was much more up to date with the world they had left behind than most of the others. Everyone pretended not to care, but she had seen the way that people devoured the newspapers that turned up on occasion in the library.

In the World of Ideas, it was possible to watch real-world events directly, but surprisingly few bothered. It took patience and skill to filter out the good bits from the dross, and most people struggled with the technology. From time to time, Hegel organised the material into news bulletins—a Hegelian synthesis, if you will. However, like most of Hegel's work, it wasn't very user-friendly. Those loyal to the Hegelian tradition lapped up the bulletins; those who disagreed with everything he said never went near them; and the largest group, which included most members of the first two, found them impenetrable. The upshot was that most inhabitants of the World of Ideas were starved of real news.

When the system had finally finished booting up, Lila addressed herself to the problem: someone whose life would be made better by philosophy—who would that be? She wasn't quite sure what it meant for philosophy to make your life better. And she was pretty sure that neither Socrates nor Wittgenstein did either. Indeed, Wittgenstein believed it was impossible, which is why he'd made the bet. Lila remembered when she'd first started philosophy. She'd adored it but it had tied her brain in knots. Everything she'd taken for granted—sitting on a chair, making a decision, even using a simple word like 'green'—had become a quicksand of doubt. It was hard for her to remember this now, living as she did where philosophy was as normal as having a bath. More normal for some people, unfortunately.

Lila typed brief instructions as to what she was looking for and then scanned the images. One showed a teenager picking his nose in a room covered in streaky black paint. Too much snot. Lila switched over and watched a girl standing on her head knitting a rainbow stripy scarf. Too upside-down. On the next screen she saw a boy in shorts balancing on one leg and trying to touch his nose with his toes. These people! On another screen, there was a boy and a girl playing a computer fighting game. Boring. Lila then watched two girls rolling on the floor, laughing hysterically. Every time one of them tried to speak, she would make a noise like a happy seal and they would collapse in a new round of giggles, weeping and pointing at each other. Lila smiled, a bit jealous, though they would never do for the bet.

Lila's attention was caught by some music. She boosted the volume and reset the main screen. A nutty-haired, green-eyed boy was playing blues guitar. His attractive face was contorted with the effort of a fifteen-year-old who carried the weight of the blues on his narrow shoulders.

CHAPTER SIX

My life is so boring,
My friends are so sad,
I got to escape 'fore . . .
Turn into my dad.

Ben heard giggling outside his bedroom door.
He sang louder.

My sisters are morons,
Their heads are just logs,
Nobody likes them,
They look like fat frogs.

I- aahhhh got the Wednesday evening,
  life is empty, family hassle,
Nothing to hope for . . . bluuuues.

Ben played without singing for a while.

Got kidnapped this morning,
They want lots of dough,
Ooooh, got kidnapped this morning,
They want lots of dough . . .
I escaped before lunchtime,
The fearless hero.

Flew over the desert,
In my own silver plane . . .

21

Aahhhh flew over the desert,
In my own silver plane . . .
Must take more photos
When I do it again.

If only.

CHAPTER SEVEN

Lila smiled to herself. He looked a little bit like someone she'd been fond of, a long time ago. Truth be told, very fond, but also—she sighed—a very long time ago. Before she'd . . . when she was still . . . Lila decided she wanted to see more of him, and downloaded the recorded footage of the boy's life.

Could philosophy be held responsible for her death? Hadn't her mind been caught up in a knotty epistemological problem when she'd lost control of the car? Lila hated to think about that episode, but whenever she did she liked to place the blame on determinism, icy road conditions and intellectual distraction, rather than excessive emotion. He'd miss me if I were gone, she'd promised herself. And he had.

Back to the job in hand. There was, after all, no going back. Lila watched a classroom scene. There was no teacher and the students were messing around. Lila quickly spotted the boy

22

in the middle of the chaos. What was that strange green paper thing in his hand?

Lila watched him playing football, walking the dog, at home with his mum and dad and sisters. She made notes of his name, his family, his age. The final clip showed the boy cycling downhill—too fast—with a smile on his face. Ben, as she would now call him, jumped off his bike and locked it to a railing.

'Where are you going, my new friend?' Lila said quietly.

He went into a fish-and-chip shop, shouted, 'Tony? I'm here,' and put on an apron and a hat.

Lila shoved her fist into her mouth in order not to shout her thought: Chips! out loud. Chips! There they were, juicily frying. Her mouth watered. It was over thirty years since she'd tasted a real, live chip. She zoomed in on the picture, hypnotised. Chips relishing their chippiness. She could actually smell the hot fat and vinegar.

Lila heard the door open behind her and hastily switched to another channel.

'Well, what's out there?' Socrates pulled up a chair in front of the screens.

Wittgenstein stood near the door, in the frayed tweed jacket and blue shirt that he always wore.

'I've found one.' Lila checked her notes. 'He's called Ben Warner; lives at 50° North, 1° West; aged fifteen and a half. His parents

23

are Fiona and Tom. Two younger sisters:
Matty is ten and Katie is thirteen. He goes to
school—'

'Too much information,' said Wittgenstein.
'Show us the pictures.'

'Here are the chips . . . clips.' Lila blushed
and keyed instructions into the machine.

The first screen showed a football match.
Lila pointed at Ben just as he slammed the ball
cleanly into the top corner of the net.

'Football. How sweet,' Wittgenstein said
with a smirk. 'I feel as if I've won already.'

'Don't let Albert Camus hear you talking
like that!' said Socrates.

'Just because he *apparently* stood in goal for
Algeria, he thinks it makes him special.'

'You're just jealous.'

'I could have been a contender.'

'No, you couldn't.'

'Whatever.'

Lila proudly showed them almost all of what
she had just seen of Ben's life.

'Why not?' said Socrates. 'Well done, Lila.'

'Why him?' asked Wittgenstein.

Hard to say. Lila just had a good feeling
about him. It was only partly the possibility of
fresh, hot chips. 'Call it female intuition.'

'Shall we hunt for someone superior,
Ludwig?'

'Choose any scum you want. It's fine by me.'

Suddenly the screen filled with the chip
fryer. Lila manoeuvred herself in front of the

24

monitor, reaching for the off switch.

'Hang on, what was that?'

'That? Um . . .' Lila tried to be casual. 'Just his summer job.'

'Having the fewest wants, I am nearer to the gods,' said Socrates, who wasn't fooled for a second.

'I am,' said Wittgenstein, 'easy to please. As I always tell my hosts, I'm happy to eat anything as long as it's the same every day.'

They looked at him.

'It's dangerous over there,' he said, and grimaced at the thought of all those ordinary, living people.

'He's right,' Socrates said. 'It's a privilege to be allowed an outside visit. Don't mess up.'

'Oh, don't be ridiculous,' Lila said. 'I'll just go and talk to him. And bring him back here.'

'You make it sound so easy,' said Wittgenstein. 'If he doesn't come then you default immediately.'

'Not fair,' said Socrates. He turned to Lila. 'Remember you have to leave things as you find them, except Ben Warner, of course. We mustn't interfere with the natural order. If we're not careful, we might lose visiting privileges. Then we could never bring Ben here.'

'That *would* be a shame,' said Wittgenstein.

'Or, worse, we might get him here and not be able to get him out.'

'That really would be a shame,' said

Wittgenstein, who thought that there were already far too many unsuitable people in the World of Ideas.

'He mustn't ever stay too long when he comes here,' Socrates said.

'*If* he comes here,' said Wittgenstein.

'*When* he comes,' said Socrates, 'you can show him round, Lila. Introduce him to the gang, get into some debates.'

'No cheating,' said Wittgenstein. 'You mustn't tell him what to think.'

'You can do all the big themes.' Socrates was warming to the idea. 'I could make up a schedule. I'll tell people to expect him.'

He was already formulating a plan of how to teach Ben the basics of philosophy. He was feeling confident about the bet: how could philosophy not improve Ben's life? It was surely better to appreciate one's lack of knowledge and learn, than to live unaware even of the extent of one's ignorance. Of course, Socrates had been fatally wrong before about people's willingness to hear this message, but self-doubt was not part of his repertoire.

'May the best man win,' Wittgenstein said, folding his arms.

'May philosophy triumph,' Socrates said, and scuttled off to make preparations.

CHAPTER EIGHT

Ben had only just started his third evening shift in the fish-and-chip shop and already the white 'hygiene hat' that Tony Swan had enforced was making his forehead itchy. Tony had pinned up a motivation notice, designed on his computer and printed on pink A4 paper. It had a big smiley face and an arrow pointing to a diagram of a boomerang surrounded by £ signs. The shop was quite small: there was nowhere to sit, just a big counter and a big window. Despite the customer-love Tony propagated, there wasn't much encouragement to linger. It was just pay and take-away.

Ben whistled 'Fly Me to the Moon' as he cleaned the equipment and started up the fryer. In fact, he wasn't very good at whistling, but his dad did it constantly and other people's annoying habits became less annoying if you made a point of doing them yourself. Also, he could only remember a few of the words, so it had to be whistled. He would never admit it, but he liked his mum's old records.

Ben didn't look up when he heard the door opening.

' "... see what spring is like on Jupiter and Mars," ' a woman sang. ' "In other words, hold my hand ..." '

' "In other words, darling, kiss me," ' Ben finished without thinking. 'Hi. Welcome to Cod Almighty!' he said with a forced smile.

The woman winced. 'Is this a Plaice of Worship?'

'Apparently, when the boss ran out of money to refit the shop, he got the local vicar to invest in the business. But he insisted on changing the name—said Fish Upon a Star promoted superstition.'

She smiled at him like they were old friends, which, Ben was pretty sure, they weren't. She looked a bit odd too in her old-fashioned clothes. Some sort of purple-velvet floaty top, as if she'd raided her mum's wardrobe from the seventies.

'Can I help you?' Ben asked, as professionally as he could manage.

'Bag of chips, please,' the woman said, looking guilty.

Ben opened a new plastic bag of ready-chopped potatoes, poured them into the metal basket and dipped it in the fryer.

She peered round to get a better view.

The shop door pinged. 'Hello, hello. What have we here? Hello, gorgeous. Don't let my tasty chips spoil your lovely figure.' Tony ducked under the counter. 'Just got some business to do,' he said, going into the back room. 'Don't go away.'

Ben jiggled the chip basket in the oil a little too vigorously.

The woman stared at the chips as he wrapped them, like a religious fanatic who'd been promised a piece of an ancient saintly sandal. She clearly wouldn't be taking Tony's advice. As soon as she had them in her hands she tore open the paper and stuffed a chip into her mouth.

'Nice?' Ben said.

'It's only that—' She shook vinegar violently over her chips and put two more in her mouth, sighing with pleasure.

'Sorry about Tony, he's just . . .' Successful with women, in fact.

'Oo uu fing het hith ship tafthes eh thame oo mee av ih ud oo ud?' she said enthusiastically.

This was really embarrassing.

'Forry.' She swallowed. 'Hot chips. Do you think this chip tastes the same to me as it would to you?'

'I doubt it. I'm already getting tired of chips. It seems more, um, exciting for you.' Cod Almighty's chips didn't usually send people into ecstasy.

'It is exciting. But what I mean is: how do two people manage to talk about, and compare, a totally private experience like tasting a chip? If we split this chip in two and eat half each'—she gave him his half—'then we are eating the same chip and sharing that experience. But what about *what it feels like* for the other person to taste the chip? We can't

29

share that—it's personal. It could be completely different for everyone. How can I know what the chip tastes like to you?' She stuffed in another couple, in case she forgot what chips tasted like to her, presumably.

Ben had never had a conversation like this before. He supposed it was what you'd call a philosophical question. His friends all agreed that philosophy was for prats. And maybe some girls, but only the ugly ones. She wasn't a prat, really, just a little bit strange. And, he had to admit, she certainly wasn't ugly.

'You could try and describe it,' the woman continued. 'It's salty, for example. But how do I know what "salty" means to you? You might use the word to refer to the same foods as me—Twiglets and anchovies—but the taste in your mouth could be different and I would never know.'

The shop bell rang.

'Just coming,' Tony shouted from the office.

'I have to go. I'll be in touch, Ben.' She reached for the chips, then moved her hands away. Then reached back, but stopped herself. Finally she grabbed a fistful, grinned and ran out.

'Wait! Who are you?' Ben said, too late.

How did she know his name? She'd disappeared so quickly, he wasn't even sure she'd been there in the first place. Some of her chips had been eaten, and Tony had definitely seen her. Ben munched on a chip and stared confusedly into space.

'Cotton ships all come in threes,' said the new customer.

'Eh?'

'Haddock, chips and mushy peas.'

'Right.'

There was a small white card on the counter. Ben grabbed it before Tony noticed and studied it while the fish was frying. 'World of Ideas', it said.

CHAPTER NINE

Socrates and Wittgenstein were waiting for Lila.

'I told you not to!' Socrates shouted.

'I know, I know, but if you'd smelt them . . .' Lila licked her greasy, salty hands.

'Is that really leaving things as you found them?' Socrates asked. 'A greedy visit to the World-of-Chips?'

'What were they like?' asked Wittgenstein.

'Hot and salty and soft but crunchy and—'

'Enough!' said Socrates, mouth watering.

'You can't go back again,' Wittgenstein said. 'Might as well give up now.'

'Out of the question,' Socrates said. 'Send him an email. You've already got his attention.'

'You were a bit weird, Lila,' said

31

Wittgenstein. 'Maybe you put him off.'

'Coming from you!'

'How will you bring him in?' asked Socrates.

'I believe it is common practice to use a wardrobe,' said Wittgenstein.

'Perhaps not,' said Lila, remembering her glimpse of Ben's wardrobe on the monitors. Dirty clothes, muddy football boots, old comic books and who-knew-what-else piled waist-high. 'I'll think of something.'

'He won't come, though,' said Wittgenstein. 'Why would he be interested?'

'I wouldn't be so sure,' said Socrates, like a man with a plan.

CHAPTER TEN

Back at home in his bedroom, Ben couldn't stop thinking about the strange woman. He picked the duvet up from the floor. A few coins, a sock and half a magazine fell out of the red cover. Ben spread the duvet on the bed and lay on top of it. He flipped the white card round and round. There was a phone number on the back, which he hadn't noticed at first. The idea of calling it made him feel dizzy.

'World of Ideas': what did that mean, anyway? There was a World of Leather on the ring road. World of Ideas: *Low prices for Communism this week? Special offer: 2 for 1 on*

Theory of Evolution flat-packs? Ben turned to his computer for some distraction. There was only one new email, from an address he didn't know:

From: lila@worldofideas.org
To: ben@mymail.com

Hi Ben,
It's me, Lila, from today in the chip shop. I suppose this all seems weird, but the most important part of being a good philosopher is to be open to ideas. Don't believe anything until you can find a good reason for it. And don't disbelieve anything, either, until you can argue strongly against it.

Being a good philosopher? What did that have to do with haddock and chips?

The world can be much stranger than you think. Or rather, stranger than what you take for granted before you properly think. For example, what evidence do you have for believing that the world really is as you experience it? You have the evidence of your senses, but we know that they can be fooled sometimes in illusions and dreams. Maybe they're tricked more often than you realise. Maybe all the time.

I was enjoying our conversation over the chips. Were you? I'd love to show you around the World of Ideas. Call the number. Lila.

The World of Ideas: was it a real place then? And where did Lila fit in? Maybe it was just another email hoax:

We have contacted you as someone whom we can trust to assist with our investment plans. My client has $3 billion and will pay you 10 per cent if you can help us relocate our money from the World of Ideas to your country. Please respond urgently.

Ben got ready for bed, and climbed under the duvet. He'd decide whether to reply to Lila's email in the morning.

CHAPTER ELEVEN

Ben was climbing up a long, winding staircase. The stone steps seemed to go on and on and get narrower and narrower. Finally, exhausted, he reached a small wooden door at the top. He somehow knew it would be unlocked and he pushed it open.

'I've been waiting for you,' said an

unfriendly voice.

After the dark staircase, it took time for Ben's eyes to adjust to the light from the candles and the large fire. He blinked and focused on the room's only inhabitant, a wizened white-haired man in a lab coat, who was grinning like he knew a secret that Ben wouldn't want to hear, which only made the old man more keen to tell it.

'Welcome to reality,' said the old man, enjoying Ben's confusion. 'Everything that you thought was real—everything about your life— was just an illusion. All this'—he pointed at photos of Ben's house and family, his school and dog—'is nothing but an illusion. *This* is real.' With a misanthropic grin, the man shuffled slowly over to the other side of the room. One leg was shorter than the other. He threw open another door on to a little room. It took Ben a while to realise what he could see, and even longer to understand it. It appeared to be *him*, lying asleep in a reclining chair. Wires were fixed to his head and some to parts of his body.

'Yes, it is you,' the evil scientist said harshly. 'This apparatus has been controlling all your thoughts and sensations for fifteen and a half long years. All those things you thought you did, well, that's just it,' he said, 'you only *thought* you did them or—if you prefer—you did them in thought alone. You did indeed have those experiences but, in terms of the ultimate reality, you have never left this room.'

Ben felt sick. There was no point doing anything if it wasn't with real people in real places. He didn't want just to have experienced his life, he wanted to have lived it. He wished he had never found out. Or was it better to wake up from the dream and live in the real world?

'We've been giving you a nice life, though, haven't we?' said the old man.

'That doesn't matter if it isn't real. It has to be real!' Ben thumped his pillow.

Pillow was a good sign. Ben was in his own bedroom. It looked like a bomb had exploded, which was a relief because that was how it always looked. Ben shut his eyes again, daring the chamber at the top of the staircase to reappear. It didn't: the view stayed black. When he looked again, his bedroom was still there. Ben's heart was beating wildly. He was tempted to go around the room touching everything to see if it was solid, but he realised that, even if the nightmare was true, everything would still seem 'real'. That was why it was so awful: there was no way to know. Problems on problems—he'd thought his life was dull, but now it might not have even happened.

Ben knew, of course, that it had to have been a dream. The nightmare, that is, not his whole life. But he couldn't deny that it had made him think, and the silly doubts were lingering. If the dream could appear so real— if our senses could get it totally wrong—then why were we so sure about the truth of everything else they showed us? Had he only assumed that the rest of life wasn't a dream because the bits from before and after falling asleep matched up, and because it lasted a long time? Life was life because he could recognise dreams as dreams. That made sense.

Ben clung to the idea that, after all, things being the way they seemed was probably the best and simplest explanation. Even so, he wished he could think of a better reason for why he wasn't going to be fooled by a mad scientist. Except, why would the mad scientist bother?

He was sure the dream had something to do with the visit and the email from the strange woman. With uncharacteristic determination he jumped out of bed, grabbed Lila's card from the table and marched purposefully out of his room. He was going to call her, and do it before he changed his mind.

Ben crept barefoot downstairs to the landing, years of practice ensuring he avoided the creaky floorboards on the first three stairs. He picked up the receiver on his dad's out-of-date cream phone and looked at the wheel. It took him ages to dial the number because he kept doing it wrong, and there were lots of 8s and 9s.

It actually rang! Ben hung up, of course,

37

before anyone could answer. Right. Time to stop being so pathetic. He dialled again carefully and this time left it till someone answered.

'World of Id—'

Ben hung up quickly. Face it, he just didn't have the guts to go through with it. Whatever 'it' was.

Then the phone rang. Ben snatched it so quickly that he banged the side of his head with the bulky headset.

'Ow,' he whispered.

'Ben?'

'Lila?'

'I'm glad you called,' she said.

'You called me,' he said pedantically. He paused. 'I've had this terrible dream and—I don't know why—but I think you had something to do with it.'

'It's not really safe to talk too much over the phone. We need to meet in person.'

'Meet? Who are you?' Ben wondered if he had a supernatural stalker. He almost liked the idea of being stalked by someone sexy like Lila.

'Ben,' Lila said. 'Give us a chance. Maybe the dream was a bit strong . . .'

'So it *was* you.'

'Sort of. We just wanted to get your attention. Make you think about ideas: like the taste of a chip, or what is real about real life.'

'Is that philosophy?'

'Yes. Please agree to meet us.' Lila held her breath.

Ben was tempted. It would be wimpy to say no when something different was finally happening. And she had invited him, not Tony Swan, or thuggy Steve from school.

'You can't come here, though. My parents—'

'No. You come to us.'

'How?'

'Don't worry, it's not far. You know that cupboard next to the bathroom where the clean towels are kept?'

'Yes, I know it.' But how did she?

'Open the door, squash inside and then shut it behind you. If you push through the towels, you'll see us there.'

'I push through the towels?'

'See you soon.'

Ben checked the old clock above the phone. It was 4.30 a.m. He crept carefully back to the upstairs landing. He opened the airing cupboard as quietly as possible, trying to avoid the noise it always made as the wooden door scraped on its frame. His parents' bedroom was just opposite but there was no sound apart from his dad's gentle snoring.

Surely real adventures didn't begin in the airing cupboard? Ben used to hide here when he was younger. He'd loved the cosy warmth and the smell of the fluffy clean towels. Even now, the familiar space made him relax. He was much bigger now but he more or less still fitted in. He could almost forget why he'd come here. He shifted around a bit: it wasn't actually that comfortable now he'd grown. The shelving at his side was loose. He wiggled round to face the back of the cupboard and pushed a bit more. The towels gave way. He pushed a bit harder, and crawled through the small space towards the light.

CHAPTER TWELVE

'Oof!' Ben said, although he really meant 'whatonearthisgoingonwhereamiisthisajokecan 'tbelievei'mdoingthishelp!'

'So, you're here.' Lila picked him up from the floor.

Ben tried to take in the scene in front of him: a kind of hall with a wooden floor, several doors, and tall windows that looked on to a beautiful walled garden. There was only a small door where the airing cupboard had been. What would happen if he couldn't get back?

'I still don't . . . but . . . how? . . . where? . . . what?'

Before Ben could make up his mind which was the most important question, a sprightly, shortish man of about seventy, wearing a dark tailored suit, bounded in, smiling broadly through his short white beard. 'Welcome to the

World of Ideas. I am Socrates.'

'Wow!' Socrates was a character in books, wasn't he? Was he supposed to be real? In which case, he was supposed to be really, really dead; or he'd be thousands of years old. Ben tried to concentrate on what Socrates was saying, and not look at his oddly-shaped nose.

'Here, in the World of Ideas, you will encounter the major questions in philosophy. Success is not about how many facts you learn, but how you think about the ideas. One requirement is that you be prepared to question ruthlessly your assumptions about the world and remain open-minded. The fact you are here at all suggests that you have this gift.'

Ben gawped at him: open-mouthed and open-minded.

'But don't be afraid to disagree,' Socrates said. 'Dissent is the engine of philosophy.' The far door banged open. 'Speaking of which—'

A younger, thinner man with a mop of thick black hair rushed into the room. 'I can't believe you started without me.'

'I started two thousand years before you,' said Socrates.

'Age before genius . . . I suppose you do have some excuse for your primitive thinking.'

'Ben, this is my colleague, Ludwig Wittgenstein.'

The philosopher scrutinised Ben. 'Pleased to meet you,' he lied. 'You may have heard of me.'

'Um . . .'

'Ignorant, petty world,' said Wittgenstein. He waved at Socrates to continue.

'I arrived in the World of Ideas after I was condemned to death for promoting my philosophical method.'

Death for doing philosophy? It didn't exactly have a reputation as a dangerous sport.

'Corrupting the young men of Athens was one of the charges.' Socrates grinned. 'I used to accost people in the streets and engage them in debate. The Athenians found it threatening—'

'But wait,' Ben managed to say. 'What happened in the end?'

'As I said, I was executed for my philosophy. I was made to drink a cup of hemlock—of bitter poison.'

'So you are dead?'

'Yes yes, dead. So what? No need to be rude. The important thing is, I saw myself as a buzzing fly—'

'Hang on. You're all dead?'

'Look, you, there are billions of dead people in the world. You shouldn't be so surprised. Here in the World of Ideas we concentrate on philosophers.'

'What happens to the others?'

'So young, so many questions. Now, where was I? I played the part of a stinging gadfly; the city of Athens was like a smug, thoroughbred horse.'

Wittgenstein passed his hand over his eyes in despair.

'I was an irritant of course,' continued Socrates, 'but for their own good—to rouse them out of intellectual torpor. It wasn't welcome.' He smiled at Ben, ignoring Wittgenstein's grimace.

Ben tried to smile back.

'They had him put down, like a sick animal,' said Wittgenstein.

'There is only one good,' said Socrates, 'and that is knowledge; and one evil—ignorance. You have been chosen to visit us because we saw you as someone who would benefit from the experience.'

Ben felt sick. What was he doing in this place?

'We hope you'll learn to love philosophy,' Lila said.

Socrates jabbed Lila with his elbow, worried that she'd give the game away. Wittgenstein gurgled—it might have been a laugh.

Ben was prepared to be inspired by Lila, and if loving philosophy was the way, he'd give it a go.

'You are our first . . . er . . . live visitor,' said Socrates. 'In turn, we believe that we will gain something from you.'

'Well, one of us will,' said Wittgenstein, under his breath.

'After all,' Socrates said, 'constant questioning is a noble path.'

43

'Except when I ask about whether you're all dead,' said Ben.

Socrates smiled. 'There are certain questions to which you cannot know the answers yet. Remember: the unexamined life is not worth living.' He shook Ben's hand. 'Good luck. Come on, Ludwig.'

'Why wasn't he wearing a toga?' Ben asked Lila. Everyone knew that Socrates wore a toga.

'Fashions move on—in clothes and in ideas,' Lila said.

'When did you die?'

'Didn't your mother teach you never to ask a woman her age? 1972.'

No wonder she was a bit weird. 'How?'

Lila hated talking about death, above all her own. 'Now, I'll be your guide. I'll introduce you to various people who in turn will introduce you to the wonders of philosophy.'

'So I'm just going to meet people and we'll talk about philosophy?'

'Exactly.'

CHAPTER THIRTEEN

Socrates ran along the corridor opening doors at random and shouting, 'He's here! He's here!' Good start—the boy had finally arrived. Why were people so suspicious of philosophy? Make them feel clever and they love you; try to make them think and they hate you.

Lila had done a good job. He must remember to tell her, he thought, then promptly forgot all about it. His assistants seemed to be getting younger by the decade, which was no bad thing.

'He's here!' Socrates burst into the library. Aristotle and Simone de Beauvoir were playing backgammon by the fire. 'I said he's here.'

'Who?'

'The boy. For the bet.'

'Socrates, I'm not getting involved,' said Aristotle. 'I sincerely hope you win and all that, but I simply don't have time to teach amateurs. I have my work to think of.'

'Your move,' said Simone, handing him the dice.

'You don't have to meet him—I've already sorted out some people,' said Socrates. Indeed, the big names were nothing but trouble. 'But you could at least show an interest.'

'And you could throw dice for your job if you're so keen to let it go,' said Aristotle, rolling a double five. 'What were you thinking—playing these reckless, childish games?'

'Haven't you had enough past to let the future go?'

'Socrates, you don't even half believe that. Anyway, there's letting go, and there's . . .

Ludwig Wittgenstein.' Aristotle moved his pieces and took one of Simone's, placing it on the bar.

She picked up the dice. 'Ludwig Wittgenstein gives me the creeps. Jean-Paul can't stand him.'

'An attribute which is not unique to Wittgenstein,' said Aristotle, who had a bit of a crush on Simone and was getting nowhere despite twenty years of backgammon and brandy in the library.

CHAPTER FOURTEEN

'Shall we go?' asked Lila.

'Right now?' Ben wasn't sure he could move his legs. 'Already?' He didn't remember exactly agreeing to join in with these weirdos. These dead weirdos. But then it wasn't as if he had anything better to do in the middle of the night.

'OK. No!' Ben realised he was wearing the scruffy grey tracksuit trousers and red T-shirt that he had been sleeping in. 'Wait, I can't meet anyone like this.'

'I'm sure no one will mind.' Lila was impatient. 'Follow me.'

Lila set off purposefully. Ben decided to follow—shabby tracksuit, bare feet and all. They walked down a wide empty corridor, identical doors down both sides. Though the floor and the doors were made of beautiful wood, they had an institutional feel. Each of the doors had a different sign: *Truth Is Beauty. Why Did You Do That? Oranges and Lemons. Surely not?*

Some of the people they passed greeted Lila, and smiled at Ben; others whispered and turned to stare. Ben adjusted his tracksuit bottoms. Did they all live here? Or rather, did they spend all their time being dead here? Lila certainly didn't seem very dead. In fact she was quicker than Ben and he had to run to catch up. She stood there, watching him.

CHAPTER FIFTEEN

Wittgenstein pulled down the metal protective helmet over his head. He peered out through the see-through panel and lit the blow torch. The metal began to glow red, then white, under the flames. He found welding very relaxing. The workshop was a haven away from the Socrates Appreciation Society.

Damn Socrates and his sneaky dream control. It was probably the dream that had got Ben hooked. Cheap Hollywood tricks. You can lead a boy to water, but you cannot make him think. It was obvious that Ben wouldn't be everything that Socrates hoped. Things would change around here when Wittgenstein was in charge. He'd get rid of all those pompous philosophers, for a start.

And why hadn't everyone heard of him? It was as he'd said: philosophy was a marginal pursuit these days. Below recreating medieval battles and embroidery, way below train-spotting. His work may not be as far-reaching as he'd hoped, but it was iconic nonetheless. The problem, however, with being iconic was that his work was abused: misquoted, never properly understood. It was no surprise really—its brilliant truth was only revealed to a precious few. He wasn't writing for the masses like that pleb Bertrand Russell. And so how to be properly respected?

Who wanted to be a household name anyway? Persil was a household name.

CHAPTER SIXTEEN

'Here we are,' Lila said, stopping in front of a door marked *The Sceptic Tank* that looked like all the others. 'This is exciting!' Lila bounced as she went to open it. 'It's the classic philosophical question: is the evidence of our senses reliable? Can we ever know the true nature of reality?'

'My dream!' Ben shuddered.

'This question's kept them busy for over

eighty-five generations, on and off.'

'So it's too much to hope that I might solve it?' How difficult could it really be, this philosophy lark?

' "Solve" is a bit ambitious. But maybe you'll work out what you think and find some better reasons for thinking it, which is not a bad start.'

'I'll try,' Ben said, although he wasn't at all sure what this involved.

'You know, believing something for a good reason is much better than believing it for no reason at all, even if it's the same thing you believe in both cases. Ready?'

Ben smiled in a not-really-but-let's-do-it-anyhow way. He had absolutely no idea what to expect. He hoped it wouldn't be some sort of classroom.

Lila opened the door, and shut it behind them. The air here had a different smell and was cooler. All Ben could see was a tall hedge. No, he certainly hadn't expected that. What was the point of a door that opened on to a hedge?

Ben followed Lila through a gap in the hedge. The path was blocked by another hedge, but Lila turned right. They were in a huge maze!

'Wait for me.'

'Come on. You'll meet two people who have different opinions, so you can expect them both to try and convince you that they are right.'

'How do I decide?'

'See who has the better arguments. You don't necessarily have to decide now. We just want to get you thinking.'

That sounded painful. 'You won't leave me, will you?'

'Don't worry, I'll stay. I'll be around for all your visits.'

'How many visits?'

'That's up to you.'

'I see,' although he didn't. 'What about this maze?'

'Good, isn't it? It gets re-done every week. Keeps us on our toes. Mentally speaking. If minds had toes. Never mind. Actually, I think we should turn left here, not right.'

After several minutes tracking the path, they reached a clearing and a large oak tree.

'Hi! You found us!' A young woman was sitting on one of the lower branches. She waved.

A young man was carving something into the tree with a penknife. He was wearing long baggy shorts with big boots and high socks, and a smart jacket over his yellow T-shirt and braces. Must be some sort of fashion victim, Ben decided.

'Hello, I'm Max Salter.' He shook Ben's hand. 'Pleased to meet you, Ben.' Formality didn't suit him.

The woman up on the branch was skinny,

unsmiling, dressed all in black and barefoot.
'Polly Cromwell. Hello,' she said, dropping an
acorn.

Max scrutinised Ben's night-time outfit. 'Is
that what they're wearing these days?'

Ben looked down at his frayed old tracksuit.
'Yes, we wear them a lot. But only for special
occasions.'

'Great look,' said Max.

'I think you should begin,' Polly said from
the tree, 'since what you have to say is much
less interesting.'

Was this the way philosophers always
behaved?

Max wasn't particularly put off, even when
an acorn caught him on the ear. 'When we say
something is "all in the mind", what do we
mean?'

'That it's imaginary?' Ben said.

'Exactly!' Max jabbed at the air with his
finger. 'That it doesn't really exist. Or rather, it
doesn't exist as an external independent thing,
only as a thought that totally depends on the
mind of the person who has that thought.'

'A thought only exists in someone's mind as
they think it,' Lila explained. 'It doesn't carry
on by itself like a tree.'

'But you know what,' Max said to Ben, 'in
one sense all of the outside world is just in the
mind.'

Polly threw a shower of acorns down in
disgust.

51

'Ow!' An acorn bounced off Ben's shoulder. 'What do you mean: all the world is just in the mind?' Ben would need to be convinced, but his dream had been vivid enough to suggest that maybe there was something to it.

'Well.' Max started pacing. 'How do you know anything about the external world, the world of solid objects and so on?' He patted the hedge that bordered the clearing.

This must be a trick question: the answer seemed so obvious. 'I see them, I feel them.' Ben held up an acorn and squeezed it. The pointed end left a shape in the fleshy bit of his hand.

'Exactly!' Max clapped his hands. 'You *see* them. You *feel* them. This is the evidence you have for believing that the objects exist—your perception of these objects.'

'Hang on,' Ben said. 'Didn't you just tell me that they didn't exist?'

'Wait,' Max said. 'This "evidence" is just in the mind—it is a mere experience, a sensation of seeing or touching something. You don't experience objects *directly*, in fact, but *indirectly* through the medium of sight, touch, sound, smell and taste—the five senses.'

'What do you mean, "indirectly"?'

'Well, let's say that you have a square table in your bedroom.'

Ben knew that it wasn't a coincidence that he did, in fact, have a square table in his bedroom.

'Now, every time you look at it, you see a square table, because you know that is what it is.'

Philosophers really did have a talent for stating the obvious. And then making it not obvious after all.

'But think of what you actually see. I'll show you, if it helps.' Max took him by the arm and led him behind the hedge.

Ben tried not to look surprised to see his own bedroom.

'I was just about to tidy up. Any day now.'

'Look at the table,' Max said. 'You almost never actually see a square shape, do you? You see different four-sided shapes, depending on which angle you look at it from.'

Ben realised that, amazingly, it was true. Why had he never noticed that? His brain had always 'told' him that the table was square. And yet he'd never 'seen' a square table.

'So that is why we say we don't experience the object directly: because we rarely see it as a square, although that is its true shape.' Max looked pleased with himself.

Ben followed him back to the centre of the maze.

'So,' Max said, 'as long as we experience objects indirectly, we must rely on the evidence of our senses to know about them.'

Ben looked up at Polly, for confirmation.

She nodded. 'I'm afraid so. That bit makes sense, at least.'

'Exactly!' Max punched the air and looked smug. 'All you can be sure of, then, are your sensations, not the objects they represent. When Descartes undertook his great, but flawed, project to prove the existence of the real world he began with the only thing he could not possibly doubt: his sensations. Thus he concluded, "I think, therefore I am."'

'So,' Ben said, 'our sensations are real—'

'Oh yes, someone experiencing it is all that is required for that.'

'But this doesn't mean that anything else is real.'

'Exactly!' Max shouted, throwing up his hands.

Ben jumped; it was scary even when you got it right.

'We know the senses can be deceived. For example, we are all familiar with optical illusions, where you see things that aren't really there, or see them in the wrong way. Look at this drawing. You "see" an object that cannot exist.

'And,' Max continued, 'amputees have been known to feel phantom pain in limbs they no longer have. Also dreams. While you have dream experiences you are convinced that they are real and it's only because we wake up that we know that what we thought was real is not after all.'

'But we do wake up, don't we?' Ben was disconcerted by the memory of his own dream.

'If some of our perceptions and experiences can be wrong and misguided, why not all of them?' Max grabbed Ben by the shoulders. 'Why not? We'd never know the difference. Think about it: there is no external way of verifying the truth about objects. We have proved that you never experience them directly, but only through sensations. So what corroborative evidence could you possibly find to justify what your senses tell you?'

Ben thought about it, once Max let go. 'What about scientific experiments? They reveal how the world really is.'

'Certainly not!'

Ben had been hoping for an 'Exactly'.

'How do you know about science?' Max said. 'You read it or you hear someone telling you about it. How do scientists discover their results? They look at their instruments. All your supposed scientific knowledge is being filtered through your senses, and so it's subject to the same doubt as ordinary experience.'

Ben felt depressed. He had grasped that philosophy was about re-examining your reasons for believing things. But there was no need to turn the whole world—square tables, ice cream, people, trees, music—into a figment of his imagination.

'So you're trying to tell me none of the world is real?' He had to get this straight.

Polly got the giggles and nearly fell out of the tree. 'That is so ridiculous.' At least that's probably what she said: it was hard to tell.

Max ignored Polly. 'That view is called solipsism: that the only thing that is real is what's in my mind. Or your mind, depending on your perspective.'

Polly dropped all her acorns. 'You don't have enough imagination to have made this up,' she hooted, hanging on to the branch for balance.

Max sighed and stretched his braces. 'I'm not saying that I invented you. Not likely.'

'I heard that.' Polly looked seriously down at Ben, and said, 'The solipsist is the one who never bothers to turn round because he can only see what's in front of him.' She jumped down from the tree.

'To be fair,' Max said, 'although there is no reason for firmly believing that there is a real world, or that it is anything like it seems to be, we don't have any good reason for not believing it either. The correct position is to doubt everything, to be a sceptic.'

Ben imagined introducing himself: 'Hello, my name's Ben. I'm a sceptic.'

'For ages,' said Max, 'philosophers have been trying to come up with an answer. No one could bear the idea that we couldn't *prove* that there was a world of objects that existed, whether or not we were there to experience it.'

'Max Salter,' Polly said, 'you've spent the last twenty minutes arguing that we don't exist. It's a project that has to be pointless. Either you're wrong, in which case you're wasting our time; or you're right, in which case why are you bothering to talk to us? You always did have idealist tendencies.'

'Really?' said Ben. Max didn't look much like a human-rights campaigner.

'Here, idealism means that you think nothing exists except experiences in people's minds—or ideas,' Lila explained. 'There are no solid objects that are there when we're not experiencing them; instead the world is just a construction out of these experiences. To say a tree exists simply means "a tree is seen".'

'Oh.'

Polly sighed. 'It must be exhausting being an idealist. Whenever you stand up, you take the chair with you.'

'I never went that far,' Max said.

'The scandal of philosophy,' said Polly, 'is not that there is no decent answer to this question, but that people still think it's worth asking.'

'But why shouldn't we be trying to answer it?' Ben said. 'I mean, if none of the world exists—'

'That's not quite true,' Max said. 'At least your experiences exist, or you wouldn't be having them. It's just that it is reasonable to doubt that there are any objects that cause these experiences, or to which they correspond.'

'That's just it, Max—that's where you're

wrong,' Polly said. 'It isn't *reasonable* to doubt it. It's perfectly true that we cannot *prove* the existence of the external world. But we've known that for centuries. Grow up!'

Max hung his shoulders like Kermit the Frog after a telling-off from Miss Piggy.

'In fact, though, it's simply impossible to doubt that the world exists as we experience it.' She turned to Ben. 'I can see you're affected by what Max says, but can you honestly say that you believe, even suspect, that these objects around you are not real?'

Ben kicked the tree trunk speculatively. It stayed where it was. 'I suppose not. But that doesn't have to mean it's true.' Ben's dream was still fresh.

'But why complicate things?' said Polly. 'We have certain experiences of objects that occupy space, move along continuous paths and exist, whether or not we look at them or touch them. What might be the reason for this? That material objects are merely a collection of sensations, or that they really do exist?'

'Umm . . .'

'Have you heard of Ockham's Razor, Ben?'

'No,' he said, trying to look clever nonetheless. He stopped slouching. Was Polly trying to humiliate him—talking about razors when he didn't shave properly yet?

'Well, it's the rule that you should always go with the simplest explanation that makes sense. Don't complicate matters needlessly.'

Polly pointed to a badger slinking its way along the bottom of the hedge. 'The movements of a badger make no sense seen as a collection of our internal experiences, but they do if we think of it *as a badger*.'

'I agree that a world of objects is the most plausible hypothesis,' said Max.

'Plausible hypothesis?' said Polly with a groan. 'Don't be pathetic—it's more than that. We have evolved to deal effectively with the world around us. We can make accurate predictions about heavy objects falling, know that inanimate things will stay where we left them and so on. We would not have evolved this way if there wasn't an external world, and one that is more or less as it seems.'

'Of course believing in a regular world of objects is common sense,' Max said. 'But the point of philosophy is to question common sense and work out whether we can justify our basic beliefs. For years it was common sense to believe that the world was stationary and flat and that the sun was a disc of light that travelled across the sky. Common sense is not always a reliable guide. We mustn't be complacent. We cannot ever know what the world is really like, independent of our perception of it. It must be true that this is beyond our understanding.'

Polly stood there, her hands on her hips.

'At the very least,' Max added, 'you have to admit that a large part of the way we experience the world depends on us, how we are constituted as humans.'

'Hmmm,' Polly said.

'What do you mean by that?' Ben said.

'Come here, and we'll try an experiment.'

Ben followed Max to a table set up at the edge of the clearing. There were three wooden tubs of water on it.

'Put your right hand into this one, and your left hand here.'

Ben put his right hand into the first bowl. 'Ah! It's freezing.' He tried to lift it out, but Max held his arm down in the water.

'Just a bit longer. Now put your other hand in here.'

Ben dipped his left hand gingerly into the second tub, bracing himself against the cold. But it was hot, only just bearable. Now what? He felt a bit foolish standing with his hands in tubs of water, Max, Polly and Lila gathered around the table.

Max was looking at his watch. 'OK, that should be long enough. Now, put both hands into the third bowl. Tell me, is the water hot or cold?'

'It's . . . well . . . it feels hot with my right hand and cold with the left. So . . .'

'Is the water hot *and* cold?' Max asked. 'How can it be both? If you experience the water as hot and cold at the same time, then surely you cannot claim that either property—hotness or coldness—belongs to the water

60

itself. You see now that some characteristics of the world are not constant: they depend on the situation of the observer. If our experience of an object can change when the object itself doesn't, then maybe we should be careful about what our senses tell us. Now come over here.' Max beckoned Ben behind the hedge.

The bedroom had gone, but Ben noticed that it was getting dark, much more quickly than usual. Max stopped under a streetlight.

Ben went to dry his hands on his T-shirt. 'Ugh!' His favourite bright-red T-shirt was a dull murky brown. 'It must be some trick.'

'Not really. It's a special kind of light called mono-frequency, which is normal in streetlights. It has a very narrow wavelength—just this yellow. As a result, all other colours look washed out.'

'Weird.' Ben was still studying his muddy-looking top when the streetlights went out and daylight returned. Suddenly the T-shirt was bright-red again.

'So, would you say that the T-shirt is red or muddy brown?'

'It's red.'

'Why do you say that?'

'Because it's normally red.'

'Or rather it looks red to normal people in conditions of normal light. But it can look different.'

'So you're saying that the red colour isn't really in the T-shirt?'

61

'Exactly! If the red can be made to disappear just by changing the light then perhaps it isn't a fixed property of the object itself. Certain properties of things depend on how they are experienced. In what way is there one true colour if it can change at different times? Even for different people: some are colour-blind and see all reds and greens as a shade of brown.'

'But can't we just choose one appearance and decide that is the colour?'

'Well, which of its colours should you choose?' said Max, leading him back around the hedge. 'We can take it even further. If no one is in your chip shop, does the fish still smell?'

Ben worried that he smelt of fried fish. 'Of course it does. Why should that change?'

'I would say that all that remains is the potential to cause a smell. The smell itself can only happen when someone experiences it. Just as to say that the T-shirt is red means it could cause a red experience in someone if the light were right.'

'That's just a matter of terminology,' said Polly. 'You're confusing the smell with the experience of smell, the colour with the experience of colour. The colour is in the object. The experience of colour is in the person.'

'My point is exactly that. Most people make this mistake all the time. They say the T-shirt is red. But really the redness is in us when we experience it, and the T-shirt just has the ability to produce this red sensation in certain observers under certain conditions. A lemon is not tart in itself, but has the ability to produce this experience in us when we put it in our mouths. Music is simply disturbances in the air unless someone hears it as a song.'

'That's not enough to show that the real world doesn't exist, though,' Polly said. 'After all, if the object goes away, so does the appearance of red. It's not all in the mind. What you're saying now is not as strong as what you were claiming before.'

'OK, so maybe we can't really question the existence of objects in general. I can admit that there is something that causes our experience of objects. But I insist that certain properties of the world are contingent.'

Ben appealed to Lila.

'Contingent means conditional,' she explained. 'That is, dependent on certain circumstances occurring, which might well not have occurred. "1 + 1 = 2" is *necessary*, it results from what "1" and "2", "+" and "=" mean; it couldn't be any other way. But the fact that you have two acorns in your hand is *contingent*. You might just as easily have had three, or none. Things happen to be as they are, but they could be different.'

'In this case,' Max added, 'it means that the way things look and feel depends on circumstances and how we are constructed as observers. I managed to show you that the way we experience objects can change, even when the objects themselves do not. This goes back to what I said at the beginning: that although we must rely on our perception for information about the world—there is no other way to learn about it—we cannot trust what our senses tell us. We must debunk the myth of a material world inhabited by objects whose properties are entirely fixed, no matter whether or how we observe them. The real world beyond our "veil of perception" might be a very different place.'

'Or it might not,' suggested Polly.

'Well.' Max sighed. 'We know that the true nature of things is stranger than how they seem. Think about objects at the quantum level. Theories about very small particles are so counter-intuitive that even those who came up with them find them hard to believe. Instinctively we can only understand middle-sized objects: from a breadcrumb to a conference centre, a mouse to a jumbo jet.'

'Mumbo-jumbo jet,' Polly said under her breath. 'Anyway, you can't bring science into it. You said that all science was subject to the same problem and could be doubted too.'

'I did indeed. But now I'm making a slightly different point. It was just an analogy from quantum physics, to try and illustrate how all of our experiences could be caused by something much weirder than we could ever imagine.'

'And where does that get us?'

'Where? Well, that's interesting, isn't it? To recognise that a part of the world we consider to be external is actually created when we experience it. And that the world beyond this intervention we make in experiencing it has to be unknowable.'

'That's interesting, isn't it?' Polly said. 'And if I refuse to be interested in the unknowable? What good does it do anyone to say that objects are "really" very different from how they seem to us, but in ways that we could never know about? I don't approve of all this talk about objects beyond some "veil of perception".'

'Oh don't be so discouraging. Ben, don't you think it's interesting?'

'It's amazing.' But Ben wasn't sure he was ready to be tied down to agreeing with either of them. Max was convincing, but he was just making his brain go round in circles. And Polly was saying what everyone normally thought but, now that he'd started doing philosophy, Ben realised that even the normal was weird.

'You're both always worth listening to,' Lila said diplomatically. 'And now we have to go. Philosophers may have been worrying about these things for hundreds and hundreds of years, but we haven't got that long. Ben needs to be getting back.'

As they walked through the maze, Ben tried to summarise what he'd heard, to see if it made any sense. 'Right. The first thing is that the evidence we get about the outside world all comes through our senses. So if we can doubt what our senses tell us, which we can, then we can doubt our whole experience of the outside world.'

'That's the basic point.'

'But, as Polly says, we have better reasons for believing it than doubting it.'

'Nevertheless, many great philosophers have been worked up about never getting beyond "good reasons" to "proof",' Lila said. She opened the door and they were back in the corridor. It was as if the maze hadn't been there at all.

'And then Max explained that many experiences of colour and sound and heat and stuff are not fixed in the object but depend on the conditions and even on us. That's more complicated.'

'Yes. If an object can appear to be a different shape and colour at different times, then you have to be careful what you mean when you say that the object *is* a certain colour or shape. Max wants us to acknowledge the contribution we make when we experience the world—we are not passive observers, even if we don't actively control what we see.'

'I hadn't really thought of it like that, but it does seem true.'

Lila smiled fondly. 'You should go now. But come back whenever you want. There's a lot more to talk about.'

Ben realised he was standing in front of the small door in the main hallway—the one that he'd come through in the first place. Lila pulled the handle and held the door open. She looked at Ben and smiled. He didn't know quite what to say and made eye contact with his toes. He squished back through the towels, with some difficulty, and opened the cupboard door on the other side.

With relief, Ben saw that he was back on the landing in his own house. He padded quietly to his room, hoping that no one would be around to ask him what he was doing. He must have been away for ages. He looked at the digital clock by his bed in disbelief: it was only 4:38. He'd discussed the existence of the real world and sensations, met Socrates, seen Lila again—and yet only a few minutes had passed. Ben hoped he hadn't imagined it all. But he was holding something in his hand: an acorn. The World of Ideas did exist. He put the acorn on his bedside table and fell asleep.

*   *   *

When Ben woke, it took some moments to remember what had happened during the night. He couldn't believe it was real, but the acorn was still there. If the World of Ideas had

67

always been behind the towels in the airing cupboard, why had he never found it before? And if it had only just arrived, then why now? Ben felt very special to have been their first visitor. They seemed to be hoping to see him again. Hadn't Lila said come back whenever you want?

Ben had to admit that he wouldn't mind doing some more philosophy. Lila was cool too. Not that he fancied her, obviously. He'd try and get back there soon, but not today: this morning he had important business to attend to.

CHAPTER SEVENTEEN

'Hello. HELLO!!' Ben held Matty tightly by the arms. 'Where is my baseball cap?' he shouted, nose to nose. 'You wore it yesterday. Now it's gone.'

She was Queen of Ignoring and he was outclassed. 'La la la la looooo la la.'

This was too frustrating—she was just off in her own world. 'You know your problem. You're a solipsist.'

'Mum!' she yelled, 'Ben called me a rude word.'

He stomped off, bare-headed. No one understood him round here.

CHAPTER EIGHTEEN

Why had Lila invited him to the World of Ideas? Ben wondered, lying in the bath. Surely someone her age wouldn't be interested in him. It was hardly that she was ugly and desperate. Ben decided that she was probably the most beautiful woman he'd ever met, not counting people in films. Maybe she *was* getting desperate, stuck with all those fusty dead philosophers. Perhaps he was in with a chance, after all? He submerged himself in the warm water, just his nose poking out to breathe.

He sat back up. Those swotty philosophers might still be tough competition, though. They *were* older than him, and Lila seemed to be pretty keen on philosophy. Ben forced his mind on to higher things. Time for some self-improvement. He pondered what Max Salter had said. 'If there is a fruit on the top of an inaccessible mountain, does it have a taste?' he asked himself. He supposed the answer was yes, even though this taste would never be experienced. Because having a taste could mean 'the potential to make someone have an experience of taste'. That was what Max had meant, wasn't it?

Then he came up with another question. He was definitely getting the hang of it.

Philosophy was easy. What was all the fuss about? What if no creature had ever evolved hearing, he wondered. Would there still be sounds? (Obviously it was silly to imagine all creatures being deaf—predators would be able to creep up on them and they'd all be eaten.) Never mind: if there hadn't been hearing, would there still be sounds?

Ben filled the sponge and squeezed it out. On the one hand, yes, there would still be sounds. If nothing had changed in the rest of the world and sounds could be 'made', then there would be sounds without hearing just as much as sounds with it. But on the other hand, if no sound was ever heard could it really be called a *sound*? An unheard sound was a sad creature.

Ben imagined a sound that became higher and higher. At first humans could hear it but then only some animals. Eventually it would be too high for dogs and cats, and only bats could hear it. But what about a sound too high for bats? Was that still a sound?

Ben decided that it depended on what you wanted to mean by 'sound'. If a sound was just vibrations in the air then it could exist without anyone to hear it. But if a sound was someone's experience of hearing something then it clearly couldn't. Ben realised that in everyday language 'sound' was used to mean both. Mostly people didn't think properly about these things and so the language worked

70

well enough. Finally, Ben decided that the answer was yes, and no. Not a very effective conclusion, he admitted, but he was pleased with himself for getting this far on his own. He thought Lila would be impressed.

'Ben? Are you still in the bath? Get a move on, will you?'

He sighed. Socrates had been murdered for doing philosophy. Nothing changes. Ben resigned himself to a life of unpopularity and intellectual honesty.

'Ben, did you hear me? Get out of the bath!'

CHAPTER NINETEEN

'But, Socrates,' Wittgenstein said, 'are we now suggesting to Ben Warner that the common man doesn't understand perception because he never finds it odd that he sees objects?'

'It's important to question our preconceived ideas.'

'He sees, hears and smells just fine, doesn't he? It works.'

'But we have to investigate and find the true essence of the world. Of perception, of justice, consciousness, memory . . .'

'If I heat you to 1000° C, then all that is left when the water vapour has evaporated is some ashes. Shall we say that this is the true essence of you?'

71

Socrates shook his head.

'Of course not,' said Wittgenstein caustically. 'Stop trying to reduce everything to its fundamentals. A nothing will do as well as a something about which nothing can be said.'

He marched off, leaving the water and ashes of Socrates to ponder its true nature.

CHAPTER TWENTY

It was late-morning and Ben was cycling to work in time for the lunchtime shift. He changed down a couple of gears to go up the steep hill into town. He was proud of his new bike, but was it a real object like it seemed, or just an idea?

Ben wondered what Lila was doing today, and whether she'd thought about him since he'd left. Then it occurred to him that his bike couldn't be nothing but an idea because he had just been thinking about something else and the bike had stayed where it was. If it only existed in his head, didn't that mean he'd have to think about it constantly when he was riding it?

On the other hand, if his body and the road were also ideas, then it wouldn't matter if you forgot the idea of the bike for a bit—you couldn't possibly fall off. But how did the road and bike manage to reassemble themselves perfectly into the usual route to work if they had disappeared along the way? He began to see Polly Cromwell's point about the razor. A real road made more sense than a series of roads-in-the-head that all happened to fit together.

Ben was so caught up in his thoughts that he only just noticed the red traffic light in time. He braked sharply, the bike skidded and he was thrown sideways on to the pavement. The ground certainly felt real enough as it scraped his bare legs.

CHAPTER TWENTY-ONE

Lila was waiting when Ben arrived. She smiled when she saw him.

He suddenly felt shy. He'd only thought about coming back and not about what he'd do when he got there. At least he wasn't wearing his tracksuit this time.

'Let's go.'

'Right.' They really were keen to get on with doing philosophy. Still, that was supposed to be why he was here. At least it covered the awkward moment when he didn't know what to say to Lila now that she was actually in front of him.

They set off again along the corridor, past doors marked *Remember Remember* and *Say*

What You Mean.

'Are you limping?' Lila asked.

'I fell off my bike.'

'If it hurts too much, you can lean on me.'

Wow! 'No thanks, I'll be fine.' Idiot!

Lila stopped at a door marked *It's a Matter of Life and Death*. That seemed dangerous. He thought it might be safer to visit *Is the Moon Made of Green Cheese?*, which was opposite. Through the door the air was warm and sticky. Far above the plants was a glass roof.

'What is this place?' It was like somewhere tropical.

'It's the butterfly house. Keep still and look.' Lila pointed to a purple-blue butterfly as big as the palm of her hand. The butterfly flew right past Ben's head as if he wasn't there.

'That's amazing.'

'We're not here just to look at butterflies. Come on.'

Lila dragged him through the leaves. As they crunched across the gravel floor, Ben heard voices.

'I'm telling you, it's a Guatemalan Warrior.'

'No, no, NO. It's an Empress Blue. Look at the bottom wing.'

The man sitting on the wooden bench was wearing a monk's habit, a rope tied round his waist. His brown hair formed a neat, round cap on his head. The other one was in jeans, a shirt, yellow socks and no shoes. Obviously he hadn't bothered to shave for a few days and

74

hadn't bothered to brush his hair ever. He stood with his nose up close to a large butterfly perched on a twig, showing off its wings.

'Why will you never admit you're wrong?' said the monk.

'Because I am never wrong. Next question.'

'Who's this then?' said the monk, smiling.

The other man kept his eyes on the twig. 'Nice to meet you, Ben. Have you seen this fine Empress Blue?'

The monk waved Ben over to the bench, away from the butterfly of dispute. 'I'm Conor Shaw and the deluded butterfly "expert" is Lewis Carnegie. So, Ben, what's the worst thing that could happen to you?'

Ben gazed lovingly at an orange-and-white butterfly perched on his knee. What a way to start a conversation. 'Death, I suppose.'

Lewis Carnegie groaned and turned away from the bush. 'That's so unoriginal. Now think harder.'

Socrates had said that philosophy was the art of opposition, but sometimes it did seem more personal than professional. He'd only just met Lewis Carnegie.

Conor leapt to Ben's defence, and then sat back down. 'Don't be unfair, Lewis. If I'm here pottering along having a lovely life, then it can't get much worse than dying, can it?'

'Pottering along—that's about right for you. Of course it can get worse than death. What about horrific pain and suffering? The death of someone you adore? Torture. If someone were to pull out your fingernails one by one, give you electric shocks, put rusty nails in your eyes . . .'

Ben winced. 'How am I supposed to decide if that is worse than dying or not?'

'My point is,' continued Lewis, not particularly put off by the idea of heavy-duty torture, 'that bad things that *happen* to you are worse than death, which, by definition, happens to no one.'

That didn't make sense. 'Death happens to everyone, obviously.' Two small white butterflies circled Ben's head. He went crossed-eyed looking at them.

'Everyone must die, of course, that's true. But death itself doesn't *happen* to anyone.'

'How can that be right?' asked Ben.

'Death, as soon as it occurs, cannot be bad for a dead person,' Lewis said. 'Because there is no longer a person. Death causes suffering, there's no doubt about that. But we hate death because we confuse the pain that many feel just before dying, and the grief of those left behind, with death itself. When I die, I cease to exist. If I cease to exist, how can death be a bad thing for me?'

'Ceasing to exist is not trival,' Conor said. 'Ceasing to exist is extremely upsetting.'

'That's totally irrational,' said Lewis. 'There will be *no you* to be upset.' He looked almost pleased by the thought of no Conor to

76

disagree with him. 'As Epicurus so wisely says, "Death is of no concern to us, for while we live it is not present, and when death is present, we no longer exist."'

'Epicurus is an old fool!'

'I'll tell him you said that.'

Conor fiddled nervously with the end of his rope; he didn't get the same kick out of upsetting people as Lewis did. 'The thought of death upsets me now and so it is a valid thing to fear. Epicurus is wrong: death is present while I am living. It is present, because it is my future and I am conscious of it.'

'The prospect of death is bad, but death itself cannot be.' Lewis was absolute. 'Death is nothing.'

'That's what worries me, silly.' Conor got up from the bench. 'I don't want to be nothing. I don't want to miss life, people, music . . . Butterflies.' He paced around, waving at the butterflies, who flapped away in panic. 'Your claim that it is irrational to fear death is simply wrong. It is how we are programmed. No species would have flourished under the pressures of natural selection if it had not had a central, powerful instinct to loathe and avoid death.'

'Hmm,' Lewis said.

Lila sat down on the bench next to Ben. In the palm of her hand was a hairy black caterpillar on a leaf.

Conor concluded, 'If you love life, it is

rational to fear death. Life is God's gift: we ought to value it.'

Lewis snorted.

Conor tried again. 'Look, if death is really nothing to worry about, would you be happy to die tomorrow?'

'Well, no.'

'Aha. Aha.' Conor stepped closer to Lewis. 'And if I offered you the choice between dying in one hour or having one more month to live, which would you choose?'

'More time,' Lewis answered sheepishly.

'Always?' Conor asked, a little smugly.

'As long as I was healthy. And happy.'

'Of course you want more living. That's why you came here, isn't it?'

'I wouldn't quite call this living,' Lewis said, burrowing his yellow socks into the gravel.

'This limbo dancing isn't for everyone,' Lila said with feeling.

'But still you remain here,' Conor said, 'not exactly ceasing to exist. Doesn't that imply you would want endless life?'

'Oh no, endless life is far too much,' said Lewis. 'You need a lot of imagination to fill up an eternity.'

'OK, so maybe at a certain point you would decide you'd had enough. But I think you'd want more than you are likely to get. So long as life is good, death is bad. If there are any things I enjoy or want to do then death will deprive me of those. And something that deprives me of good things is to be despised.'

'So there is a negative side to death,' Lewis conceded, 'but at least you've clarified that the problem is lack of life, not death. And lack of life only matters because of what we can do with it—life has no value in itself.'

'Life is sacred—you couldn't be more wrong.'

'We only desire life above all else because, without life, there *is* nothing else. And, obviously, this only matters from the perspective of the living. I still maintain that being dead, once it happens, is nothing to worry about. Because there's no one to worry about it.'

'Don't believe you. I'm convinced that something of me will continue after death.'

'I can't disprove that, but there really isn't any evidence that it does.' Lewis sighed. 'Why not get a life before death instead? As far as I am concerned we are just our bodies, complex beings perhaps, but purely physical ones.' I am most complex of all, he thought to himself, and even I will disappear completely before long.

'As you say, you can't disprove it. By definition, we can never know whether there is life after death until it happens. And I have faith.'

'Assuming you know anything about what happens after death is mere arrogance. Just like your inability to imagine a world without yourself in it.'

'Arrogance? That's rich, coming from you. And anyway, I can imagine the world without me in it. I can imagine the world before I was born, for example.'

'Of course you can't. Now you mention it'—he clapped his hands as if he had an idea—'if non-existence after death concerns you so much, why aren't you bothered by all those thousands of years that people were around and you weren't; before you were born?'

'I am quite bothered by that actually,' interrupted Ben. 'It's weird to imagine the world before I was thought of.'

'But that's different,' Conor said.

'Why?' asked Lewis. 'I thought you were arguing that the main problem with death, or being dead, is that it is a period of time in which you don't exist.'

'In which I *no longer* exist. It's not symmetric. Once I have been born there is a specific person who cares about dying. There wasn't before.'

'That's just my point.' Lewis ran his hand through his hair but it got stuck in the tangles. 'There will be no person who cares after you die. Ow.' He extracted his fingers.

'But there is one to care now.' Conor jumped up and down to prove he existed and cared about it. His belt rope flopped up and down.

'There nearly wasn't. Think how unlikely it was that *you* were born and not someone else.

80

Some slightly different timing, a different successful sperm, and your parents would have had another child, not you.' Now Lewis was winding him up.

Conor shuddered. 'I'm part of God's plan. I can't be so contingent.'

'I've learnt that one,' said Ben. 'It means . . . erm . . . well, when Max Salter used it, it meant that in some way that colour wasn't really in the T-shirt, but partly created by me and the light. Or something. It seems an odd way to worry about the meaning of life.'

'Contingent means it doesn't have to be this way: things could have been different,' said Lewis.

'And what if Dad hadn't gone to that party where he met Mum?' said Ben, worrying about his contingency.

Conor sighed overdramatically. 'Why should we strive for anything then, if we're all going to end as nothing?'

Lewis rolled his eyes.

'I mean,' Conor sighed again, 'what would be the point of it all? That's why there must be something more.'

Lewis picked his nose.

'Firstly, don't confuse the *end* of life with the *aim* of life. Life ends in death but it is directed to all sorts of goals along the way. Secondly, and more importantly, the fact that we will die is what gives our life meaning.' He examined his fingers and flicked something

81

green to the ground.

'Don't be ridiculous, Lewis.'

This did sound perverse. 'How can it be death that gives life meaning?' Ben said quietly.

'If not meaning exactly, then at least it makes it precious.'

Ben looked at him suspiciously.

'Look,' Lewis explained, 'because we don't have unlimited life, we have to make choices, which imply sacrifices. Being a concert pianist means not being an explorer. Being a surgeon means not being a fashion designer. With an eternity at our disposal we could do everything; the only decision we'd have to make would be what we did when. But the choice would be empty: if we're not choosing *between* options, why would we care about any particular person or project? The scarcity of life is what makes it valuable.'

'Everyone works better with a deadline,' said Lila flippantly.

Conor wasn't particularly comforted by this. 'But if you look at it from this bleak eternal and external perspective, we are no better than these butterflies that live for a few months and only know the inside of this hothouse. I want my life to be more meaningful than that.'

'You can always find a point of view from which your life is meaningless,' Lewis said. 'Luckily for us, we cannot maintain that perspective.'

'Humph.' Conor tried, and failed, to catch the tiny pink butterfly near his head.

'What is man?' asked Lewis. 'Nothing in relation to the infinite, everything in relation to nothing. Man is wonderful, creative, loving, evil, lazy, cruel, imaginative, boring . . . No wonder we can't stop taking ourselves seriously.'

'But,' Conor said, 'when I do something, I want it to have a purpose, a reason that will make it meaningful. Even cleaning my teeth has a purpose, which is to prevent toothache. As with the small, so with the large: I want there to be a purpose to my life, to all human life.'

'"I want" never gets, Conor. There is no such purpose. Your life can't be *for anything* in that sense. Personally, I can live without being as important to the universe as teeth-cleaning. Face it, if silly human activities matter at all, it's because they matter to humans. What other benchmark can there be? Why do you need external approval from God or Martians or people in three hundred generations?'

'So as not to feel pointless, like a butterfly.'

'What is the point of a butterfly?'

No one said anything.

'To make more butterflies, perhaps,' Lewis continued. 'And what's the point of those butterflies?'

'To make more butterflies?' suggested Ben, wondering how many life-cycles Lewis was planning to go through.

'So one butterfly is only important if all butterflies are important. And to butterflies—except the melancholy ones—butterflies are incredibly important.'

Lewis splatted a small white butterfly dead between his hands. The others gasped.

'That was a rare Costa Rican Snow Queen!' Conor said.

'Nah. Cabbage White. Common as muck.'

'Or, the importance of butterflies is to give us pleasure with their beautiful wings.'

'If that's so, then we need to ask: what's the point of *us*? Tell me, what would be so awful if the human species were wiped out?'

'What an obvious question.'

'You won't have any trouble answering it then.'

'No more human life!' said Ben.

'Ye-es, but why would that matter?' persisted Lewis. 'There would be no humans to mind.'

'There'd be no more technological development, no more works of art,' said Conor.

'But these things are only useful to and appreciated by *humans*. Imagine we didn't know in advance that we'd be wiped out so we wouldn't be upset about the prospect while we were alive, and we all die painlessly and suddenly. What would be so bad? The planet and other species would probably be better

84

off.'

Ben tried to think of something brilliant to say. It was obviously a bad thing. It just was.

'So you're saying we really are like butterflies then?' Conor said. 'But human consciousness and welfare and ideas and certain experiences are the most important thing. I can't imagine anything more important.'

'Of course you can't—you're human,' said Lewis. 'On the one hand wiping out humans is the worst thing possible—for us, of course. But from another point of view it's totally unimportant. I suppose what I'm saying is that we are like butterflies from one perspective, but that it doesn't matter.'

'It *does* matter.'

'Asking about the meaning of life is like asking about the meaning of carrots. They just are.'

'Humans are important to God. God would mind if we were all extinguished.'

'I imagine He would,' said Lewis, with a mocking smile. 'Of course, if you use the trump card "God" then this can give human life external meaning. But what if God doesn't exist? Or He does, but He's wasting his time? Being part of God's purpose only gives our lives meaning if we accept the importance of God's purpose. And if we don't, it doesn't help. What's the meaning of God?'

'*What?!*'

'What if it's just our human prejudice that we are the special chosen species? After all, if horses had hands, they would draw gods that looked like horses.'

Would the horses they drew have hands as well, or would they look like normal horses, with hooves? Ben wondered.

'It's perfectly obvious that we're the important species,' said Conor, giving Ben and Lewis a disgusted look. 'No other animal is capable of having this discussion. The horse doesn't think: I am a horse, and it's really terrible that one day I'll be dead. Its mind is not that complex.'

'Ah, how do you know?'

'Oh, please! Next you'll be saying that caterpillars build their cocoons out of a sense of architectural beauty.'

'Maybe they do.'

'I have,' said Conor through clenched teeth, 'an urgent appointment. Somewhere else. Goodbye, Ben.' He strode off, tunic swishing against the plants.

Lewis smiled triumphantly, but he looked lost without his opponent.

'We'd better be going as well,' Lila said to Ben. She stood up, scattering a host of pale-pink butterflies that had been resting on her shoulders.

She led Ben back through the butterfly house towards the door. He looked over his shoulder to catch a final glimpse. He saw

Lewis pick up a fat reference book from under the bench. With Conor gone, Lewis would secretly memorise the names of all the species in the hothouse.

Lila opened a door hidden behind some ferns, and they were back in the cool corridor. Ben wondered what was behind all the other doors. Perhaps he'd find out eventually. Soon they reached the main hallway by the door that led to the airing cupboard and his house.

'Thanks for coming,' Lila said, smiling.

Ben tried to think of something clever to say, so that he could stay a bit longer with Lila in the World of Ideas. 'Bye,' he said, all of a blank, stepping sadly towards the pile of towels.

CHAPTER TWENTY-TWO

'Ugh! What's wrong with these people?' said Wittgenstein. 'How can they keep asking such pointless questions? *What does it all mean?* Look, has this problem developed at all since you lot were thinking about it in Athens? Does anyone ever make any progress with this kind of philosophy?'

'It's not always about progress.' Socrates shook his head. 'Old ideas, yes, but new people to have them. A philosophical question is one that will be asked by each generation. Ancient

Greek drama, if we must call it ancient, remains meaningful now—as does our philosophy.'

'Didn't someone put you in a play once?' asked Wittgenstein.

'Aristophanes. *The Clouds*,' said Lila helpfully.

Socrates gave her a black look.

'It wasn't very flattering,' she added.

'No indeed,' said Wittgenstein. 'As I recall, he had you suspended in a basket, worshipping the clouds and sounding off about gnats' farts.' Wittgenstein uttered his bark-like laugh. 'Which all helps to prove my point that philosophy is not like art. Let us concentrate on the types of problems that can be solved— those about logic and language, for example. This, I've pretty much completed. We must stop bleating about the rest. Give philosophy peace from the questions that cannot be answered: What is good? What is the world really like? It's all so much babbling in baskets.'

'Whether they can be answered or not, these questions must be asked,' said Socrates. 'I will not give people peace. We must be flies—'

'Not again.' Wittgenstein held up his hands and backed away. 'The point of philosophy— the only point—is to *release* the fly from the bottle.'

'That might be your point—it isn't mine.'

'To provide solutions to certain questions and liberate the fly from having to ask them.'

'I don't want to be free from philosophy.'

'In this case, *I* am the fly. One should only attempt philosophy if one has a calling, a talent that can't be ignored. And if you don't'—he nodded in Socrates' direction—'in many ways that is a blessing. It allows you intellectual peace.'

Socrates wasn't much blessed with intellectual peace just at that moment.

'If deep thought is madness, God preserve me from sanity,' mused Wittgenstein.

'God certainly will,' Socrates said, as he and Lila left Wittgenstein alone with his genius.

CHAPTER TWENTY-THREE

The next day, Ben was in the garden, throwing balls for Whistle, who was part lurcher, part retriever, part something else, but all dog. Could Whistle worry about the meaning of life? He probably had no idea that he was going to die. Ben couldn't decide if that was a good or a bad state to be in. If Lewis Carnegie was right, knowing that life was short made you get on with it. On the other hand, Whistle would probably spend his last hours simply chasing tennis balls, if you gave him the chance.

Lewis had claimed that there was no way that death could be bad once it happened. So why was it the worst crime to kill someone? Why wasn't torture, or severely injuring someone, worse? The victim would have to live with the outcome. Perhaps murder was bad because of how it affected those left behind. But would they really rather have a badly injured and psychologically damaged torture victim to care for than to have to deal with the fact that the person had died? Ben didn't know how to answer these questions.

'Ow!' he shouted as a tennis ball hit him on the head.

'Oops. Sorry,' said Katie. 'I was just practising my serve. It's a bit out of control.'

'My guess is that your aim was right on target,' said Ben.

He went inside the house, feeling for a lump on his head.

CHAPTER TWENTY-FOUR

Ben decided to escape into the World of Ideas. Not that it was safe there, either—you might get hit on the head with acorns if someone didn't like your ideas. Happily, he discovered that once again the towels gave way at the back of the airing cupboard. He lunged through into the World of Ideas, landing at

Lila's feet.

'Ready for some more?' she asked.

'Nearly,' Ben said from the floor.

This time Lila stopped in the corridor in front of a door marked *Mind Over Matter*. He followed her into an orchard. She closed the door behind them and set off through the trees, as if there were nothing to be surprised about. Which, if you were her, there wasn't.

The ground was covered in dappled sunlight and apples that had fallen from the trees. It seemed to be autumn, although it had been summer that morning. Ben looked back to where they had come from but he couldn't see the corridor or the door, just more rows of trees.

'Now,' Lila explained, 'here is one of the greatest mysteries in philosophy. Indeed, one of the strangest contradictions in all of life. That which you feel closest to, your own private thoughts and experiences—what we might even call the essence of you—is one of the hardest things to understand or explain.'

'Do you mean that we don't understand our unconscious? Freud, or whatever? We want to have sex with everyone, but we don't want to want to have sex with them?'

Lila laughed. 'Something else. I mean what our thoughts and experiences actually are. What do you think the mind is?'

'Whatever's in my head?'

'Yes. Everything we might call "mental

experiences": sensations such as the taste of a chip or a horrible pain, a belief that you are called Ben, the desire to play football, feeling happy. All these make up the mind.'

'Seeing these apple trees, hearing you talk, wondering what I'm doing here.'

'That's it. In fact the mental encompasses lots of different types of things. A *belief* that snow is cold is not the same as *feeling* cold snow on your fingers. But nonetheless they all have something in common in being elements of the mind. The big issue, as you will see, is how they relate to the physical world of objects. In particular those special objects: bodies and brains. Is your mind something more than your brain or not?'

How could you answer a question like that? Presumably, Ben was about to find out.

They weaved their way through the gnarled old apple trees. Ben could hear strange noises: clanking, shuffling, grunting and shouting, which got louder as they came to a gap in the trees.

'En garde!'

'A hit!' The man removed his wire-mesh mask. 'That's 5–2 to me.'

His opponent took off his own mask and threw it crossly to the ground.

'If I could just get round your—Ah, hell-oo.' He scurried over. 'I'm Jack Cavendish—lovely to meet you.' He smoothed down his blond hair, which was sticking out all over the place without the constraint of the mask. The smoothing didn't make any difference, it being the wrong sort of hair. 'Call me Jack.' His cheeks were rosy from the exertion.

The other fencer came over more slowly, studying Ben through piercing blue eyes. He had a sharp nose and slightly receding dark hair. 'Oliver Whitby.' He offered his hand. 'It's an honour.'

'This is Ben Warner,' Lila said on his behalf, because he'd suddenly gone quiet.

Oliver's foil glinted in the sunlight.

'So, welcome, welcome,' said Jack Cavendish. He undid a series of buckles and flaps on his padded top and pushed down his long white socks. 'Er . . . where shall we start?'

'What have you talked about so far?' Oliver Whitby said in a businesslike manner. He loosened the collar a little on his fitted white jacket.

Ben looked at Lila. She nudged him. He whispered, 'We've, we've been talking about what the mind is. Mental experiences and stuff.'

'Ah, yes. The what-it-is-like-ness. It's wonderful.' Jack's eyes were shining.

'It is?' Ben wanted to find it wonderful too, but he wasn't absolutely sure what Jack meant.

'How my sensations feel to me, and yours to you,' Jack said gushingly. 'The pain of toothache, the sound of a trumpet, the smell of baking bread. Everything that makes it like it is to be you from the inside. That's the really extraordinary aspect of the mind.' He, and his hair, bounced with excitement.

'Right,' said Ben, feeling very special for having all these wonderful experiences.

'Any purely scientific explanation of molecules and electrochemical impulses just can't capture the experience of tasting chocolate,' said Jack. 'It's so obvious that there's more to the mind than the brain.'

'It's not at all obvious to me.' Oliver Whitby's tone was as sharp as his fencing foil. 'Not obvious and, worse still, wrong. There's nothing in this world but physical matter, and we have absolutely no evidence to believe otherwise.'

Jack parried back. 'No, no. I feel totally convinced that the essence of consciousness just must be something non-physical. It's not a brain blip: it's the smell of a rose!' Oliver gazed at him coldly, but Jack continued regardless. 'You could monitor the brain activity. You can "see" as much of that as you like, even point to which neurons fire when I see a sexy woman, but you can't observe from your scientific perspective what it *feels like* from my point of view, from the inside.'

Oliver Whitby gave a derisory snort. He picked up a fallen apple, tossed it into the air and sliced it in half with a swish of his foil.

Jack, unfazed, picked up a slice of apple, wiped it on his sleeve and munched it. He said, between bites, 'A deaf person could learn all there is to know about neuroscience, but they would never know what it felt like to hear a saxophone.'

Oliver stuck the point of his foil in the ground and turned to Ben. 'So what do you think?'

Ben found Oliver a bit scary, even now he had got rid of the sword. Ben tried to convince himself that nothing living inside the airing cupboard could be that frightening.

'Well, I hadn't really thought about it before.' He paused.

Jack looked at him expectantly. Oliver seemed as if he knew exactly what Ben would say and wasn't going to be impressed.

'But, I suppose—' Ben tried his best—'I feel that my mind must be something more than my brain. It's true that my thoughts do feel like something to me, and that makes them more special than a physical process like moving my arm or breathing.' Ben waggled his arm as a demonstration.

'An elementary mistake,' said Oliver Whitby. 'Don't worry, Jack has the same confused view, and he isn't the only one. But perhaps I can make you see what's wrong with it. The fact that it doesn't seem that way to us is not enough to believe it's not true; our intuition is wrong about all sorts of things. Think about bright-red.' Oliver gestured towards Lila's red trousers. 'That seems like a strong colour, not a radio wave of a certain frequency. And consider water.' He emptied the water bottle over Ben's hands, while Jack looked on thirstily. 'That does not feel like an enormous number of hydrogen-oxygen molecules jiggling around, but it is. My point is that we do not necessarily perceive the true nature of the world. Our thoughts may appear to be special mental things—whatever you can possibly mean by that—but this does not mean that they really are.'

'Maybe I can't assume that my view—the obvious one—is correct,' Jack said, 'but you haven't proved anything either. So I will continue to think that my mind is where "I" am, and that "I" am more than just my body and my brain, however complex they may be. Let us not attempt to doubt in philosophy what we do not doubt in our hearts. How can the lump of grey matter alone produce something that is aware of itself as a thinking person? My *soul* can't be physical.' Jack puffed himself up, as if being a bit taller would make his point more convincing.

'Jack, Jack,' Oliver, who remained taller, tried to mollify him, 'just wishing it to be true cannot make it so. Hunger is not bread. What sort of philosophy are you teaching this young man? One must question everything and believe only what there is good cause to believe. It would be nice to be convinced that our minds are something special, something not entirely material and therefore not governed by physical laws, indeed something that might last beyond the death of the body. But this is just a wish—childish superstition, nothing more.'

Jack Cavendish looked a bit taken aback.

'Tell me more about what sort of thing this non-physical mind might be,' Oliver said.

'Well . . . it would be sort of mental stuff.'

'Mental stuff?'

'Different from physical stuff. Obviously.'

'Obviously. Have you any idea what sort of stuff there could be that is entirely different from all the stuff we have handled so far? In the first place, if it has no physical properties then it can't have a location. How can it be nowhere?'

'It—'

'And clearly this "mental stuff"'—anyone would think there was a bad smell under Oliver's nose—'interacts with physical stuff?'

'Of course. Events in the outside world cause thoughts and sensations. Equally, a thought—such as a decision to make a phone call—can cause movement in the physical world: you move your arm and dial. So mental stuff must interact in both directions with physical matter.'

'How?' Oliver leant forward on a bent knee to stretch his thigh. 'The physical system of actions and objects is a closed, self-sufficient system. How can something "outside" it, like this crazy mind of yours, have any connection with the world?'

Jack looked less certain. 'I don't know.'

Oliver looked at him quizzically.

'We can't know, but it does.'

Oliver shifted round and stretched his other leg. 'Then your mental stuff doesn't really contribute anything to the explanation. We still need to understand what this mental substance is, how it is affected by the physical world and causes actions there. You have just moved the explanation to a different level, but you haven't really accounted for any of the strange aspects of mental states.' Oliver sniffed and pushed his elbows back, stretching his chest. 'Mental things really are different from the brain, you say?'

'Yes,' Jack said.

'So if you say, "I heard the phone ring and then I answered it," the "I" is different in each case. The mental-you hears the phone and the physical-you answers it.'

'Err . . .' Jack looked deflated.

'The only way around this is to say that the mind is the brain and no more,' Oliver concluded.

The two men glared at each other. It was as if they hadn't stopped fencing at all.

Ben glanced at Lila. She smiled encouragingly. 'So . . . er,' he said quietly.

'Mmm?' said Oliver.

'Go on,' said Jack kindly.

'I was just wondering . . .' Ben looked up from the floor and turned to Oliver. 'If you don't like what Jack's saying, what do you think the answer is?'

'Happy to oblige.' Oliver cracked his finger joints. 'Your mental life is just a peculiar perspective on the state of your brain. The thought that you will play tennis tomorrow is just a particular state of your neurons. Smelling a rose is just a particular electrochemical pattern in your brain.'

'That's it?' It was hard to imagine that thinking about this was just a complicated chemical reaction.

'Different combinations of synapses allow for more possible brain states than there are particles in the known world. You both accept that mental events are intimately related to brain states?' asked Oliver. 'Plenty of evidence for that—drugs such as antidepressants, alcohol and hallucinogenics can induce different mental experiences. Damage to a particular part of the brain can result in the loss of certain faculties, such as face recognition. So why not go the step further and admit that all your mental life is just the activity of your brain, and nothing else?'

'I never said that it didn't depend on the brain,' Jack protested. 'But why can't I assume that there are these other mental things, which are caused by—and cause—activity in the brain?'

'There is no "ghost in the machine",' said Oliver. 'There's just a machine. If you can find an adequate explanation that includes only one type of thing—physical, electrochemical impulses in the brain—then why extraneous talk of mental events if they don't really explain anything?'

'Ockham's razor!' Ben was excited. 'If two theories can explain the facts, always choose the simplest one.'

'That's it,' said Oliver, looking quite impressed.

'But your theory seems to leave out what Jack liked so much, the aspect of what something feels like,' Ben dared to say. 'It seems to me the most important bit of our minds.'

'Yes,' Oliver admitted, 'until science comes up with an explanation, it's hard to reconcile with our concept of what a mind is, but that's just our human prejudice. To take an example, think of our perspective on the world. We cannot ever seriously believe, at an instinctive level, that we live on the surface of a vast globe that spins at high speed through a vacuum. This is just not what we experience in our daily lives, but it is the true explanation. In the same way, we have a unique perspective on our brain activity—we experience it, say, as a sensation of the colour blue—but this doesn't mean that it isn't just a neural impulse.'

'You'll never convince me,' Jack said. 'Ben,

you need to think carefully before you accept Oliver's analogy of water not seeming like H_2O molecules when we touch it. In the water case, you can argue that there is a "true" nature of water, and how it feels when we swim in it or drink it is just a peculiar effect of the way *we experience water.*' He picked up the empty bottle and a few drops dribbled out. 'But in the world of our experiences themselves, you cannot draw the same line between how it seems and reality. *How it seems to us* is the whole point of an experience. Seeing blue is nothing without the sensation of seeing blue.' He looked at Oliver. 'I can't believe that you don't get this. Mental things are not the same as objects in this important way: a full account of a *sensation* of cold water must include *how it feels* to the person with his hand in it, even if an account of what water is can just talk about molecules.'

Ben looked at Oliver, but for the moment he was quiet.

Jack thrust home his advantage. 'Any physical explanation that ignores this part of the experience is leaving something out. It is as hard to work out how a physical process can produce conscious experience, in fact, as it is to find a place for mental stuff in the physical world.'

Oliver Whitby would not admit defeat. 'Maybe so, but that doesn't mean that physical stuff doesn't produce these experiences. We just can't explain how. Yet, I must stress two things.' Oliver addressed Ben, who concentrated hard on looking clever. 'Point one: just because something seems that way, doesn't mean it is. And point two: we must consider which explanation we have the best reasons for believing.'

'But physical matter can't be the whole story,' insisted Jack. 'You seem to think that the way it feels is just a side issue, not *the whole point of an experience.*'

'Maybe I do,' Oliver said, 'and anyway, what does it *feel like* to believe that today is Wednesday?'

Jack scrunched up his face. 'Touché.'

'Mmm? Beliefs like that are a crucial part of the mind. Or at least they should be. It's not all *smelling freshly cut grass . . . listening to drums . . . watching a sunset.* Most of our mental activity is knowing that Madrid is the capital of Spain, deciding to go for a walk, thinking that—'

'All right! But there's still that bit that you haven't explained. And it's absolutely crucial.'

Lila took Ben's arm. 'I think that's enough for now.'

Ben didn't know what to believe. He wanted them both to be right, and wrong, at the same time.

Oliver and Jack were glaring at each other.

Oliver broke the silence. 'Hope to see you again, Ben. Now, it was 5–2, remember, Jack?' He zipped up his collar, picked up his foil and waved it in a perfect figure of eight. 'Duellist v. dualist, eh?'

'You're not going already?' asked Jack, looking despairingly at Oliver, who was already practising lunges. Jack pulled up his socks and tied the laces on a shoe.

Lila led Ben back the way they had come through the trees. 'Bye, and thanks,' he called over his shoulder, but Jack was occupied with doing up the complex fastenings on his jacket, and Oliver couldn't hear him through his fencing mask.

'So?' Lila said.

'Phew. That was fun. I think. Interesting, anyway.' Ben kicked a fallen apple. It bounced satisfyingly off the tree that he'd aimed at. 'What did Oliver mean at the end?'

'Oh that. A dualist is basically someone, like Jack, who believes that mind and body are different; two things, a "duo". Oliver, on the other hand, prides himself on being a better fencer than anyone else.'

'And Oliver thinks that the mind is the brain—there's only one thing. So he's a unionist? Monoist?'

'Actually, he'd probably be called a *materialist.*'

'Oh.' Ben paused. 'Someone who likes shopping?'

'Meaning that everything is made of matter. That is to say that the mind is just part of the physical world. Or maybe you could say he's a

103

reductionist.'

Ben sighed. '*Meaning?*'

'A reductionist explains one thing in terms of another: a rainbow is nothing more than light refraction and prisms. The stripes of colour across the sky are irrelevant.'

'So, according to Oliver, all experiences can be explained solely in terms of brain processes. And he thinks that Jack still believes in the pot of gold at the end of the rainbow.'

'Yes, that's more or less it. Explaining the rainbow doesn't stop it existing, just makes us understand it differently.'

'But does it make it less beautiful?'

Lila shrugged. 'Some say yes, some say no.'

Ben's brain was hurting. Or was it his mind? He'd always thought that his mind was somehow something separate from his body, although obviously the brain was important. To be honest, he'd never really thought very hard about it. To imagine he was *just* his brain was really hard to do. But then he had just learnt that doing philosophy wasn't about believing what you had always believed, or even what you wanted to believe. It seemed that there was no good reason to claim that there was anything more than the brain. And yet, that couldn't be the full explanation, could it?

'What do you make of all this?' Ben asked Lila, as they walked back along the corridor.

Lila was tempted, but she remembered the

rules of the bet.

'I'm afraid you have to work out for yourself what to think. I can only help you understand some of the ideas. When you first do philosophy, you're at the mercy of any plausible argument. You'll realise that you're getting somewhere when you start to disagree. And, when you can produce good reasons for disagreeing, then you'll know that you're doing well.'

Ben couldn't imagine reaching that stage. 'I feel like I agree with bits of what both Jack and Oliver said. But they obviously disagree with each other, so . . .'

'You know, a few people have argued that the mind–body problem—that is, how the two aspects are related—is absolutely closed to human understanding. We can either see the inner "subjective" view, from awareness of our experiences; or the so-called "objective" view, from a scientific study of the brain. Unfortunately, they claim, we will not—cannot—ever connect the inner view with the objective view and see the truth about how things really are. Just as a badger most probably can't understand about molecules, so perhaps we are under-equipped to comprehend the link between the physical world and our consciousness. In which case there may be nothing mysterious about the answer in itself, except that we humans will always be in the dark.'

Ben felt depressed at the thought.

'You play football a lot,' Lila said, then checked herself. It wouldn't do to let on how much she knew about Ben's life. 'Do you like football at all?'

'Yes. Why?'

She picked up a football that just happened to be bouncing towards them. 'Imagine that the volume of the football is everything that you know. All the space outside the football is everything that you don't know.'

'I only know a football's worth of what there is to know?'

'Not to scale.'

'Possibly it is,' Ben said bitterly.

'Anyway, the surface area of the football is everything you know that you don't know. As the football inflates—that is, your knowledge expands—so does its surface area. Do you see? The more you know, the more you realise that you don't know.'

'Learning philosophy feels like that.'

'It's still a good thing to be aware of the scale of your ignorance. Socrates says it's the key to wisdom.'

'I'm not sure it's a good thing to be totally aware of my ignorance. It's pretty exhausting.'

In a panic, Lila looked at her watch. She knew that if Ben stayed too long on any one visit he might get trapped inside. Whilst that was fine in itself, it could impede future movement between the two worlds. If he got truly stuck, his family would be left with nothing more than a missing-person file. Much as Ben seemed to like visiting the World of Ideas, it wasn't fair to make him a permanent resident so young. Lila herself had arrived here far too soon, but there was nothing anyone could do about that.

Lila pushed Ben roughly through the door to the airing cupboard, grabbing his ankles. 'See you soon,' she called, as his feet disappeared.

Did she really mean see you soon? Ben wondered. In which case, why shove him away like a fat parcel through a narrow letterbox?

*　　*　　*

That night he dreamed about fencing. He was winning a convincing, crowd-pleasing victory over his friend Joe, who had never even thought about what happens in your brain when you see a sexy woman. Then Lila gave him an apple from the orchard and smiled. He woke feeling happy. He lay in bed, half-asleep, trying to understand how dreams could be nothing more than the workings of the brain. But they seemed so different. Of course, Oliver Whitby would say that it didn't matter how they seemed.

CHAPTER TWENTY-FIVE

Oliver and Jack had got Ben thinking, he realised, as he walked Whistle to the park. What was it like to be a dog? He knew that dogs had amazing hearing and smell compared to humans, but couldn't see as well as people. He tried to imagine what that would be like. It was really hard, of course. But then he realised that it wasn't hard, it was impossible. Ben was imagining what it was like to be himself with better hearing and smell, which wasn't the same at all. He couldn't escape from being human. The dog wouldn't think that it was strange to smell all these things that were beyond human noses. Being a dog was normal, for a dog. It was like an alien asking what it was like to be a human. If you had to ask, you'd never know. It couldn't be explained. Ben watched Whistle with admiration. 'What's going on in there, little friend?' Not much, it seemed, as Whistle began growling at a round predator, known to humans as a football.

'Ben! Want to play?' said Joe.

Ben tied Whistle to a tree and ran over to the others. The process inside his mind and body: outside movements happened, his brain organised them as sights and colours and sounds. This in turn created a decision to move (if it could be called a decision—it wasn't really conscious) and his body obeyed.

'Ben!'

'What's wrong with you, you were miles away.'

'No one's going to pass to you if you're asleep.'

The unexamined life might not be worth living, but the over-examined shot at goal wasn't up to much either. It is a truism that thinking and football players don't mix. Ben embraced an everyday perspective on the world, and scored with the next pass he got.

CHAPTER TWENTY-SIX

'Shall I explain it to you once more?' said Wittgenstein.

'Please do,' said Lila. They were waiting for Socrates. Lila was going to demonstrate how they could watch Ben on the monitors.

'The world is the totality of facts, and not things. It's all about logic. Propositions. But not unhelpful ones such as "This is good". You can't really analyse what that statement means.'

'No?'

'No! But then I changed my mind and came up with a much better idea.'

'Go on.' Lila started up the monitor system.

'You don't explain what "red" is by saying

that red is a colour, something of a certain category, you say, "This book is red." You have to show it, not say it. The meaning of a word is the way that it is used. Meaning does not come from a correspondence between a proposition and a fact. All this, of course, is an amazingly basic version of my insights, but you have to start slowly.' He looked at her pityingly. 'You've heard of my private-language argument, I presume?'

'Of course.'

'Explain it to me.'

'Er. Well, I'd love to hear your version. Direct from the philosopher's mouth.'

'Very well. The traditional view of language is that it describes a private experience: "I am in pain" is a public identification of a certain private sensation, owned by and only known to the possessor. Clearly such a language is unintelligible if the words are labelling secret things that cannot be shared. If this is the case then the rule for the use of words cannot logically be followed by another person. And it doesn't even make sense to the speaker. You cannot ask yourself "Am I in pain? Is this the right word?" If you know how to ask about pain then you know what pain is, and—'

'Sorry I'm late,' said Socrates, running breathlessly into the room.

'Ludwig was just explaining his work to me,' said Lila.

'Ah? Then I really am sorry I'm late.'

'As usual,' said Wittgenstein. 'Your trouble is that you want to sit on six stools at once but you've only got one arse.'

'So kind of you to point it out. This time my arse was positioned on the matter of reviewing the latest batch of applications.'

'Any good ones?' Lila was always keen to get new people into the World of Ideas.

Unlike Wittgenstein. 'Please don't tell me that Derrida man is coming.'

'We could hardly say no, could we?'

'Couldn't you?'

'I don't know why you want my job—you'd be hopeless at the administration,' Socrates said. Lila bit her tongue. 'Look, he's an important philosopher; people here are expecting him; applications are down lately—have been for a while, actually—and we can't afford to be choosy.'

'One can always afford to be choosy,' said Wittgenstein.

'Come and look,' said Lila, pointing at Ben on the screen.

CHAPTER TWENTY-SEVEN

Ben was sitting in the park with his friends after football practice. He held up the football. 'Imagine that the volume of this ball is everything you know. All the space outside it is everything you don't know.'

The others were looking at him as if he were mad.

'So as you learn more things, the ball grows and the what-you-don't-know space shrinks.'

Joe started to laugh.

'But,' Ben persevered, 'imagine that the surface of the football is everything that you know that you don't know. As your knowledge—the volume—increases, so does the surface. So the more you learn the more you realise you still have to learn. Part of true knowledge is understanding the extent of your ignorance.'

There was an embarrassed silence, broken by sniggers.

Ben knew what they were thinking. It made sense too: why wonder about the process of kicking the football when what mattered was whether you scored a goal? Who cared how a dog's mind worked as long as he didn't get lost? It wasn't as if philosophy made life easier. So far it was quite hard work. People in the World of Ideas understood. At least Lila didn't think he was an idiot for wondering about these things.

'The unexamined life is not worth living, by the way,' he said suicidally, and walked off, feeling like a prat. Maybe the examined life wasn't so great after all.

CHAPTER TWENTY-EIGHT

'See,' said Socrates, pointing at the screen, 'it's affected him. He's infused with philosophy. Like a tea bag.'

'Can't you see it's not working?' Wittgenstein said. 'He's swimming a lonely path.'

'You can't swim a path.'

'You can. But ideas are not tea bags.'

'Pedantic git.'

'Pompous old fart.'

CHAPTER TWENTY-NINE

Lila seemed pleased to see him the next day, which made a nice change from everybody else. And he was pleased to see her, which also made a nice change from everybody else.

'What are we doing today?'

'We're going ice skating.'

'Oh.'

'I thought you'd like it.'

'I do, I love ice skating, but I was expecting you to say, "Does God know He exists?" or something like that.'

Thousands of stars were twinkling above the ice. There was a sign telling everyone to skate anti-clockwise, but someone was resolutely skating in the other direction. This contrary behaviour was generating much abuse and a few crashes.

'By the way,' Ben asked, as they were lacing up their boots, 'what do you do here, when I'm not around?' That came out wrong. 'I mean, you surely can't talk about philosophy all the time.' He wondered if she had a boyfriend. Some famous philosopher, probably.

'Of course we don't just talk about philosophy. Well, quite a lot, but we do lots of normal stuff, obviously.'

There was nothing obvious about it. He hadn't seen much evidence of 'normal stuff' in the World of Ideas. 'Such as?'

'What do you do when you're not here?'

'Normal stuff, obviously.'

'Such as?'

'Never mind.'

Ben skated round the edge, quickly gaining confidence. He caught glimpses of Lila as she sped backwards and forwards. Then he heard shouting from the middle of the ice.

'I *do* exist! Of course I do,' a man in a green bobble hat was saying.

'Ah. You would say that,' said the man who had been skating in the wrong direction, 'but I choose not to believe you.'

'Then who are you having this conversation with?'

'Which conversation?'

114

'Argh!' Green-bobble-hat pushed wrong-direction, hoping that brute force would prove his existence where reason could not.

His contrary opponent crashed on to the ice and shrugged. 'Shit happens. Sometimes you just fall over.'

Bobble-hat skated away in despair: his knockdown argument had failed.

Ben hoped no one would push him over for saying the wrong thing. He tried to skate in a way that wouldn't attract attention.

Lila grabbed Ben with her soft cool hands and pulled him along. She skated elegantly backwards guiding Ben forwards behind her. His hands tingled where Lila had touched them.

'I've heard,' she said, 'that all mammals have the same number of heartbeats in their lifetime.'

'What?' Ben's right foot slipped, but he managed to stay upright.

'Well, an elephant lives much longer than a mouse. But since the mouse's heart beats much faster, it has roughly the same lifespan in terms of number of heartbeats. About 800 million.'

'Why does that matter?'

'Well, it affects their subjective view of time. A lifespan "seems" as long to both an elephant and a mouse, although the difference in years is huge, because creatures mark time by their heartbeats. Think of the passage of time like frames in a reel of film. Having a faster heartbeat is equivalent to being able to detect more frames per minute. If a mouse runs round an elephant then to the mouse it's just running, but to the elephant it's so fast that he can hardly focus.'

'And if the elephant's walking, then to the mouse he's hardly moving.'

Lila nodded. 'Which is very practical, since the mouse needs to keep out of the elephant's way.' She paused. 'That must be why it's so hard to swat a fly.'

'So a mouse sees life as a slowed-down film, and an elephant as a speeded-up one.'

'Yes, relative to us in the middle. But of course they wouldn't understand what you mean by "speeded-up", since that is just how they see the world.'

'Is it the same for humans?'

'It could be. When you're frightened your heart speeds up. And then time seems to slow down.'

'Gives you more time to react.'

'Not exactly. You have the same number of minutes. In terms of the objective, shared measure of time, nothing changes. But with more heartbeats per minute, it feels longer.'

'But if it feels longer then that's all that matters. That's what you need to react quickly to danger.'

'So should we measure time in heartbeats?'

'Yes. Well, no—that would be weird. I don't

know any more if time means the number of minutes or how it seems to us. Well, how it seems to us is obviously important: that's what the mouse-and-elephant story shows. But then everyone would have a different timescale and it would be chaos. We need some outside way of measuring time or we could never catch a train.'

'True. Minutes and hours are very useful conventions.'

Ben watched Lila disappear into the throng and braced himself to skate alone. He sympathised with the elephant as he watched the other skaters whizzing past him like giant speedy mice.

CHAPTER THIRTY

Matty was pretending she was in a music video.

'That's so lame,' said Ben.

'Yo!'

He snatched his baseball cap off her head. She'd been wearing it sideways.

She stopped singing. 'I'm *bored*. Bored bored bored bored BORED.'

Ben remembered something that he'd heard in the World of Ideas. 'The cure for boredom is curiosity. But there is no cure for curiosity.'

Matty stared at him. 'You're pathetic.'

'Supper's ready,' said his mum.

'Spinach,' she announced as they all sat down.

'Ugh.'

'Carrots, and cabbage.'

'Ugh. Ugh.'

'Don't be silly,' his mum said. 'How else will you get your five portions of fruit and vegetables?'

'I had some chips at lunchtime,' said Ben.

'Potatoes don't count.'

'Why does spinach make your teeth furry?' asked Matty.

'How come potatoes don't count? Where does it say five portions a day of fruit and vegetables, except potatoes?'

'What makes it a vegetable *in biology* is not the same as in magazine articles which tell Mum what to tell us to eat. It's a different kind of vegetable-ness,' Katie said.

'Don't be a smartarse, Katie,' his mum said. 'It's unattractive.'

'I read in the paper that it's gone up to eight portions of vegetables,' his dad said.

'Eight? Let them eat chips.'

'You know how food tastes horrible after you've cleaned your teeth?' Ben said.

'I hate cleaning my teeth,' said Matty.

'They'll all fall out and you'll be an ugly old bag,' said Katie, effortlessly driving her sister to the brink of tears.

'The thing is,' Ben persisted, 'it's a question

of how much of the taste is in the food, and how much is created by you when you eat it.'

His family looked blank. He can't have been explaining it very well. These ideas were amazing—everyone had to learn about them. Ben had forgotten that a couple of weeks ago, his reaction would have been the same.

He tried again. 'If I put my finger in this mashed potato'—Katie and Matty laughed—'then it feels warm.'

'Stop playing with your food,' his mum said.

'OK. Think of it like this.' Ben got up and went to the freezer. 'If I had just eaten some cold ice cream'—he spooned some raspberry ripple into his mouth—'then the potato would feel very hot.' He ate some potato and it really did feel too hot after the ice cream. The combination was also pretty disgusting, but Ben didn't let that put him off his stride. 'And if I had just drunk a fresh cup of tea then the potato would feel cold.'

'Don't talk with your mouth full.'

'What's your point exactly?' asked his dad.

'Well, it shows that to some extent the property of temperature is affected by what we bring to the potato as someone having the experience, and not all about the potato.'

'Why can't you just say, "This is delicious"?' his mum said.

119

CHAPTER THIRTY-ONE

Ben woke up early and sat bolt upright. The chips! After four visits they still hadn't told him the answer to that problem. What if chips taste different to everyone and we never knew?

He had to go back and ask. But was he allowed to visit whenever he wanted? He'd got in several times already but maybe he couldn't just turn up. He sent Lila an email.

It was nearly an hour before she replied:

Dear Ben
Thanks for your email. Of course we should talk about the chip problem— good that you asked. Before you come, though, try and work out what you think about it. The question to consider is whether my personal internal experience of looking at a clear blue sky, for example, is the same as yours. Why might we assume it is and what if it isn't? What do we actually mean when we say 'I see blue'?
See you soon,
Lila x

She'd put 'x' at the end!

Socrates had said that it was more

important to think clearly than to know the answer. Right. So, why wouldn't two people see the same thing when they looked at a blue sky? Unless one of them was colour blind. They wouldn't both call it 'blue' if they were seeing something different.

Then again they might see all blue things as being one colour, and call them blue like the rest of us, but might see them differently from the inside. If they used the right word—'blue'—then we would never know! Ben felt he'd got somewhere with this thought, even if he was only describing the problem. Still, that was how philosophy worked, he told himself authoritatively.

Thinking like this had made him hungry. But why was muesli so difficult to eat quickly? He'd been eating for ages but his bowl wasn't getting any emptier. He was due to mull over how we experience things: no time to chew oats and raisins. Ben left the half-empty bowl in the sink and ran to the airing cupboard.

'What's the rush?' his dad said.

'Rush?' How could he explain about the World of Ideas?

'You're running up the stairs like a loony.'

You might think philosophy would make you more imaginative, but he couldn't think of a single thing to say. 'Got to go.' Brilliant.

Ben sauntered round the corner as casually as he could manage and waited for the sound of his dad going into the bathroom.

The coast was clear! He climbed into the airing cupboard.

CHAPTER THIRTY-TWO

'Ouf!'

Lila helped him up. Would he ever get the hang of emerging with dignity? It wasn't something he'd ever needed to practise before.

This time Lila didn't set off towards the corridor, but opened one of the entrance-hall doors instead.

'I thought we'd go to the café and chat,' she said.

Palm trees and cream- and pastel-coloured buildings flanked the wide avenue.

'The meaning of a statement is the method of its verification!' squawked a large blue-and-orange parrot perched on a fountain.

'Religion is the opium of the masses!' screeched a green parrot.

A man with a cheeky moustache and a goatee beard bowed and kissed Lila's hand, winking at Ben. 'Bonjour, Mademoiselle Lila.'

'Bonjour, René.' She was blushing.

Ben rolled his eyes. 'Who was that?'

'René Descartes.'

'He thinks therefore he is?'

'Brilliant. He's so handsome, don't you think?'

He's slimy, Ben thought, but kept quiet: contradiction wasn't always encouraged, even in the World of Ideas. Lila could fancy anyone she wanted, for all he cared.

'And'—Lila's eyes were shining—'he invented co-ordinates.'

'What?'

'You know in maths, when you plot things on a graph, you have the x and y coordinates: so much along and so much up? These two numbers will give you the precise position on the page.'

'I know.' Ben remembered lots of boring lessons measuring graph paper.

'Well, Descartes invented that method. That's why they're called Cartesian coordinates.'

'Is that what they're called? It seems so obvious.'

'It is, once you've heard the idea.'

They sat down at a table on the terrace, next to some people speaking Latin.

Ben looked at the menu:

Eggs (fried, poached, scrambled); eggs and beans; eggs, beans and chips; eggs, mushrooms, beans, chips, fried bread. Any of the above with sausage. NO OTHER combinations available.

He'd never been in such an elegant greasy spoon. The inhabitants of the World of Ideas liked to feel classy, but they had cheap tastes at heart.

'I assumed you didn't get chips over here,' he said, remembering Lila's desperate behaviour in Cod Almighty.

'Oh not proper chips. The food here all tastes the same. The only difference is in the texture.'

'But—' Ben was distracted by a commotion at the door. A man with curly dark hair and a black beard was shouting aggressively and waving his arms.

'I'm sorry, sir, beans are a popular dish. We can't take them off the menu just because you have a problem with it.'

'But it's evil.' The man, immaculately dressed in a white linen suit, wailed in frustration. 'Cannibal!' he shouted at a customer, who covered his plate with a piece of toast.

'Poor love,' said a jolly woman. 'We have this nearly every day.'

Ben turned to Lila. 'What on earth was that about?'

'That was Pythagoras.'

'The triangle guy?'

'Yes, among other things. He has lots of brilliant ideas, and some wacky ones. He claims that the souls of dead people grow in beans.'

'You're not serious?'

'Very. One day when he was being chased by

a hostile crowd, he let them catch him rather than trample a bean field.'

'I didn't realise philosophy was such a dangerous business in Ancient Greece.' Ben made a face.

'Do you want to know the specials?' asked the jolly woman standing at their table.

'Why not?' said Lila.

'Of course it all depends what you mean by "know". You may suppose that the special today is carrot soup, but—even if it is carrot soup—this isn't knowledge as such. You'd have to have spoken to the chef to know, rather than guess, that the special was carrot soup. Now, you couldn't possibly know that the special today is carrot soup, because to know something it must be true. And today it's mushroom soup.'

'I'll have a mixed juice,' said Lila, winking. 'Ben?'

'Actually, I'm not thirsty. Anyway, I've been thinking about the question.'

'Great. And?'

'Well . . .' He felt pleased with himself. 'I've had some ideas. We assume the "inner" experience is the same for every person. We don't normally think about whether blue looks different to different people, do we? I think the reason we don't question it is because we could never know. I mean, you can't see what I see. Or rather you can see the same sky, but we can't check *how* you see the same sky. Um

. . .' It was difficult to be as precise as you were supposed to be in philosophy. Surely Lila knew what he meant? Ben waved his hands to suggest that there were lots of good ideas lurking behind his words.

'You can never experience my "inner blue" because if you did it would be your "inner blue" and not mine?' Lila offered.

'Yes.' At last, someone who really understood him.

'And we assume that the experience of blue in different people matches, because it is caused by the same thing in the outside world—the sky—and because all people have more or less the same physical construction. It seems reasonable to assume that we would all have very similar sensory experiences in the same circumstances. Although we do know that people prefer different colours and foods, so maybe they can experience things differently.' Lila waved at the waitress, who brought a drink over to their table. 'Here, taste this.'

Ben sipped cautiously: you couldn't be too careful in the World of Ideas. The drink was so disgusting that Ben almost gagged when he swallowed. Lila drank down the rest of it without flinching.

'How could you?'

'There's this stuff called phenol-thio-urea—which tastes incredibly bitter to about a quarter of people, and of nothing to the rest.

So it's not implausible that people have different inner experiences caused by the same outward stimulus.'

'I certainly know which category I'm in.' Ben snatched the toffee that Lila offered him to take away the taste. 'The thing is,' he said, sucking the sweet, 'now I've realised that we might have different experiences, it seems weird. We might all see, smell, hear and taste the world in our own special way. We can't compare our inner feelings directly.'

'And comparing other outer things doesn't solve it. We might all agree'—she pointed at the tablecloth—'that we call this "blue" because it looks like other "blue" things. But how do you know that all blue things don't look to you like "orange" looks to everyone else?' The tablecloth suddenly became orange.

'I'd still talk about it in the same way, wouldn't I?' Ben felt worried now. Maybe he was missing out on something that everyone else, except him, could experience. 'It doesn't get us very far, though, if we say it might be different but we could never tell. If it really doesn't make a difference then it, well, it doesn't make a difference.'

Lila nodded. 'Good point. However, there is a way in which it makes a difference. I'll give you an example. What do we mean when we say, "I see blue" or "I taste chocolate"?'

'I suppose we mean that we have a certain feeling: a blue-type thing, or a chocolate taste.'

127

'That's what most people assume. And it makes sense—we use the words "I see blue" when the sensation of seeing blue happens to us. But if, as we're speculating, the blue experience is different for each of us, then the word "blue" means something different to each person: because we each attach it to a different inner feeling.'

'Can that be right? That would be confusing.'

'Wouldn't it just? Some people might accept that "blue" means something different to everyone, that it's a private concept. But others say that this is ridiculous: a language is useless without general agreement about meaning. That's what words are for: they work because we all use them to refer to the same thing. Asking you to get the butter is no good if we don't both call it "butter".'

'So how do you solve it? I mean, it isn't meaningless when we talk about "blue", is it?'

'Well, some people claim that seeing blue has what is called a "functional" relationship to the world and other mental states. To take an example, "smelling bacon cooking" doesn't mean having an experience that *feels* like a certain thing, it simply means the experience that's caused by bacon cooking, which causes you to want to eat bacon and to say, "Is that bacon ready yet?"'

'What's the difference between that and saying that "smelling bacon" refers to the smell itself?'

'Well, according to this theory, the defining feature of a mental state is not how it feels from the inside, but its relationship to these other things—objects (bacon), beliefs (there is bacon), actions (asking for bacon). There *is* something that it feels like to smell bacon, but this just helps you identify that you are smelling bacon and to talk about it. It is not what it *means* to smell bacon.'

'Surely smelling bacon is exactly what it means to smell bacon?'

'You might think so, but not everyone does. It's a neat solution to the problem that otherwise we can't speak properly about inner matters.'

'I think I see. But does it makes a difference? Do I have to choose between them?'

'You do really, and here's how it makes a difference.'

Lila paused as a short, pale man with a pointy nose and a sour mouth approached the table next to them. On spotting Ben and Lila, he scowled and moved away.

'Not at your usual table, Mr Kant?'

'*No*,' he said, gesturing with his cane and turning his back.

Lila checked her watch. 'Bang on!' she said, shaking her head in amazement.

'What is?'

'Immanuel Kant,' she whispered. 'He's so

129

regular with his morning stroll and coffee that you can set your watch by it. I always think I might catch him out but it never happens.'

'Why didn't he want to sit near us?'

'He doesn't ap—No reason really.' Immanuel Kant was completely opposed to the bet on moral grounds, and thought Ben should have been left alone, and also that it wasn't healthy to consort with the living. So Lila couldn't very well explain. 'Where was I? Yes—the difference between the two meanings for "seeing blue". If we all experience the same thing when we look at a cloudless sky, then it doesn't matter. But what if you experience "orange" in circumstances that cause everyone else to see "blue"? We have agreed this might be possible. So, would you want to say that you were seeing blue or orange when you look at the sky?'

'Blue. No, orange. I don't know. So if I believe that the inner state is important, I have to say orange.'

'Yes, and if you prefer the functional explanation then you are seeing blue.'

'OK. Both seem a bit disappointing. I mean, if I say "blue" then I'm ignoring the fact that it feels different for me. That the experience is what everyone else calls "orange". And that has to matter.' Ben thought some more. 'And if I say "orange" and everyone else says "blue" then we can hardly start talking together about the colour of the sky at all. If a word does

130

mean something different for everyone, that's silly. I hadn't realised it was this complicated.'

'And that's the answer to the chip problem,' said Lila.

'That's not an answer.'

'OK, perhaps not. It's a way to think about the question. Then you can decide which explanation you prefer.'

'How—what's that noise?' He looked out of the window.

'Who's that?'

'Plato.'

'He's here?' Ben had heard of Plato. And now he'd seen his sports car, he was even more impressed.

'Can I meet him?'

The car revved loudly and zoomed off with a screech of tyres.

'I wouldn't bother. He's very full of himself. He wanted to run the place as some kind of utopian republic, but his ideas were very unpopular. He was insufferable for ages when he couldn't have his own way. Less than a Platonic Ideal, you might say. Ha ha.' Lila punched Ben playfully. 'Well, perhaps you wouldn't say, but the point stands: you won't learn anything from him these days.'

'What is a Platonic Ideal?'

'Actually, it's got nothing to do with behaving well. The Platonic Ideals, or Forms, are the perfect example of each type of thing: a paradigm. So an object is an apple if it

131

resembles the paradigm form of "apple". And a red apple gets its redness from the ideal form of "red". We never experience these ideals of "red" or "apple" directly, we just perceive an example. However, Plato thinks that you can have knowledge of these ideal forms through philosophical thought.'

'Only through philosophy?' These people really rated themselves.

'For most people, it is as if they have been chained in a cave since birth. They see shadows on the cave wall and believe this is reality. But reality is what produces the shadows: the forms outside the cave. The philosophically enlightened few, however, know about the real world outside the cave.'

'What a weird idea.'

'Actually, Plato and Socrates had a big falling out. You see, Socrates had been a sort of mentor to him. And so Plato wrote a very moving account of Socrates' death—made him seem much more noble than he really was. But afterwards, Plato destroyed everything that Socrates had written—'

'No way!'

'Yes! That's why none of Socrates' original philosophy survives. Plato re-wrote it himself with Socrates as a character.'

'You can't just use Socrates as a character in a book!'

'As the ideas that Plato wrote for Socrates got sillier and sillier, he got more and more annoyed with Plato. When Plato finally arrived in the World of Ideas, Socrates gave him a real earful. So he said, anyway. They made up later.'

'Are all the big philosophers here?'

'More or less.'

'Will I meet famous ones—I mean, apart from Socrates and . . . er . . .'

'Wittgenstein.'

'Apart from them?'

'No.'

'Really? Aren't I important enough?'

Too important, thought Lila. Ben had no idea that he would decide the future of the World of Ideas. 'It comes down to this,' she said. 'If you were to meet, shall we say, an established philosopher, they'd just want to tell you about their favourite theory. "If you want to know about free will, I'd advise you to read my book": that sort of thing. You're much better off starting with a general introduction.'

'OK.'

Ben had enjoyed his discussions so far. He probably wouldn't have understood the great philosophers anyway, which would have annoyed them. It didn't seem to take much to annoy a philosopher.

'By the way, can I borrow some of that bitter stuff?' he said.

CHAPTER THIRTY-THREE

How were you supposed to work out which fish was 'first in'?

Tony poked his head round the cold-room door. 'Louise from Quick Getaways next door gave me some old travel posters. I thought we could put them up to cover the chipped tiles. Do it now, will you? There's Sellotape somewhere in the office.'

Ben found the Sellotape under the sofa. Work wasn't the pleasant change from school he'd expected. He still had to turn up on time, five days a week, talk to people he didn't particularly like, and do what someone else told him to do.

He stuck up a picture of Gran Canaria (*Discover the difference!*) next to the window, then another on the tiles by the drinks fridge: *Greece: Pure History*. He thought of Socrates.

There was, at least, one important difference between work and school. With £3 an hour, Ben could buy things—admittedly not much. This meant that other people also had to go to work: to make and sell the stuff that he wanted to buy.

What if people just held on to their money, instead of pointlessly moving it round and creating other jobs? If other people didn't earn money then they wouldn't be able to pay for fish and chips, and Ben wouldn't have to serve them. Then he could play the guitar or go to the beach all day. If other people were earning money, then Ben needed some too—this was how the world worked. But if everyone stopped, people could just swap things when they got bored. Yes!

He taped Mickey Mouse over a large brown-sauce stain on the counter and went back to the cold store.

'Hello.'

Ben jumped back and hurriedly pushed the door shut. He opened it a few inches and peered into the dark.

'Hello?'

'Sorry, didn't mean to scare you. No need to shut me in the freezer though,' said Lila.

'No need to *be* in the freezer.'

'Actually, yes. I had to come and get you—there's a special event. Follow me.'

Ben would have followed Lila to . . . well, at least into the cold store.

'Leave the door propped open so you can get back in.'

CHAPTER THIRTY-FOUR

'Today,' said Lila, 'we're having a symposium.'

'What's that?'

'It was a Greek drinking party. From syn

135

(with), and posis (drinking).'

'Are we going to the pub?'

'Not exactly. It all started off—' Lila waved her hand—'thousands of years ago, as a convivial meeting where people would get together to have a few drinks, do some chatting. There was once a Symposiarch who would decide how watered-down the wine should be—depending on whether the focus was debate or, well, drinking. Over time, however, some did more chatting than drinking. Then after a while those who were doing more listening than chatting stopped drinking and did more talking. And in time everyone was so busy talking that they forgot about the drinking. And the dancing girls.'

'Dancing girls?'

'Well, no. Not any more. At least not the symposiums that I'm invited to.'

'Ah.'

'Basically, our symposium is a discussion forum that happens here every so often. Actually, "discussion" might be overstating it. Everyone gathers in the large hall and then each person has one minute to give their opinion.'

That didn't seem very much. What would he say in one minute? But, on the other hand, what would he say if he had to talk for an hour?

'What's it about today?'

'Happiness.'

'I didn't realise that being happy was a philosophical issue.'

'Anything can be a philosophical issue. Art, music, the news, right and wrong, God, jokes, even sex.'

Ben could feel himself blushing, which wasn't fair. He hadn't even been thinking about sex. Well, she had been the one who mentioned the dancing girls.

Lila led Ben into a large auditorium. They found some seats near the back with a good view of the speaker. The crowd was applauding Socrates at the lectern. Wittgenstein was nowhere to be seen.

Socrates waved for silence. 'Since the best way to have a good idea is to have lots of ideas, we're going to do just that. The US Declaration of Independence cites three inalienable rights: to life, liberty and the pursuit of happiness. Can I sue if you make me unhappy? What is happiness anyway? And so, over to you. The usual rules apply. Please welcome our first speaker.'

A nervous-looking young man in a shirt and tie approached the podium. There were cheers and claps and also some hissing. Once the crowd was quiet a man at the side of the stage turned over a sand-timer and banged a large goat-bell—still attached to the goat, who bleated its assent.

'What do you most want in the world?' the speaker began, adjusting his tie. 'What do you most want?' he repeated, growing in confidence. 'To be a successful musician, perhaps, or a renowned philosopher?' The audience laughed knowingly. 'But is that really what you most want? So much so that you would sacrifice relations with your family, or your health? Sometimes what you most want in the whole world is for your agonising earache to stop. What does this show? That there is no *one thing* we want most in the world, except happiness. Why do you value friendship? Because it makes you happy. Why do you value financial success? Because it makes you happy. Happiness is the only thing that is valued for its own sake. Happiness trumps everything! It is a simple fact that happiness is everyone's aim and yet, paradoxically, we can only reach it by aiming at anything except happiness—by seeking whatever it is that will provide it. Searching for happiness itself is the most unhappy pursuit of all.'

A loud klaxon noise filled the hall, marking the end of his time. The young man left the podium, waving. There was some scattered clapping.

'Next!' came a shout, and a glamorous woman wearing lots of jewellery came forward. The adjudicator turned over the timer again and chimed the goat bell.

'Sometimes what you want most in the whole world is indeed that your earache should stop. At that moment nothing could make you happier than the pain disappearing. And what does *this* show? That happiness can Never Be Achieved.' She jabbed her finger at the crowd, her bracelets rattling. 'If what you want most is for your ear to stop hurting, then you imagine you will be gloriously happy when it does. And you are, for about ten minutes—until you *forget* how bad the pain was. Now what you want is a glass of wine, or a jam doughnut—this is what will make you happy. Or you want to be seduced by your next-door neighbour, or win an Olympic medal. Since we always want something, actually getting it doesn't satisfy us. Some might counter that happiness is not achieving our goals, but striving for them. But desperately hoping for earache to stop or craving something we haven't got makes us miserable, not happy. Therefore we can never be happy, except for fleeting moments before the next craving arrives. Happiness is entirely—'

Honk honk. Time was up.

'—unobtainable. It is a myth—'

Honk honk honk honk. The adjudicator waved the woman off the stage. Rules were rules. 'Next speaker please!'

A man in a badly-fitting suit and a lopsided tie walked up to the podium. He was going for the crumpled-linen look—in grey rayon. He jangled his keys in his pocket as he waited for the crowd to be quiet.

'Good to see so many of you here, albeit that the opportunity cost of time for the dead is negligible. I hear it said that happiness is to be valued above all things. This is true in a purely trivial sense. Obviously what we choose in life is what we most want, given economic and social constraints.' He adjusted his glasses. 'By revealed preference, our actions demonstrate what it is we most value. Evidently, you do what you most want to, otherwise you would do something else. And thus to call what we most value "happiness" makes it an empty concept. Therefore'—there were gasps from the audience—'given that we are rational and after our best interests, it follows automatically that we act according to our preferences and make ourselves as happy as possible. As such—'

The gasps grew to shouts and some laughter.

'It's an economist! Who invited him?'

'Get out!'

The adjudicator squeezed the horn hurriedly and another assistant ushered the speaker out of the back door. The speaker allowed himself to be nudged offstage by the goat.

A wise-looking old man, his long white hair shoved up under a baseball cap, was already standing on the podium, smiling serenely at the crowd.

'The world of the happy man is utterly

different from that of the unhappy one. Happiness is a skill. Anyone can be content, but the faculty to realise it is deficient in most of us. Don't pursue it—embrace it. It is a mistake to think that happiness is something that you deserve but lack. Many good things are just the absence of bad things—health, security and freedom are fine examples—and we are not experienced at appreciating what is lacking. Happiness is the state where we don't want anything to be different, therefore if we accept things as they are, we can let ourselves be happy. Decide to be happy and you will be. The smallest things can bring happiness if we let them. A piece of bread can give more pleasure to a hungry man than any luxurious banquet to a man sated. You can choose happiness or you can fruitlessly search for it.' He leant forward gravely. 'Although, since happiness is a skill, it is inevitable that some will have a greater talent for it. Happiness might be just a matter of luck, a gift for some, denied to others. But anyone can do better with practice.'

Honk.

Was that it? Ben wondered. Happiness was just a matter of deciding that you were happy? He'd better start practising, in that case.

'Next!' called the adjudicator, 'and silence please in the audience.'

It was Lewis Carnegie from the butterfly house. He'd put on some shoes, although he still hadn't brushed his hair. The timer was turned, the goat-bell was struck.

'The most fundamental element of happiness is unhappiness. Happiness is a complex, mixed emotion. People often prefer things that give them pain rather than pleasure: that is why we choose love over mere sexual gratification, the hard truth over ignorance. To demonstrate my point, assume a society structured to ensure that all life is pleasurable and gratifying. In this Brave New World there are no physical hardships, no hunger, tiredness, desperation. Pleasure, comfort, ecstasy are only meaningful through contrast. We can have no satisfaction if we haven't previously endured a lack. I reject lazy contentment: boredom is the death of happiness. I want suffering so that I may truly be happy. The right to pursue happiness? Let us preserve the right to be miserable. For without unhappiness, happiness is meaningless.'

Could that be true? That happiness was nothing unless you experienced unhappiness to compare it to? It sounded mad to think that misery was an important part of being happy, but it made a strange World-of-Ideas kind of sense.

Socrates was back at the podium. 'And now it is my great honour to present to you a very, *very* special guest, visiting from our Eastern Branch. No doubt you've all guessed who it is.

Big welcome for Siddhartha Gautama.'

There was an enthusiastic murmuring from the crowd and some clapping as the guest came on to the stage. He was wearing white flowing robes with an orange sash.

'It's Buddha,' whispered Lila.

In person? Ben couldn't believe it. He didn't look anything like those fat gold shiny smiley statues. He was skinny and serious.

Buddha approached the lectern and patted the goat, who wiggled and rang its bell to mark the start of the minute. He smiled at the crowd, closed his eyes and stood in silence for what seemed like ages. The audience was silent too. Buddha opened his eyes.

'If we can rid ourselves of all desire then there will be no sorrow. The path to enlightenment and eternal peace is eight-fold. Right opinion, right resolve, right speech, right conduct, right—'

The klaxon interrupted noisily.

Buddha shot the horn-squeezer a dirty look.

'Sorry, didn't mean to interrupt.'

'As I was saying,' Buddha continued, ignoring the rules, 'the noble eight-fold path.' He paused to milk the moment. 'There is also right conduct, right employment, right thought and right contemplation. And if you weren't all in such a rush, I'd tell you what these involved. Good day to you all.' He bowed and walked off the stage.

'Lovely,' said the adjudicator. 'Err . . .

lovely, lovely. On with the next speaker. One minute only, if you please.'

It was Conor Shaw.

The goat had escaped its rope. The adjudicator chased it round the stage before giving up on the bell and squeezing the horn instead.

'The only way to happiness is through God. There is no "fulfilment" on purely human terms—just pathetic self-gratification. How can life be meaningful without an external, eternal purpose? Happiness is to be found in living according to God's word and performing His will. Happiness in this life is a distraction, to divert weak men from the true happiness to be found in an afterlife with God.'

'Heaven is the ultimate hedonistic possibility,' came a shout.

'Why fabricate a sense of meaning in your life,' Conor Shaw continued, 'when there is one readily available in God?'

Two people on Conor's side had set on the heckler, fists flying.

Now his cause was boosted by several supporters. 'You can't get away with that, you bastard,' one shouted, pulling his opponent's jumper.

'Happiness is not about pleasure, but *good*,' yelled Conor. 'Come on! Hit him back. *Hit back!*'

The honk announcing the end of the minute instigated a temporary truce. Some agnostics put themselves in the middle to keep the sides apart.

A man with bright-blue eyes approached the stage. He was losing his hair but was still young and handsome in a funny-looking way. The goat bleated.

'There is a myth that having greater wealth and more success will make us happy. Deep down, everyone knows it is a myth. Yet we still long for these things, and think that we will be the exception to the rule. But I'll tell you why more doesn't make us happier.' He put his hands on the lectern. 'Your absolute level of wealth or success is irrelevant. What matters is how we compare to those around us. In the evolutionary world, we selected the best option available to be our mate. When everyone is better off and has more wild boar to eat, you will still select the best of the bunch. The way to be selected is simply to be doing better than everyone else, no matter the average standard. People offered a pay rise of 5 per cent, in circumstances where no one else gets a rise, prefer it to receiving a pay rise of 10 per cent when everyone else gets 15. Reading articles about luxury hotels that we can't afford makes us sick, although it shouldn't affect us whether or not such hotels exist. We are conditioned to prefer *relative* to *absolute* success, provided we have enough to avoid cold and hunger. Give everyone in the street a better car and no one feels better. Give one man a better TV and he is definitely happier.'

Honk. 'Next contributor, please.'

A man in a patterned shirt stood up. His hairline was receding but his sideburns flourished. The crowd were booing and cheering in equal measures.

'Is he famous or something?' Ben asked Lila.

'John Stuart Mill? He's quite well known. And, to be fair, he has never shirked the attention. He likes to think of himself as the authority on happiness, among other things. They say he could read Ancient Greek by the age of three. He was a late starter with Latin— couldn't read that till he was eight.'

'No way!'

'Shush,' said the man next to him.

'What is happiness? Quite simply it is pleasure and the absence of pain. And when I say pleasure'—he raised his voice over the braying crowd—'I do not mean just base pleasures. If you think the pursuit of pleasure involves ignoble instincts then it says more about your view of pleasure than mine.' There was a roar of agreement. 'What matters is the quality of the pleasure, as well as the quantity. One can recognise a higher pleasure because any person who has experienced both will prefer it. This is why philosophy is superior to playing fruit machines. It is obvious that some kinds of pleasures are more desirable than others. Pleasures of intellect and imagination

146

are above those of mere sensation. Contentment is the enemy of happiness because it prevents us from trying to achieve greater pleasures, which are more fulfilling but harder to reach. Those with a lower capacity for the higher pleasures will find themselves more easily contented. But a small amount of higher pleasure is far more valuable than a mass of base pleasure. And so I say to you: better to be Socrates dissatisfied than a goat satisfied.'

There were cheers and cries of 'Nonsense!' from the audience. The goat pawed the floor; Socrates bowed and indicated that they should be quiet for the next speaker.

A middle-aged man in a black polo-neck was waiting at the podium. He had auburn hair and an intense expression. The adjudicator, having finally caught the goat, rang the bell to mark the start of the minute.

'A great philosopher, if there is such a thing, once said that happiness is the fulfilment of human potential through the faculty of reason. He claimed that well-being consists primarily in intellectual activity. Bullshit! Wisdom, knowledge and learning have often been cited as the key to a fulfilling life. But only because philosophers write the definitions.' The audience began to slowly stamp their feet. 'Just be happy: stop talking about it. Find happiness in beauty, in nature, in other people. Not learning, but living, is the key.' He spoke louder. 'Anything worth living for must also be worth dying for. And no one dies for their pet theory of causation.'

The crowd began to chant: 'Po-et! Po-et! Po-et!'

'What's that all about?' Ben asked Lila.

Now people were storming the stage and throwing bread rolls.

'That's John Donne, the poet. Poets and philosophers tend to row. They each think that the other one is wasting his time with empty words.'

John Donne moved to the front of the stage and proclaimed loudly:

And new philosophy calls all in doubt,
The element of fire is quite put out;
The sun is lost, and the Earth, and no
*   man's wit*
Can well direct him how to look for it.

'I see what you mean,' said Ben. 'He thinks it makes the rainbow less beautiful.'

'Plato excluded poets from his ideal Republic, which annoyed them,' explained Lila.

'What did he have against them?'

'He kept them out on the grounds that immoral stories would corrupt young minds. Not that the poets wanted to be involved, so they said.'

'I thought philosophers were supposed to be

open-minded.'

'Hmm. I think Plato thought that he couldn't trust anyone else to be open-minded. Mind you, he also said that the best form of government would be one made up of philosophers.'

'Really?'

'And then, when Keats said, "Philosophy will clip an angel's wings," there was a huge fuss. Socrates wouldn't let any poets in here for years. If you ask me, though, it's really because poets have always been more successful at pulling than philosophers.'

John Donne had stopped speaking and was throwing some of the rolls back at the crowd. 'Useless philistines!' he shouted, just avoiding a head butt from the partisan goat.

'Poetry is pointless!' someone yelled, as the poet beat a hasty retreat.

'Order, please! Please!' Socrates shouted, a bread roll narrowly missing his head. 'Don't sink to his level. Coleridge himself admitted that "no man was ever yet a great poet, without being at the same time a profound philosopher". We can also take comfort from the fact that to ridicule philosophy is really to philosophise,' he said, somewhat desperately, 'albeit in a rather unsophisticated manner.' The goat was mildly munching Socrates' sleeve.

Socrates picked up a couple of bread rolls from the stage and tucked them in his pocket.

'Our guest was wrong about one thing, however: people do die for ideas. Different ideas—about other people, customs, political systems, God—are exactly what people kill for. But this is a topic for another day. I'd like to thank you all for participating in this enjoyable and—constructive—exchange. See you next time, when the topic will be Justice. If you'd like to speak, please sign up on the list outside my office.'

CHAPTER THIRTY-FIVE

'Tony?'

'I'm busy.' He was doing the easy crossword in the easy paper.

'I've just seen a mouse in the kitchen.'

'Nah—we haven't got mice. If I can't see it, it doesn't exist.'

'Actually, lots of things exist that we can't see.'

Tony gave him a look. 'Leprechauns?'

'Well, music, for a start. But also you can never hold equality, democracy or dignity in your hand, but that doesn't mean they don't exist.'

'They don't exist in this restaurant.' Tony laughed.

'Much less common than mice.'

'Haven't you got some frying to do?'

CHAPTER THIRTY-SIX

'Well, thanks for visiting,' Socrates said to Siddhartha. 'It's always enlightening.'

'I don't really approve of that method of debate,' said Buddha. 'You can't rush these things.'

'Indeed. The Symposium is just an experiment,' Socrates bluffed. 'Quite a good intellectual discipline, though. These lot can go on for ever, if you let them.'

Buddha was, as usual, unimpressed. Socrates felt uncomfortable. He remembered being trapped for hours listening to Buddha's long anecdotes.

'So what do you think of our other experiment?' Lila asked Buddha.

'The visits of the young man?'

'Yes,' said Socrates. 'It's going quite well, I think.'

'Obviously I haven't met him,' said Buddha, 'but we've been doing it for years.'

'Doing what?'

'Inviting guests, of course.'

'Really?' It seemed the Eastern lot had always done everything. 'And?'

'Mixed results. But a success on the whole. All those who pass a test get the chance to visit.'

'What's the test?'

151

Buddha laughed and shook his head. 'Classified information. But I will tell you this—'

Socrates smiled expectantly.

'At night all cats are black. But not all goldfish are good swimmers.'

'Er, quite.'

'And now I must take my leave. See you in twenty years. Your turn to visit us next.'

Buddha and his monks dressed in orange robes bowed to Lila and Socrates in turn. Socrates went to shake hands but then hid his hand behind his back, and bowed.

The visitors climbed into a barge filled with colourful rugs and rowed back across the calm river. Socrates waved until Buddha became a tiny blob and was quickly out of sight.

'At night all cats are black?' he mused.

Lila shrugged. 'Not all that glitters is goldfish.'

CHAPTER THIRTY-SEVEN

'Hi, Ben.'

'What can I do for you ladies?' It seemed Tony's counter-top manner was infectious.

Clare giggled. 'We'd like some fish and chips, silly.'

'Uno momento.'

'Susie and I are just hanging out for a

while,' Clare said. 'Do you want to join us?'

Susie concentrated on the tower she was making out of the ketchup sachets on the counter.

'I've got to work late,' Ben said.

Susie's tower fell on to the floor. She left it there.

'Tomorrow?'

'Maybe.'

As Ben wrapped their food, Susie started opening and closing the shop door, making the bell ring. 'Pay for the food, Clare, then we can go.'

'I don't really want to go,' Clare said.

'I don't really care,' said Susie.

'Happiness can only be appreciated in contrast to unhappiness,' said Ben. Clare smiled at him as they left.

Ben picked up the ketchup sachets. Clare had made a large water-lily flower out of a paper napkin. He put the ketchup in it, and placed the flower next to the till on the counter.

CHAPTER THIRTY-EIGHT

'Listen, right,' said Alex, captain of the football team. 'I know that we're gonna win the match on Sunday.'

'How do you know?' said Ben.

'What do you mean? I just know, yeah. Because they're rubbish, and anyway their captain's away this week.'

'By the way, to say that you know something means both that you *believe* it, and that it's *true*.'

The others stared at Ben suspiciously: he felt himself going red.

'And for it to count as knowing, there must be some link between the fact and your belief. So, a lucky guess that you're wearing red underpants.'

'Why you talking about my pants?' said Alex.

'Never mind. Err—something I believe—that just happens to be true—is not real knowledge. If I believe that there's a hurricane in Florida because the fairies told me, it's very different from believing it because I saw a proper weather report, even if in both cases there really is a hurricane. Only the second can count as *knowledge*.'

'Shut up, OK?'

'OK.' Ben paused, but he couldn't resist. 'I'm just saying that you can't possibly *know* that we'll win the match on Sunday. It's just a *belief*, which may or may not have some rational justification.'

'Are you playing in the match, Ben?'

'Yes.'

'Good. Now piss off till then, will you? You're scary.'

Didn't they realise that they were chained in the cave, seeing only the shadows made by reality? Why had Lila arrived and made him worry about these things?

CHAPTER THIRTY-NINE

'Ow! Ow!' Ben got his left foot caught on the cupboard shelf while the rest of him fell through into the World of Ideas.

'Are you OK?' Lila asked. The airing cupboard had seemed like the perfect place for the secret entrance, but it hadn't quite lined up properly on both sides.

'Of course.' His leg hurt where his thigh had been unnaturally stretched.

They were back in the corridor with all the doors. Lila paused in front of one labelled *Self-doubt*.

'Before we go in, you need to think about this question. It's quite a tricky one today. What are you?'

What sort of question was that? 'I don't get it. How is *what am I?* different from *who am I?*'

'What do you mean when you talk about "yourself"? And why are you the same person today that you were yesterday and will be tomorrow?'

'I . . . er . . . I . . .'

'Exactly. What is "I"?'

'Right. Well, I am me, and I am the same person as yesterday because . . . because I am. What else can I say?'

'You can rely on philosophers to think of lots else to say. Do you remember René Descartes' famous conclusion?' Lila went misty-eyed.

' "I think therefore I am"?'

'That's it. René realised that you could doubt that the external world was real, and he aimed to prove that it did exist. He started with the one thing that it was not possible to doubt: that he himself was having these doubts. And if he was having these thoughts then *he* must exist, so that was a good start. *But—*'

'But?' That didn't sound good.

'Some say that all he could be really sure of was that *thoughts were being had*, not that someone was having them.'

'What?' 'Thoughts being had'—and no one to have them? These philosophers must drive themselves mad!

'As it happens, the "I" is fairly controversial. The people we're about to meet will explain more. Now, just before we go in, you need to think about the difference between consciousness and self-consciousness. Having sensations makes you conscious—most creatures can be said to have that. But self-consciousness means—'

'Feeling embarrassed in public?'

'No, not that.' Lila smiled. 'Although this kind of self-consciousness would be necessary for being embarrassed. It means being aware of yourself as a conscious being, different from other conscious beings. That thought you had earlier: I am me. That you are a person, different from the other people. We don't know whether, or which, animals can get that far, but all humans over a certain age have this important thought. That certain movements and experiences have a special property for you in the world, namely that they are *yours*.'

'Why my pain is much more important to me than anyone else's pain?'

'That's it. So today's issue is all about what this "being a person" means. It's more complicated than it seems.'

'Yes yes yes,' said Ben.

Lila pushed open the door on to a beach. The sun was low in the sky.

'Let's take off our shoes,' she said.

As he walked, Ben's toes sank into the sand, still warm from the daytime sunshine. The sound of the waves was relaxing. Ben thought he knew who he was, but he wasn't sure he knew how to talk about it.

'I still think we need six turrets.'

'The structure can't support six turrets.'

'Hello,' Lila called.

The man and the woman looked up from their sandcastle and smiled as though they had

157

been expecting guests.

'But then it won't be symmetrical,' said the woman.

'Don't be so square,' the man said. 'Why can't we have a wonky castle?'

'Wonky?' She turned to Ben. 'Hello. I'm Delphine LeFevre.'

She had a nice accent. Ben hoped she'd say 'wonky' again.

'Welcome.' The man indicated a place on the rug for Lila and Ben to sit down. 'I'm David. David Sherborne.'

'Do you think it can be wonky?' Delphine asked Ben, winding up her red mane and tucking a blue chopstick through it, to hold it in place.

He grinned.

'So,' David said, 'what are you?'

'I'm Ben Warner.'

'What makes you, *you*?' Delphine said, wiggling her toes in the sand.

Ben thought of the fencing Oliver Whitby and Jack Cavendish. 'I am my mind,' he ventured, 'my feelings and thoughts.'

'Just so!' said David. He jumped up from the rug, and narrowly missed stepping backwards into the sandcastle. Delphine yelped and grabbed his hand, pulling him forwards. 'You are the contents of your mind,' David continued. 'Your feelings and thoughts and experiences. Making that decision, tasting a banana, feeling sad. That's you. Nothing

158

more.'

Ben was pleased that he'd got the answer right. But something jarred. 'Wait a minute. Surely I'm not *just* my mental things? I didn't mean that.'

'Then you should be more specific.'

These philosophy types were very demanding.

'I'm Ben, which is different. I mean, I suppose, that my personality is more or less my thoughts and feelings, but I am something else too.' Of course he was.

'Actually,' David said eagerly, 'I would say that we are indeed just a sequence of thoughts, experiences and actions. There is nothing in me beyond what I think and feel and do. Why do I need to say that I am anything else?'

'I'm not sure.' He wasn't just a stream of thoughts. Wasn't he something separate which sort of *had* the thoughts? He looked hopefully at Delphine.

'I don't believe, David, that you really think that's true. I am not my thoughts, I am something that thinks.'

At last some common sense. It was like a conveyor belt. First there were the experiences moving along the belt: seeing the bluey-green sea, feeling cold, being hungry. That seemed to be David's view. Then there was a factory worker selecting the experiences, choosing the relevant ones and putting them into a big box. That was better—now someone was organising them. Was there a little man in overalls in his head?

'My thoughts are not *me*, they are *mine*,' Delphine said. 'I could have had completely different experiences and still be me, so I must be something else other than my experiences.'

Ben watched a small crab scuttle across the sand, chased by a slightly bigger crab.

'Not at all,' David said. 'If you'd had different experiences you would have been a different person. It's natural to think you are more than your thoughts and sensations, but it's wrong.'

'Look, David, there must be something that *has* the sensations. Let's call it a "self". An experience without a someone to experience it is impossible—like a surface without an object. It can't exist separately.' Delphine tried to stand up, but she had buried her feet in the sand. She collapsed back on to her bum. 'It's not that a pain happens somewhere, it's that someone gets hurt.'

Ben tried to imagine a pain floating around, looking for an owner, someone who could feel hurt. It made him dizzy.

'Perhaps so,' David said, pushing his glasses up his nose. 'You might be able to say that there is a thinker, in some logical sense, for all thoughts. Obviously a pain happens to a person, not to no one. But that doesn't mean that there is more to the person than having a pain and other experiences. If you take away

160

my seeing this beach, my feeling the sand between my fingers, my hearing your voice—'

'Or your own, more likely,' said Delphine.

'My thought that you are an idiot, for example, then there is nothing left of me.'

'Of course there is. What about your memories?'

'They're still an experience in the present.' David took off his glasses and cleaned them on his sandy shirt, which made them even grubbier.

'OK then,' Delphine said, 'are you really saying that when we are in dreamless sleep—with no conscious experiences—we do not exist?'

'Yes. I'm nothing if I'm not having an experience. What's wrong with that?'

Delphine looked despairingly at Ben. 'Can you believe it? A grown man of forty—'

'*Thirty-eight!*'

'Whatever—desperately trying to prove that he doesn't really exist. That he is nothing more than a sensation of warm sand and a belief that he is cleverer than me.'

Lila was carefully putting shells round the sandcastle as crenellated battlements. She looked over and gave Ben an encouraging smile.

'Be careful what you're saying,' said David. 'Aren't you actually trying to claim that "you" are a peculiar soul-type thing? Something different from your mental activity, or your

161

body, for that matter. So where exactly does your "self" live? Face it: we have a mind that includes things, not a self or soul that does things.'

Ben tried to decide whether he was just a series of experiences or whether there was some mysterious thing that managed the experiences. How was he supposed to decide? He definitely felt like he was a special other thing. But then it was quite hard to explain what this other thing would be like. There obviously weren't little men in overalls living in his head.

'But I feel it,' said Delphine. 'I'm aware of the fact that "I am me" as well as my other experiences.'

'But you never really observe this self-thing when you "look inside" your mind. You just have various experiences. So why believe in it?'

'Look. I can't be just my mental activity because my thoughts and experience change constantly, but I stay the same person throughout.'

'Maybe this idea of yourself as a whole thing, which lasts through time, is just the fact that the word "I" comes as a side dish with all your experiences.'

'What do you mean by that?' asked Ben. He imagined a smart waiter: 'And here is a serving of "I" for you, sir.'

'It's just that you never say: This is a pain, I wonder who feels it. If you're in pain, you

162

know it. We already agreed that your experiences are special, *to you*. So every time you have an experience, it's accompanied by an idea of "I". For example, you see the sea and you automatically think: *I* am seeing the sea. There is a constant thought: I am here.'

'So now you agree that there's a "me" that's more than my experiences?' said Delphine triumphantly.

'Not a weird, separate thing. Not at all. Just that all your thoughts are linked in a way that makes them yours. But this could be as straightforward as them all depending on the same brain. And we get confused because we think that the "I" that comes automatically with all your experiences represents some special thing. But it's just a *relationship* between all your perceptions.'

'I strongly believe that there's a separate "me" such that it makes sense to feel responsible for what I did in the past and care about what happens to me in the future.'

Lila stood up. 'Ah, now you're moving on to a different question. I think we should take a break. Ben, do you fancy a swim?'

'I can't go swimming. I haven't got any trunks.'

'Aha!' Lila handed him a green pair and indicated a red-and-white stripy canvas booth along the beach.

Had he, he thought, as he pulled on the trunks, had to learn that he was him and that

163

other people were other people? Obviously oysters didn't think: I am an oyster. Did Whistle think: I am a dog? Maybe Whistle *was* just a series of thoughts and feelings: Ooh a lamppost! Food! Postman! Was he like that, or was there something more?

Lila, in a tiny purple bikini, waved to him from the water's edge. Ben was seized with the conviction that Oliver was right: there *was* no distinction between mind and body. Thoughts were physical creatures. If his heart sped up when he saw Lila in a bikini, and his lifetime was marked by a set number of heartbeats, then maybe if he kept looking at her he wouldn't live as long. Ben decided that it was a risk worth taking. He ran down the beach and straight into the sea.

Lila stood, the water up to her thighs.

'Come on,' Ben said. 'It's not that cold.'

Lila rose to the challenge and dived in.

'Did you understand that?' she asked.

'More or less. Mostly more, sometimes less.'

'Well, David Sherborne is another reductionist.'

'Like Oliver with the mind.' He was trying to concentrate. Lila was close enough to touch under the water.

'Yes. And so he believes that there is nothing more to us than the contents of our mind: no mysterious soul or self. But Delphine sticks to what we might call the common-sense view, that is, the one most people would have before doing any philosophy. She claims that we as people, or souls or whatever, are something more than our thoughts and brains.'

'Right.' Ben was trying to keep his head above water.

'But,' Lila continued, floating effortlessly, 'as you've begun to notice, the common-sense view is not that common here.'

'And there isn't always much sense in it.'

'True. It can be quite hard to argue for. Not that those who take the other view don't also have some fighting to do. Basically, if your standard view of the world is challenged, you either have to defend it effectively or you have to adjust.'

Ben splashed Lila.

She laughed and splashed him back, much more fiercely. 'So what do you think about the self now? Can you argue for your previous view or will you have to change it?'

Water had gone up Ben's nose. When he stopped coughing, he said, 'Really, I don't think I can stop thinking of myself as a separate thinking thing which *has* thoughts and experiences.'

'Yes, I think that feeling is pretty hard to lose.'

'But'—Ben's feet touched sand again—'I'm not so sure that I'm allowed to think it any more. I don't know if I could defend it if I had to.' Not that he would have to. He was hardly likely to be asked to describe the essence of a person in Cod Almighty, nor even at school. 'Can you tell me anything about what you think?'

Lila swam closer conspiratorially. 'For what it's worth, I think the best analogy is with a nation.'

'What do you mean?' For once she was going to tell him what she thought. She must think that he was making progress with his philosophy.

'Well, a nation is just the combination of its geography and its people and its history, and yet it is true to say that a nation itself is something other than these things.'

'So there doesn't exist any other entity apart from the brain and thoughts and experiences, yet a "self" could be something different from these?'

'That's it. It's sort of constructed out of the other things: it's real and yet not a separate thing.'

'Like a beehive.' Ben was excited. 'It behaves like a unit—a hive—but there's nothing more than organised bees.'

'Nice image.'

CHAPTER FORTY

Delphine and David were still arguing.
'You'll flood it,' Delphine was saying.

'You were the one who insisted we needed a moat.'

'I know. But not like that.'

'Nice swim?' Delphine asked. 'I was in there all afternoon, but David doesn't like getting his ears wet.'

'I have a complicated ear infection,' he said, fiddling with his sandals, which he was wearing over black socks.

'Anyway—now for another problem. What it means to be the same person over time.'

'George Orwell once wrote: "What have you in common with the child of five whose photograph your mother keeps on the mantelpiece? Nothing, except that you happen to be the same person,"' David said, by way of introduction.

'What David means,' Delphine said, 'is that to some extent it's a problem about change and staying the same. We can say that you are the same person as when you were born and as you will be in ten years. This is what is known as an "identity" relationship: over time you are always the same person.'

'Are you, though?' said David.

'I always feel like me at every age,' said Ben.

'Have a look up there,' said Delphine, and pointed to the sky, which was dark orange with the setting sun.

There was a huge projection covering the whole sky.

'That's me as a baby! How embarrassing: I

was really fat.' Then him at four years old. 'Hey, that's the house we used to live in.' The images were very familiar and yet he didn't feel that the person he saw was him exactly. Now him in Cod Almighty. Then with a girl he didn't recognise. 'Where's that?' he asked as the sky went blank.

'You in the future. Far too dangerous to show you that,' said David.

'So what do you think the answer is?' Delphine asked.

'Er . . .' Ben was overwhelmed by seeing his life in the sunset. 'Just remind me what the question was.'

'What is it that makes us say you're the same person in all those pictures?' Delphine said. 'It might seem a trivial question, but it's very important. We all take it for granted that we can tell one person from another. You care about what will happen to you in a particular way that, however noble you are, you do not feel about other people. If a certain person is going to be in pain tomorrow, you care deeply whether this will be "you" or not.'

'Also,' David said, 'to have an on-going relationship with someone else, it matters to know that this is always the same person.'

Ben agreed. How could you be friends with someone if you weren't sure that they were the same person each time you saw them? It would be exhausting starting again each day.

'Right then,' Delphine said. 'What is it that

makes you "you"?'

'I think I understand the question now.' There was a long pause. Ben waited for one of them to answer before he realised that they were expecting him to come up with a suggestion. Better attempt something. 'Right. Since, as I say, I always feel like me, then being the same person is something from the inside. What about that "self" thing that Delphine was talking about before?'

'Let's try and stay away from incoherent ideas of souls that haunt the body. Also, if you say this, you are assuming too much and explaining nothing. It would be equivalent to saying, "I am the same person because I am the same person."'

That seemed to Ben to be quite a sensible thing to say, although he could see that it wasn't really progress.

Delphine tried to make him feel better. 'But you were on the right lines, thinking about something from the inside that makes you the same person over time.'

Ben tried again. 'So if it's something internal, can we say that having the same mind is what makes me the same person?'

'Almost,' said David, 'although we need to be clearer about what we mean by the same mind. What you really mean, I suspect, is that it is a matter of psychological continuity.'

Ben nodded intelligently. How could that be what he meant to say? He had never heard of

169

it. It sounded good, though.

'Each individual thought or experience might be transitory,' David said, 'but they overlap and run together. There is a linked sequence of thoughts. It's hard to explain, but I think the concept of psychological continuity is clear enough.'

Ben was glad that he'd come up with such a clever idea.

'Think of it like this,' Delphine said. 'One ancient Greek philosopher argued that you never step into the same river twice because it is constantly moving.'

'I beat Heraclitus at tennis yesterday, actually,' David said.

'And yet it does make sense to call it the same river,' Delphine said, 'because of the continuous flow of water. The river at one time is connected to the river at the very next moment. Psychological continuity is a bit like that.'

'A *stream* of consciousness, you might say,' Lila said. She had wrapped her skirt back around her and had a faded pink beach towel round her shoulders, darkened in patches by her dripping hair.

'What about memory?' asked Ben.

'Definitely, memory is the key,' said David. 'If we didn't have memories, we'd have no past and then we'd be no one. We'd also have no future if we couldn't make new memories. Each day with your wife would be your very first meeting. So, memory is it. If I remember doing something then it was I who did it. If I don't, it wasn't.'

'Oh no,' Delphine said, 'that can't be right. Memory on its own doesn't make you the same person. All the things you did but have now forgotten—we'd have to say it wasn't actually you that did them. And if you feel like you remember something, but it didn't actually happen—we'd have to say that you did it, which is wrong.'

'But why not say that? My personality is shaped by my experience, whether they are real or not. If I am hypnotised and wake up with a memory of being Henry V winning a glorious victory at Agincourt then this is really something I remember, and it's now part of my mental history. And if I can't remember stealing apples as a child then it is surely right to say that I am no longer the same person as the boy who did that.'

'It can't be right to say that! So someone with amnesia becomes a completely new person?'

'Yes.'

'But they'd still have some of the same personality, wouldn't they? And suppose you don't remember parking your car yesterday—'

'That's quite likely, actually—'

'Let me finish. If you don't remember it then you are not the same person as the one who parked your car yesterday.'

171

'Correct.'

'Well, who the hell was it doing the parking then?'

David thought for a moment. 'It was me then, but it's not the same person I am now.'

'Oh please,' Delphine said. 'That's absurd. Look, didn't we just agree that we need to have a clear idea of a single person who lasts through time. It's either Person A or Person B, and a moment of forgetfulness can't suddenly change it. Your position is too vague.'

'Why does it matter so much to know when it is exactly the same person?' asked Ben.

'One reason,' Delphine said, 'is that we want to be able to hold people responsible for what happens. Imagine some crime has been committed. We want to put the suspect on trial. But it's only right to do that if it is the same person incriminated by the evidence. If David's idea were generally accepted then murderers could claim that they didn't remember the event and therefore the police had the wrong person.'

'Why should you be held responsible for things you can't remember?' asked David provocatively.

'Mon dieu! What are you saying?' Delphine turned to Ben. 'I think we need to consider another criterion for what makes you the same person from one day to the next. Any suggestions?'

Ben thought about it and came up with a

clever idea. 'If what makes it a true memory is that *you* did it, then that usually means that your *body* was there. So could we say that having the same body shows you are the same person over time?'

'The body is certainly used as evidence when memory is faulty,' Delphine agreed. 'In the case of the murderer who claimed not to remember, we would prosecute the person whose body was at the crime scene. It's how we recognise other people as being the same person we spoke to yesterday.'

'Note, though,' David butted in, 'that we can't mean *exactly* the same body. Apart from your brain, the physical material in your body is renewed every seven years. So you probably don't have many of the same molecules that you were born with in your body now.'

'Ugh, weird,' said Ben.

David continued: 'Think of a wooden ship that is constantly being rebuilt. First they replace the deck planks, then the side panels, then the hull is re-timbered. Gradually nothing of the original wood remains, but it is still the same ship. By analogy we can talk about you having the same body throughout your life, because the elements always belong to a common organisational structure, and only change gradually.'

'So,' Ben said, feeling like he was getting somewhere, 'we mean physical continuity similar to the psychological version?'

'Exactly,' said David, 'although I don't think it's as important as psychological continuity. The body might be good evidence of being the same person, but it is definitely not what we mean by a *person*.'

'It's not so obvious,' Delphine said. 'After all, our body is the limit of us in the outside world. It represents the boundary of what we control directly. And our personality is shaped by how people respond to our bodies.'

'My personality is shaped by how I respond to your body,' David said, with a wink.

'You Englishmen have no idea how to seduce a woman,' said Delphine, smiling.

Ben laughed, but then realised that maybe she meant him as well.

'OK. If you really think the body is that important, what happens with a brain transplant?' said David. 'Imagine it is medically possible and you swap brains with someone. Which one is you afterwards: your body with their brain, or their body with your brain?'

'Brain transplant,' Lila said. 'The only time where it's better to be the donor than the recipient.'

'It's like those films where people swap bodies,' said Ben. 'But since the person is in the "wrong" body in the films, it must be the brain and not the body that's the person. Or rather,' Ben was getting more confident now, especially as he hadn't been interrupted, 'it's the psychological continuity with their life in the other body. But definitely not the body.'

David had been listening carefully. 'But might it then be the *brain* that decided if it was the same person or not? We get psychological continuity from one moment to the next because our experiences depend on the same brain at all times. So that would mean that psychological continuity is the same as brain continuity.'

'Of course,' Ben said, 'if the mind is just part of the brain, as Oliver said, then there it would be the same.'

'It's not that simple, though,' said Delphine.

'Is it ever?' said Ben.

'What about multiple personalities in the same brain?' Delphine continued. 'You cannot always have the simple equation of one brain, one person.'

'If the self is a nation, then that's more like Bosnia,' said Lila.

'OK, try this one,' Delphine said. 'Imagine that technology has advanced and you can control your body by radio link-up from your brain. It would be possible to keep your brain safe in a laboratory while your body moves around. In this situation—where are you?'

'I don't know,' Ben said.

'Think about it. Surely you would feel that you were where your body was. That is your perspective on the world.'

'But I thought we had decided I couldn't

just be the body, because of the brain transplants?' It had always seemed simple to know that he was one person, and that everyone else was the same person each time he saw them. 'Anyway, none of those things— brain transplants, radio-controlled body—can actually happen.'

'That doesn't matter, in fact,' Lila said. 'It is logically possible, and if you're going to do philosophy you mustn't be afraid of the absurd.'

Ben had noticed that much. He was sitting on a beach inside the airing cupboard. 'These are called "thought experiments". They're very useful in philosophy because they test your intuitions about a problem by taking it to imaginary extremes. Generally, it is normal for brain, body, memory and psychological continuity to go together so it's not difficult to think about a single person. But if we want to identify which of these is most important to being a person, as we are trying now, then we want to isolate each one and see what our intuition says is important.'

Ben nodded: It seemed to make sense.

'Remember,' Delphine said, 'that we are trying to find something that enables us to say this person and that person are the same.'

'Which isn't possible,' said David. 'Try this.' He smiled. 'Imagine a futuristic brain operation in which your brain will be cloned into two identical brains and each put into one of two identical bodies. Which is you?'

'Which is me?'

'Imagine it's possible. Also imagine that one of them will be tortured and you have to decide beforehand which one. You care in a very special way about one person—you.'

Ben didn't really want to imagine future torture, but he considered the question anyway. 'Neither of them is me.'

'Neither? That would mean that you had died. Why would you have died? You've just been cloned, that's all. So are you saying that *you* wouldn't feel anything if either of them was tortured, even though they both have your body and your brain?'

'No. One of them is me, then.'

'At the start the two people are identical. How could you choose which one of the two would be you if they start off the same?'

'I don't know.' How could he know? 'I have to say both of them are me. It's the only option left.'

'I think that's the most reasonable way to think about it,' said David. 'But although they start off identically, as soon as they start having experiences they will be different people, do you see?'

'Yes.'

'Does that mean, then, that you—one person—are *the same* as two different people?'

'Typical!' Delphine said. 'I might have known you'd try something like that.'

David smiled. 'It makes most sense to say that I am both of the new people. But then you have to relax the idea of identity.' He looked seriously at Ben. 'You can't always give a definite answer to the question about whether it is exactly the same person. Much as Delphine wants to believe that you can. It seems the easiest question in the world—'

'But things are not always what they seem,' Ben said.

'It's like a road splitting in two,' added Delphine. 'If you had to say which branch was the old road, it would be difficult but it doesn't much matter. It's not a very interesting question. But to say which one of those people is me in the future seems very important. IS very important.'

'I think the best way to think about it is as a question of survival,' suggested David. 'A part of me survives in each person but neither of them is exactly me. In fact, given that we change all through our lives, you don't even need to think about weird imaginary examples. A bit of the five-year-old you survives in you now, but you are not the same person, and a bit of the fifteen-year-old you will survive in the forty-year-old.'

Ben had always assumed he was one definite person who could be alive or dead but not something in between.

'So,' added David, 'it would be better to say that a heavy smoker is harming someone else—the person they will become—not themselves at all. Which might explain why people often don't care about risks in the future.'

'Why not say these are exactly the same people who have changed, rather than different people?' said Delphine.

'Superficially, your view seems simpler. But when you see how hard it is to say when one person begins and ends, my view seems quite appealing. See it my way, and relax. For example, death simply means that there are no future experiences that will be connected to my present ones in the way that past events are. That makes it much less depressing, don't you think?'

'No I don't, actually. I think it makes life much more depressing. I want to last—as me.'

'In a few minutes, you'll be a slightly different person. From the perspective of you now, that seems sad. But in the future you will care about the new person you are then. There will be no need to be sentimental about your old self.'

While they had been talking the sun had sunk below the horizon and the blue sky was fading to black.

'We should go,' Lila said to Ben. 'Our imminent selves ought to be somewhere else.'

He nodded. But was he the same person who had arrived in the World of Ideas a few weeks, or even two hours, ago?

The waves lapped gently at the edge of the almost finished sandcastle as the four of them walked away.

'You're all red.' David touched Delphine's cheek. 'I told you to put proper sun cream on.'

'I suppose I just didn't care about that person who'd get sunburnt in the future,' she said.

Delphine and David had their arms round each other. They hadn't stopped arguing since he met them, and now they were . . . practically cuddling. Another weird relationship.

CHAPTER FORTY-ONE

Socrates picked his way through the tall grass towards the wooden shed, swatting away the swarm of flies, with no sense of irony.

'Ludwig! Ludwig? Are you all right?' he shouted at the closed door.

'Piss off.'

'Are you planning to stay there for months like last time?' Ten years earlier, Wittgenstein had built himself a small wooden hut. His thinking box. It was beautifully made and very sparsely furnished. So people said—no one had been allowed to look inside.

'I'm working.'

'Anything interesting?'

The sigh was audible through the wooden

walls of the shack. 'It would be simply intolerable to explain my thoughts to you. I refuse to blunt my ideas on the stony ground of your stupidity.'

'Thought you might want to talk.'

'I most certainly do not.'

'I've brought you some biscuits.' Socrates waited for a reply which didn't come. 'I'll just leave them outside then.' Socrates couldn't understand people who didn't like a good chat. 'Ben's been here again. A few times, actually.'

'And?'

'I think it makes him happy.'

'You would say that.'

'Yes, I would, because I always tell the truth.'

There was a muffled sound from behind the door.

'Was that you admitting that I'm winning the bet? Maybe you should stay in there a while longer.'

The door of the wooden shed twitched open. 'I'm not giving up yet,' Wittgenstein shouted at Socrates' retreating back. He picked up the biscuit packet and munched on a jaffa cake to help him think. After three biscuits, Wittgenstein shut himself back in the shed, looked up a number in his book and made a phone call.

'Hello? Hello. Yes. Can I speak to Niccolò Machiavelli, please?'

. . .

181

'What do you mean he's busy? Do you know who I am?'

. . .

'Who am I? I'm Ludwig Wittgenstein.'

. . .

'The most famous philosopher of my generation.'

. . .

He swallowed hard. 'Never mind. I'd like to make an appointment.'

. . .

'None of your business what it's regarding. Of course it's urgent.'

. . .

'Next Thursday morning? Um. What day is it now? Sunday? OK, Thursday at 11.'

Wittgenstein was determined to wipe that smug smile off Socrates' face.

CHAPTER FORTY-TWO

Ben was making cheese on toast, his favourite, maybe because it was the only thing he knew how to cook—apart from fish and chips, which didn't count.

'God, I've got a splitting headache. Where do we keep the aspirin? I can never remember.'

'You know, Dad, it's perfectly reasonable for me to suspect that you don't have a headache at all.'

His dad groaned and opened drawers at random.

'Well, exactly. You're showing all the outward signs of a headache. And I know that, when I behave like that, I *do* have a headache. But I can never test what you're feeling inside, so I can never be sure.'

'Not now, please,' his dad said, still pretending to look for aspirin but, as usual, hoping someone else would do the difficult work of actually finding them.

'But to assume all these inner experiences also happen in other people just because of what happens to me isn't strong evidence. I mean, to base conclusions on only one example is generally not good science. If I go into only one room and it's painted blue, I would be silly to assume that all other rooms must be painted blue.'

'Please give me an aspirin.'

Ben opened a drawer and handed him the tablets. He looked around mock-helplessly. Ben got a clean glass out of the cupboard, filled it with cold water from the tap and handed it over. His dad swallowed the pills gratefully.

'So when the aspirin works,' Ben asked, 'will you still be in pain?'

'Obviously not.'

'But the problem in your body that caused the pain won't have gone away; you just won't experience the pain. So it depends whether pain is literally just the experience, or some sort of connection between something wrong with your body and outward signs of pain.'

'I'm going to lie down.'

'But if it's really just the inner feeling,' Ben shouted after him, 'then I have even less reason to believe that you are in pain.' He might have shown more interest. After all, here was philosophy that was acutely relevant to his present condition.

Ben took his cheese on toast into the sitting room.

'Let me have a bite,' Katie said.

'No. Make your own.'

'Mum won't let me use the grill.'

Ben pointed to the photo of his sister on the mantelpiece. 'Is that you?'

'Of course it is. Don't be stupid.'

'Well, your body is different—all your molecules change every seven years.'

'It's still me, then, because that photo's only two years old.'

'Duh! But what is it that makes it you? That you remember that day? That you have had continuous thoughts that link you with the person in the photo? That there is a continuity between your body then and now, even if some molecules have changed?'

'Dunno.'

'Don't you care?'

'No.'

'But to say you are—'

'No.'

'The same person—'

'No.'

'It matters because—'

'No. No. No,' she sang, dancing round the room.

Ben sighed. 'Stay in your cave then, seeing only shadows. I have emerged into the light.'

She gave him a funny look. 'Will you be buying a tambourine?'

'Just go away.' Ben made a point of putting the last piece of cheese on toast in his mouth, even though it didn't quite fit.

CHAPTER FORTY-THREE

Few people realise that the newly dead grieve as much as the living for the life that has gone. It shouldn't be surprising: they have, after all, lost so much more. For those left behind, there are new people, new distractions. Life goes on. In Lila's case, life went on—without her. She didn't doubt that she was the one who had been left behind.

When Lila Frost, aged twenty-four, arrived in the World of Ideas, after a corner taken too fast on a dark slippery road, she was full of the furious grief of the separated lover. An invitation to join the World of Ideas seemed small consolation. She quickly mastered the observation technology and kept a constant watch on those gathered round the Lila-shaped hole. She wept along with them, which helped. This sort of thing was strongly discouraged by old hands in the World of Ideas. Every authority on the subject formed a (rare) consensus that this was a Bad Thing. And yet no one had dared to interrupt her fierce, red-eyed vigil in the monitor room.

In time, however, exhaustion replaced ghoulish fascination with life back home and Lila weaned herself off this unhealthy pastime. In parallel with her family, she grew tired of grief. The first time she had seen her lover laugh was like an electric shock. How could he be happy, when she was here weeping? And yet, she had gradually let go. Time—even the version in the World of Ideas—really does heal all wounds. It was twenty-six years and four months since she'd even checked up on him, and at least twelve years and eight months since she'd thought seriously about him.

So why was she thinking of him now, after so many years of good behaviour? She knew why. It was because Ben reminded her of him. It wasn't just that he looked similar but something in his manner. She remembered *his* patient face as she wittered on about her philosophy, determined, out of stubborn love for her, to understand. Ben was much younger, of course, but there was something familiar in his earnest look as he willed himself to grasp each new idea. Lila realised that she was now closer in age to Ben, physically, than to . . . *the other one.* He must be married by now. Maybe he even had children—something she'd never do.

She wondered if he ever thought of her. A cold hand reached into her chest and squeezed her heart. She took a deep breath and the cold grip loosened, leaving a dull echo of cramp. Come on, Lila, there's a death to be lived.

CHAPTER FORTY-FOUR

'Didn't I tell you we'd win, Ben?' said Alex.

'I didn't think we wouldn't win, just that it wasn't right to say that you *knew* we would win,' Ben explained pointlessly.

'Great goal, shame about the dodgy chat.'

If only he could tell them about seeing Lila in her purple bikini.

'Eurrrrrech!' Alex spat out his Coke. 'Disgusting! It's all bitter. Give me some of yours to take away the taste.' He grabbed Joe's drink and gulped it down. He spat it out even more violently. 'That's foul as well. I can't believe you drank half of it.'

'Tastes fine to me.'

'You nutter. You must have no tongue.'

'It's a new flavour,' said Ben. 'Special citrus

variety.'

'Really?' asked Alex.

Lila, watching in the monitor room, laughed at the look on Alex's face. Then she spotted something else on the edge of the screen. Oh no, what was he up to?

'Ben, that old tramp's waving at you,' said Mike.

'No he isn't.'

'No really, look.'

Something about him was familiar. Oh God. It was Socrates. Not here, please! 'Probably some mad bloke, I'll see what he wants.'

'Hello, Ben.'

'What are you doing here?'

'I thought I'd come and see you.'

'Over here,' Ben insisted, leading Socrates further away from his friends.

Socrates narrowly missed being knocked down by a roller-blader. He beamed. 'This is fun.'

Ben was flattered that Socrates had visited him in person. But he wished he hadn't turned up like this in public. Worrying about appearances wasn't Socrates' style.

'I thought a little chat might be helpful. How are you getting on with the project?'

'The project?'

'Us, you, the World of Ideas, philosophy. Are you making good progress?'

Would there be an exam at the end? Oh no, that wasn't fair.

'Of course, learning philosophy isn't about progress as such,' said Socrates. 'If it's about anything, it's about learning a new way of thinking.'

'I think I'm getting somewhere, although perhaps I'm going round in circles. Or backwards. I used to know who I was and what the world was like: and now I don't know anything.'

'Yes! Admitting your ignorance makes you wise.'

'Really?'

'As I said to the jury in Athens . . . Never mind. As you see, it's about the journey, not about reaching any particular destination. And, um, do you think this journey, this intellectual trip we've led you on, has made your life better?'

'Better?' What did he mean? Ben still didn't have any money, or a girlfriend. Or freedom. He still had parents and sisters and a crappy boss. 'I don't know.'

Whilst it wasn't quite the positive response that Socrates was hoping for, 'I don't know' was nonetheless significantly better than 'no'. 'I don't know' had potential.

Ben was still thinking about the question. Better? Well, it was better than sitting at home all day, and Lila was more interesting than any one else he'd ever met. Ben looked over at his friends, to check that no was watching him and the old tramp. Luckily everyone seemed to be distracted. Ben blushed at the memory of talking to them about philosophy. See the wrong film, wear the wrong trainers—it wasn't hard to be laughed at.

'Philosophy hasn't made me very popular,' he said.

'Tell me about it!'

'Oh, of course, you would know.' Ben was embarrassed; he wasn't about to be put to death for annoying people with his philosophy.

'If ignorance is bliss, then it follows that it is foolish to aim for wisdom. But ignorance isn't bliss—it's just ignorance.'

'What's wrong with ignorance? Is knowledge really so blissful?'

'Philosophy isn't practical, like growing food or building houses, so people say it is useless. In one sense these basic tasks are much more important, it's true, because we couldn't live without them.' Socrates looked at Ben. 'We eat to live, but we live to think. And also to fall in love, play games and listen to music, of course. Remember that the practical things are only about freeing us up to live: they're not the point of life.'

'The thing is,' Ben said, 'aren't philosophers a bit full of themselves? I mean, the view seems to be that a true understanding of life can only be reached through philosophy. That people who don't get it are sort of inferior and . . . well, don't get it.'

'We're not very good at the spin, are we?

190

But surely our position is the most humble of all. I am wise enough to know what I do not know. Anyone who thinks they have nothing to learn will obviously learn nothing. How can it be arrogant to advocate thinking, especially when we don't claim to have the answers? However, this is where we get into trouble.'

'*We?*'

'When you question people's views, they take it as a personal criticism. You don't get a rational response, just hostility. So, to belong, we accept and we don't examine why.'

'So I should stop doing philosophy if I want to be popular?'

'Popular with whom? Anyway, it's too late for you to stop. You won't be able to help asking these sorts of questions now you've started.' He patted Ben on the arm. 'Don't look so worried. To think well about things, and revere the unknowable, is a pleasure and a privilege.'

'I suppose so. I just wish it didn't make me such a freak.'

Lila, still watching in the monitor room, thought that she had better get Socrates out of there. She didn't think he would stand up very well to teenage questioning. After all, his dialogues with the young men of Athens hadn't made him many friends.

'My mother was a midwife. Did you know?' said Socrates.

'No.'

'Of course not. Anyway, I see my role in the same way.'

'Err . . .'

'Giving birth to ideas.' Socrates laughed. There was a loud beeping noise. 'Oh bugger! It's that thing again.' He pulled a pager out of his pocket. 'Now where are my glasses?' He patted all of his pockets. 'Will you read that for me?'

'It says *URGENT. Debate on the nature of freedom out of control. Come to ZOO immediately.*'

'Better rush. Come and visit us again soon.' Socrates looked around him, then ran into a phone box and disappeared.

Ben walked slowly back to his friends.

'Who was that?' asked Joe.

'It's our next-door neighbour,' said Ben. 'He's a bit strange.'

'So are you. Must be why you get on so well.'

Ben whisked the ball from under Joe's feet. Joe ran after him but Ben was faster and got away.

Ben's mind still snagged on the thought that Socrates had been dead for hundreds of years. What did he know about the world? And even when he'd been alive he'd pissed people off so much with his philosophy that they'd had him put down. Ben wouldn't have missed the chance to visit the World of Ideas. But, he started to think, enough was enough. He was

192

glad he'd met Lila, but he'd have to kill himself to be with her, which was hardly a stable basis for a relationship. And he wasn't ready to commit himself to an eternity—literally—with one woman. No, sexy though Lila was, it was time to move on to someone his own age. Clare, perhaps, who was at least alive.

Could he be happy with Clare if he decided that he was happy? If he started fancying her then that would make her—by definition—fanciable. Damn! The World of Ideas had got him *thinking*. Stop thinking about philosophy! What would Lila say? No. Stop thinking about Lila also.

CHAPTER FORTY-FIVE

Immediately after returning from the ambassadorial visit, Socrates went to sort out the problem at the zoo. It had been messy, but the situation had stabilised by the time he arrived. He wasn't sure why Lila had bothered to page him for such a minor incident. Isaiah Berlin had been giving a lecture on freedom, and someone had let the animals out of their cages to make a none too subtle point about captivity. Jean Jacques Rousseau had been chased by an angry puma and John Rawls had concussion after tripping over a loose penguin.

Ludwig Wittgenstein was on a different mission. He crossed the busy main road and went into a modern, glass-fronted building. The atrium was filled with lots of plants that were real but looked fake. He took the lift up to the twelfth floor and told the receptionist his name.

'Take a seat, please. Mr Machiavelli will be with you shortly.'

Indeed he was. In person, Machiavelli was just as charming as he needed to be. No energy wasted, but no profits lost either. He had an impish face, with some faint designer stubble. He had a beautiful smile, when he used it. He wore a dark Armani suit and a yellow shirt with a darker yellow silk tie.

'I expected you to be tall,' said Wittgenstein, by way of greeting.

'Why?' said Niccolò, trying not to look insulted in front of a potential client. I expected you to be rude, he thought to himself.

'I just did,' said Wittgenstein, losing interest.

Machiavelli led Wittgenstein into his office, which had a fine view of the city below and some fine art—possibly real—on the walls. 'How can I help you?'

'I need some advice.'

'I doubt you can afford my fees.'

'I had money—lots of it. I gave it all away.'

'That doesn't count. I need you to give some

of it to me.'

'Money corrupts.'

'Not nearly as much as the lack of it.' Machiavelli took a deep breath. 'I'll make an exception. You can have an initial consultation on the house, so long as you don't go telling people I've been giving advice for free.'

Wittgenstein's eyes widened in shock. There was no way he'd tell anyone he'd been *getting* advice for free. Wittgenstein did not, simply did not, need to borrow other people's ideas. He waved agreement impatiently.

'So, what's the problem?' said Machiavelli, settling himself behind his vast desk.

Wittgenstein placed himself in the leather chair indicated by his newly hired, unpaid, consultant and explained the terms of the bet.

'I thought I had it made, but Socrates actually seems to be making some progress with the boy.'

'Philosophy is making his life better?'

'I don't know about that. But Ben does keep coming back. And who knows what Socrates can convince him of. He's very persuasive.'

'First rule: don't leave matters to chance. Don't let your future depend on others.'

Wittgenstein was desperate.

'Indeed,' said Machiavelli, 'it's rather too late for that.'

'So what shall I do?'

'*La fortuna é donna*. Fortune is a fickle woman. Don't beg for her favours—grab her and force yourself on her.'

'I say—'

'Metaphorically speaking. What I'm saying is, you need to sabotage the bet.'

'Right. And how do I do that?'

Niccolò Machiavelli was no fan of Socrates either. Talking to him could be profoundly annoying: *You must be right, Niccolò. Just explain to me again why the end justifies the means. I'm sure I don't get it because I'm stupid, not because it's not a good idea.* Nevertheless, the thought of Wittgenstein being in charge was even worse. It would be intellectual fascism, and the trains certainly wouldn't run on time.

'I don't really have any suggestions,' Machiavelli said, looking at his watch in a pantomime manner. 'I'm afraid I have an appointment with a proper, paying, client. I'm sure you'll think of something. Remember, if you cannot be both, it is better to be feared than loved.' Machiavelli pressed the intercom, 'Liz, please show Mr Wittgenstein out.'

Wittgenstein left with his prejudices about consultants intact. He decided to take matters into his own hands. Control his own destiny. He wasn't taking that charlatan's advice, mind you; it just seemed like a good idea. If Ben didn't visit then he would hardly be behaving like someone who loved philosophy. Wittgenstein headed off towards his workshop to make sure that he didn't.

196

CHAPTER FORTY-SIX

Ben was trying to forget the World of Ideas, but he couldn't. He used to just skip through life, and now he was bogged down in a swamp of uncertainty. Was the dog real? If I swap brains with Alex—please, no—which one would be me? Am I worth less than a butterfly?

These questions were particularly unwelcome while he was working. Friday evenings at Cod Almighty were the worst because people were drunk and threw chips around. On a good day. They were nearly as bad as philosophers and poets.

'Stop that, my boss is in the office.'

Joe threw a handful of chips at Ben's head.

'Ah, missed!' Ben threw them back.

'Right.' Joe scrabbled on the floor for a missile. 'This means wa . . . wallet!'

'What?' Ben looked up from preparing his arsenal of tartare sauce.

Joe held up the wallet. 'Look what I've got!'

'One of the customers must have left it.' Ben reached out. 'I'll put it behind here. He'll probably come back for it soon.'

'There's £80 in here. I'd better take the whole thing. It'll look suspicious if he claims it and the wallet's here, but the money's gone.

'You can't just take it.'

'Why not? It's a five-fingered bargain.'

'I work here. They might suspect me.' Was that really the best reason that Ben could find? 'I should put a notice up, or give it to the police.'

'If he does come back, you just say you never saw anything. He'll assume it was another customer who picked it up and took it. Or that he left it somewhere else. He's probably been to loads of places this evening. Think what we can do with £80.'

'You can't just steal his money: it's wrong.'

'Don't be such a girl. It's not really stealing, is it? It's not like I mugged him. He dropped it. He must be loaded to go round dropping his wallet without noticing.'

'He will notice!' Ben realised that he wasn't going to stop Joe from taking it. And he'd possibly be tempted to help him spend some of the money. Ben felt grubby. Or maybe he was just worried about getting into trouble, and not about doing the right thing. That wasn't much of a conscience worth having.

'Conscience is the inner voice that warns us that someone may be looking,' someone whispered.

It sounded like Lila, but that would be impossible. OK, not impossible. Just because something didn't normally happen, or hadn't happened before, didn't mean it was impossible. He'd learnt that much. Just not very likely. However, where Lila and that lot

198

were concerned, the unlikely was likely.

'What did you say?' Ben asked Joe.

'Just that I'd better be going before your boss comes out. Promise you won't tell anyone.'

Ben hesitated.

'*Promise,*' insisted Joe.

'I promise.'

'Good. Now stop worrying.'

Telling an anxious person to stop worrying was as futile as ordering someone to fall in love with you. However, the voices in Ben's head, or wherever they in fact were, had given him an idea. Lila had said that right and wrong was a subject in philosophy. Maybe a visit to the World of Ideas would help. He'd half-promised himself he wouldn't visit any more, but now he had a proper dilemma. Time for philosophy to prove its worth.

CHAPTER FORTY-SEVEN

Ben felt the usual excitement as he opened the airing-cupboard door and smelt the warm towels. He squeezed in between the shelves and pulled the door closed behind him. He was uncomfortably squashed for a second, which became several seconds. That was strange: the back of the cupboard wouldn't yield. Maybe he hadn't pushed it in the right way? With great difficulty, he disentangled his left arm from between his knees and gave the back wall a firm push. It didn't budge. The World of Ideas was closed. Ben was disappointed. He'd hoped to get some advice about Joe and the money before he went to sleep. But then a more worrying thought occurred to him. Maybe that was it: he'd had his time in the World of Ideas and he wasn't allowed back any more.

Ben sighed, and realised he had a much more immediate problem. He'd clambered carelessly into the cupboard, certain that he'd fall out easily on the other side. Now he was lodged tightly in between the shelves. He tried several ways of untangling his legs and arms before admitting defeat. The only way was to ease the door open with one foot and then push himself backwards with one hand and the other foot. He thudded bum-first on to the carpet in an undignified heap.

Could he really have learnt everything there was to know about philosophy? Nice idea, but he doubted it. Did they know he'd been thinking about not going back? Perhaps they were bored of him and had found a visitor that they liked more. Wouldn't Lila have said something to let him down gently? Or was she doing what girls did: just stopped speaking to you for no reason and you had to work out why? Ben decided to send her an email:

From: ben@mymail.com
To: lila@worldofideas.com

Hi Lila,
Didn't you say something before about right and wrong? Maybe now would be a good time to learn. My friend's taken this wallet and I don't know whether I should do something about it. I'm sure it's nothing to do with me really, but best to check. Can I come and visit you? There must be someone who could give me some advice.
Ben

Ben waited a couple of hours for a response but there was nothing. Several times he approached the airing cupboard wondering whether he should try again to get in without permission from Lila, but he turned back. If they'd replaced him with someone else then it would be awful to turn up and not be welcome.

Fine. If that was how it was going to be, he would work it out on his own. Yes. He would. Where to start? It didn't seem quite the same as the problem of the self or the mind. It affected what he'd do in the real world. Typical philosophers—they disappear just when they could be useful. Well, if they didn't want him, he didn't want them.

Stealing was wrong, he knew that much. Why was it wrong, though? A surprisingly difficult question. It was illegal, for a start. But that couldn't be the answer. It was illegal to drive the wrong way down a one-way street and that didn't have much to do with immorality. And it used to be legal to keep people as slaves, which was obviously wrong, so it was clear that moral and legal rules couldn't be exactly the same thing. If stealing was wrong it had to be for another reason.

Ben thought for a while. Well, I wouldn't like it if someone did it to me, he decided. So perhaps being moral was just treating everyone else as if they were you, more or less. He was getting used to having these conversations with himself. No one outside the World of Ideas wanted to join in. And even there they couldn't be bothered, it seemed.

CHAPTER FORTY-EIGHT

'Now,' Lila said, 'on Monday, you have a meeting.'

'What are we now?' said Socrates.

'Friday. So, *in three days* you have a meeting with the logical positivists.'

'What do they want?'

'Not sure. And next week, there's—'

'I used to be the rebel,' Socrates said. 'Now I have an *agenda*.' He sighed. 'Where did it all go wrong?'

'Perhaps when you became a rebel who wanted to win elections,' said Lila. 'By the way, I think there's a problem with the connection.'

'What do you mean?'

'Ben got stuck.'

'In here?' Socrates went white. 'What have you done with him?'

'Not that, luckily. He tried to get in and the door didn't work.'

'Sabotage! Do you think Ludwig Wittgenstein . . . ?'

'No!' Lila paused. 'Surely he wouldn't. It's probably something technical.'

'Call the helpdesk.'

'It's frustrating because Ben really wanted to visit. He's got some problem about his friend stealing money.'

'An ethical dilemma, is it? That's interesting.'

'Socrates, what are you planning?'

'You'll see. Just make sure he can get in next time.'

CHAPTER FORTY-NINE

I wandered lonely as a cloud,
That floats on high o'er vales and hills,
When all at once I saw . . .

Someone was shouting and banging outside

the classroom.

'Continue reading, Ben,' said Miss Price.

> . . . *I saw a crowd,*
> *A host, of golden da—*

The door to the classroom slammed open. It was Matt Cobb, who'd been expelled two years ago for fighting with the teachers. He was waving a toy gun around.

'What are you doing here, Matt?'

'Shut up, you stupid bitch.' Matt pointed the gun at Miss Price.

'Why don't you put down the gun, and we can—'

Matt lurched round and shot Amy Gardiner, who sat next to the door. The toy gun worked. There was loads of blood and she fell sideways.

Her best friend, Jenny Wilcox, started screaming.

'Shut up, shut up!'

'You shot her!' She screamed even louder.

'I said SHUT UP.'

She screamed. He shot her. She shut up.

The whole class was silent now. Ben didn't dare even move his head in case he drew attention to himself. Fear had stiffened his hands and he dropped the poetry book. It thumped on to the floor and Matt spun round at the noise.

'Swot with poetry book,' said Matt.

'Don't shoot me,' Ben said pointlessly.

'OK. I'll make a deal with you. Either you can watch me shoot the whole class one by one. See their scared little faces . . . OR, I'll let them all go, not that they deserve it. On one condition. You have to shoot her'—he waved the gun in the direction of Clare at the next desk—*yourself*. Reckon you've got the guts?'

'Ben,' said Clare in a wobbly voice.

'Ben? Come *on*, Ben,' his mum shouted through the door. Ben gulped for air. 'Get up, will you? I told you yesterday that we had to set off at ten for lunch with Granny.'

Heart pounding, Ben levered himself out of bed. He checked his email but there was still no reply from Lila. He would have to go to the World of Ideas. Before he had a dilemma, now it was a philosophical emergency. And he was pretty sure who was responsible for the way he was feeling.

He put a jumper on over his pyjamas and went downstairs to the kitchen.

'Dad, can I ask you a question?'

'Of course you can, mate.'

'If you could save thirty people from being killed by killing one person, what would you do?'

'What?'

Ben sighed. 'If you had to kill one person—'

'Right, I thought you said that.' He looked at Ben curiously. 'I don't think I'd have the courage to kill someone myself. I'm not sure if

205

that's a good thing or a bad thing.'

'Would you feel more guilty about killing one person yourself, or letting thirty others die?'

'The family of the one person might blame me more. They would want to know why that person had been sacrificed for the others.'

'But if you could definitely save the thirty people?'

Before Ben's dad could answer, the phone rang. It's Lila, Ben thought. But that was ridiculous. They got loads of phone calls in this house, mainly for his sisters.

Ben grabbed the phone.

'Hello?'

'There's a problem with the airing cupboard. Try the utility room behind the washing machine.'

'Sorry, wrong number,' said Ben, and hung up.

There was a noise from the utility room.

'What's that?' asked his dad.

'I think the dog's knocked something over. I'll go and clean it up.'

Lila was hiding behind the propped-up ironing board, which didn't conceal her at all, especially since she was wearing a bright-pink dress. The clothes pegs lay scattered on the floor. Lila beckoned Ben to follow her, and crawled into a hole behind the washing machine.

CHAPTER FIFTY

'What's the problem with the airing cupboard?' asked Ben, stretching.

'Well, it never quite matched up, did it? You always fell over.' Lila hadn't yet managed to open the door, which was welded shut, though she had managed to develop a theory about why the welding was there.

'And this is better?'

'What do you want? Stretch limo?'

'Anyway, I've had a terrible dream. A philosophical one.'

'We'd better get on with it then,' said Lila.

She led him down the corridor past a door marked *Why?* and stopped outside *Right and Wrong*, which opened on to rolling grassland. Ben had never seen grass so green, or a field so yellow with buttercups. A fat tame rabbit hopped fatly, tamely past.

'This way,' said Lila, setting off up the hill. It was quite a climb. Finally they reached a wide space on the brow with stunning views in all directions: gentle hills, pleasing arrangements of trees and Battenberg-cake fields. An enormous red-and-white-checked cloth had been laid out, and two men were unpacking a picnic from a large, old-fashioned wicker hamper.

'Where's the bread? You didn't forget to

pack bread, did you?'

'No, I did not forget to pack the bread. Despite taking responsibility for packing everything else. Just look harder.' He was very neatly dressed in a clean, pale V-necked jumper over an ironed shirt, trousers with a crease and shined shoes. His fine blond hair didn't quite cover his large ears.

'Aha! Ugh! Why did you get wholemeal? No soggy bagels?' His shirt was done up wrongly, and he was wearing odd socks. One of his shoelaces was undone.

His tidy companion sighed wearily. He looked up. 'Hello there, welcome. I'm Ian Faulkner.' He shook hands with Ben. 'I hope you're hungry.'

'Mmm,' said Lila.

'Hi. I'm Jeremy Cox.' He brushed away some crumbs and shook Ben's hand.

Ben decided to get down to business right away. 'I've got this dilemma. Two dilemmas, actually. I need you to tell me what is the right thing to do.'

Jeremy was burrowing in the picnic hamper. 'We . . . ll,' he said, shaking his head. 'Now that's a question. Mmm, hummus.'

'Look, there must be a right thing to do,' Ben said, taking a carrot stick and dipping it in the hummus. It tasted of cheese. He tried the carrot and the hummus separately. They both tasted of cheese—fairly mild—but with different textures. Lila was right about the food here—it did all taste the same. Ben hid the rest of his carrot in the long grass.

'I definitely think there's always a right thing to do,' said Jeremy.

Ian, who was sawing efficiently through the healthy loaf, shook his head.

'But?' Ben prompted.

'We both have different views on what it is,' said Jeremy.

'We don't always agree on how to work it out.'

'This is just confusing,' Ben said, 'and annoying. I mean, everyone has always said, "Don't do that, it's wrong," or, "This is the right thing to do." That doesn't make sense if there isn't a right thing to do. Or there are several.'

Ian adjusted his shirt cuffs. 'I believe that certain things are intrinsically wrong: betraying a promise, stealing, killing, and such like.'

Ben looked at Jeremy. Surely he wasn't going to deny that these things were wrong?

Jeremy pulled his head out of the picnic hamper. 'Hard-boiled eggs? Isn't there any pâté? Or fatty cheese? I believe that nothing is ever wrong in itself. Lying, stealing, even killing, *can* be right. It depends on the circumstances: only the consequences of the action matter. Of course, this type of behaviour produces bad consequences on the whole, so it will usually be wrong to do these things. But not necessarily.'

Well, both of these views made sense. Some things were just bad, of course they were. And it was obvious that you had to think about the consequences of your actions. 'So what's the difference?' he asked.

'According to his way of thinking,' explained Jeremy, 'there are certain rules for acting. Do not kill, do not steal, etc.'

Ben nodded. He was familiar with these rules.

'It's definitely wrong to steal, so you probably shouldn't have made that promise not to tell,' Ian said. 'However, now that you've made the promise, it's wrong to break it. If people decided it was OK to break promises then promises would never be believed in the first place—they'd be just so many useless words.'

'Bu-ut,' said Jeremy, 'it's obvious that as soon as you have more than one rule of behaviour they might contradict each other. As you say, it was wrong to make the promise and now it's wrong to break it. That's not very helpful, is it? It's the same if you talk about rights: the right to life, the right to trust people who make promises. More than one single right brings the possibility of conflict. Then what do you do?'

Ben thought he understood the problem. 'If I tell on Joe, then I'll break my promise. Promises shouldn't be broken. If I don't, I'll be letting him steal, and stealing is wrong. If I kill

Clare then that violates her right to life. But what about the right to life of everyone else Matt is about to kill instead?'

'That's just it,' said Jeremy. 'How does the system of rules help you know what to do?' Ian opened his mouth to answer, but Jeremy barged in. 'And there's an even bigger problem with your argument. Imagine,' he turned to Ben, 'that some thugs come to your house. They are after your dad, they say he owes them money. They want you to tell them where he is, but you know they'll beat him up really badly. Do you tell them?'

'Not if I can get away with it,' said Ben.

'Of course not. But then you'd be telling a lie. And telling a lie is wrong, always wrong, isn't it, Ian?'

'Absolutely, yes. Lying is always prohibited.' Ian pointed at Jeremy's shirt, drawing attention to the mismatched buttons.

'But surely it is ludicrous to have rules for behaviour that cannot be broken *whatever the consequences*,' said Jeremy, undoing his buttons. 'Wouldn't it be right to protect your dad from the thugs, even if it meant lying? Surely it's sometimes better to break the rules? But then your view is just silly.' Jeremy refastened his shirt buttons, flashing a patch of dark curly chest hair.

Ian was spreading cream cheese evenly over a slice of bread.

'If you can say that breaking a rule is OK,'

Jeremy continued, 'if you do it to avoid a really bad outcome, then what is the point of having rules? Either the rules are inviolable and that is why you have them, or they can sometimes be broken, in which case the rules aren't rules after all.'

'In a proper moral dilemma,' said Ian, wiping the knife clean, 'whatever you do involves doing something wrong. Obviously there's not an easy answer. If there were then it wouldn't be a real dilemma.'

'With horns that could catch you,' added Lila, giving herself horns with two sticks of celery and miming a bull.

'Whatever you do is wrong?' said Jeremy. 'That's not much use, is it?'

'But it's true, and you can't gloss over it,' said Ian. 'Stealing is wrong, breaking a promise is wrong. Two wrongs can't be turned into a right.'

'I say that there's something seriously wrong with a moral code that can't tell you which option to take,' said Jeremy.

'And I say that there's something seriously wrong with a moral code that always thinks it has an easy answer,' said Ian.

They stared at each other. Ian pushed his finger deep into an egg as he tried to take off the shell.

'So,' Ben said, 'why bother with the rules if you can find reasons why you might want to break them? I mean, I wouldn't want to help them find my dad and beat him up.'

'You need rules,' sad Ian, 'because otherwise all that matters are the consequences, and not the nature, of the action.'

'What is so wrong with considering the consequences of your actions?' Ben asked. 'No thanks,' he said, refusing the offered egg. 'If murder is wrong then that must be because the consequences are bad—someone dies.'

Ian was about to bite into the egg but spoke instead. 'It's not that considering the consequences is bad in itself. What I object to is the results you get when consequences are the only consideration. If something is only wrong because of bad consequences, then—if the consequences change—the thing might no longer be wrong.'

'Which is as it should be,' said Jeremy.

Ian shook his head. 'For example, it could be right to kill someone.'

'Just so,' said Jeremy.

'If there are no rules, no absolute prohibitions, then anything is possible. It's a horrible, horrible theory.' Ian popped the whole egg into his mouth.

Jeremy was struggling to cut a slippery tomato with a blunt knife. He seemed harmless enough. 'Are you going to tell me about the horrible, horrible theory?'

Jeremy gave up on the tomato and handed it to Lila. She found a sharper knife and sliced it easily. 'The only thing that matters about an action is the consequences,' he said. 'An action is bad if it affects people in bad ways and good if it affects people in good ways.'

'And how do you decide?' asked Ben.

'You work out the consequences of all possible actions and then you do the one that produces the greatest happiness for the greatest number of people,' explained Jeremy. 'You have to consider not just your own happiness, but also the well-being of everyone who could be affected by your actions. If I value my happiness, which obviously I do, and everyone else values theirs, which is a fact, then it makes sense that it would be a good thing to maximise the overall happiness in the world.'

'So,' Ben said, 'you have to see how happy a particular action makes some people and compare it with how unhappy it makes others, and then also check it against other possible actions?'

'Yes, and do the best one,' said Jeremy.

'Sounds reasonable so far,' said Ben.

'Not at all,' said Ian, having dealt with the egg. 'Have you thought about how difficult it is to know all the possible consequences of your actions? And how do you know what makes people happy? You'd spend so long working it out, you'd never do anything!'

Ben remembered the Symposium: describing happiness wasn't as easy as it sounded. He'd heard ten different views in ten minutes.

'Firstly,' argued Jeremy, 'you only have to take into account all the consequences you could reasonably know about. And secondly, there are some obvious things that help happiness—not being tortured, being alive to enjoy family and holidays. Think of the bigger picture. It doesn't have to be about whether you prefer reading or ice skating. Pass me that cheese, will you?'

'In that case,' said Ben, ducking as Ian lobbed the Brie at Jeremy, 'it doesn't sound so different from not stealing and not lying. These things make people unhappy.' He looked at Ian. 'Isn't it similar to what you were arguing for?'

'It's very different,' Ian said, struggling to open a jar of chutney. 'For example, stealing makes some people unhappy and others happy.'

'How can you object to making people as happy as possible,' asked Ben, 'assuming you knew how to do it?'

'Let's think about your dream,' Ian suggested, handing the jar to Lila. 'At that moment in the classroom, what do you think you should do?'

Ben winced at the memory of the two girls scrunched in a pool of blood. 'I don't think I could bring myself to kill Clare. Or anyone really.'

'Quite right,' said Ian. 'And you shouldn't. You don't want to be a murderer, like Matt. You mustn't pander to his sick ideas.'

Lila opened the jar easily with a pop and rolled her eyes at Ben, who smiled.

'But do you want the deaths of thirty people on your conscience? You are responsible for all the outcomes that you could have prevented,' said Jeremy.

'You think I ought to have killed her?' Ben said.

'Yes.'

'Murderer!' said Ian, waving his knife.

'No, you're the mass murderer.' Jeremy reached for the chutney before Ian could get any. 'Surely the outcome of thirty people living is the best?'

'Of course it's better when fewer people are murdered, but not at any cost. And that is what I cannot accept. A death can never be "good" because the consequences are "good". But your moral code says that it is *right* to kill!' He snatched back the chutney. 'If I have to choose the lesser of two evils, I choose neither.'

'But you have to do something. Prissily saying that you don't want killing on your conscience ignores the fate of the thirty classmates. And you are responsible for that fate, since your refusal to act directly results in their death.'

'It is my duty to avoid committing an evil

216

act—murder—but it cannot be my duty to always prevent other people from doing bad things. I am only responsible for things that I do, not anyone else. Inaction has no moral weight, only action.'

'Absolutely not. Look, Ben, when the UN Force was in Kosovo their orders stated that they were not allowed to help villagers escape when under attack.' Jeremy prided himself on keeping up with world events whenever possible. 'Since the aim of the attackers was to get rid of these people from the area then if the UN assisted this movement they would be contributing to the "ethnic cleansing". But more people died because of this policy than might otherwise have done. That's just wrong: they could have saved these people and they didn't.'

'No, no. They saved as many lives as they could within the acceptable limits. It would be absolutely wrong for the UN to play a part in the ethnic cleansing, which was an evil project.'

'Well, I don't buy that.'

'Thankfully, you are not in charge.'

'Thankfully, *you* are not in charge.'

Ben was inclined to agree with both of them, no matter what Plato said about philosophers running the world.

'Going back to Ben's classroom problem,' Jeremy said, 'what if you could save 20,000 lives? Or 200,000? Just by killing one person. Surely you have to prefer a world where more

217

lives are saved?'

'But once you allow killing of innocents at all, as a means to other ends, you are on a very slippery slope. If it's acceptable to sacrifice one person for a greater good, why not ten or 10,000 if the greater good is important enough? This was Stalin's view: *The death of one man is a tragedy. The death of millions is a statistic.* It's a slippery slope because once you relax the principle in one case, you have to also relax it in similar cases and there's no obvious place to stop.'

'It's perfectly easy to hold tight at the top of the slope. We can factor all these possible bad effects into our calculus of happiness. In working out the greatest happiness for the greatest number we balance the positive effects against the negative ones. Do we only have strawberry yogurt? Not peach? Obviously I don't generally think killing people is the way to achieve the best outcome. Just that you have to be more flexible than absolute prohibitions allow.'

'I only like strawberry yogurt, and I packed the picnic. I oppose the very notion of the calculation where one person's life, or future happiness, can be traded off against that of three others. If a young woman is suicidal then wouldn't it promote her happiness to kill her? Surely you especially ought to if her organs could be donated to others and save several lives at the cost of one?'

Jeremy looked uncomfortable, and not just because the yogurt had spattered all over his shirt when he opened it. 'There are bad side effects from killing people like that: society would be less secure, the family would be upset. The overall consequences of killing her are not positive. I would at most have a duty to make her happy, not to kill her if she's unhappy.'

' "Side effects" aren't enough of a reason! I want my life protected even when the side effects go away. Killing her should be wrong because it's a Bad Act, not dependent on whether she has a family who will mind. We shouldn't decide who lives or dies, it should be a matter of nature.'

'Why?' Jeremy's attempt to wipe away the yogurt had produced a big pink smudge.

'It goes against justice and human dignity to use the life of an innocent person to produce a benefit that this person cannot share in, especially if they don't have a say in their own fate. You hide this by creating a "social entity" that appears to make a sacrifice in one place and receives benefits in others. But there is no big social entity—it's just different people— and in your world the boundaries between people, as individuals, are broken down. What justification can be made to those who lose out in the happiness stakes?'

'What do you mean by that?' asked Ben.

'Just that, if you were the one who sacrificed

your happiness for the general good, you'd be miserable. Would it be any consolation to know that other people were better off as a result?'

'It might be—for some,' said Jeremy.

'What happened to doing unto others as you would they do unto you? Where everyone is protected by the system?'

'Nothing can be more important than happiness. Not even justice.'

'No.' Ian shook his head. 'Your idea of the greatest happiness is founded on a big mistake. You say we value happiness most of all, and therefore we want as much of it as possible. If you want to maximise happiness then anything is acceptable if it contributes to this goal.'

'Yes. I don't see what is wrong with that.'

'But this fundamentally misunderstands what it means to value something. The way to value friendship is not to sacrifice one friend to make four more.'

'Humph!' Jeremy glowered at Ian.

'You're playing God with people's lives.'

'We're all playing God with people's lives,' Jeremy said, scraping out the last of his yogurt. 'Our actions—more rightly, inactions—affect people all the time. If you walk past a homeless child, you have failed: you could have helped and didn't, so you must take some responsibility. No man is an island.'

'In that case, your theory is just too demanding,' said Ian, opening his yogurt very carefully. 'If I could share my money with one person who was really poor, I'd increase their happiness by more than mine would decrease. So the overall happiness count is up. In your world where there is always one best possible action, sitting doing philosophy rather than keeping lonely old people company is not just slightly self-indulgent, it's *morally wrong*.' Despite his efforts, some yogurt fell on to his leg. 'How is anyone supposed to live up to that standard?' He looked down in horror at his trousers. 'You said earlier that you don't have a duty to kill the unhappy girl, but you do have a duty to make her happy. I think that's still a lot to ask.'

'I demand heroism!' said Jeremy, throwing down his spoon. 'Actually, there's nothing noble in renouncing your own personal happiness to be a martyr unless there is a good chance of increasing happiness or reducing pain for others. There is no gain in denying pleasure for the sake of it. The greatest happiness for the greatest number includes yourself. However, in an unequal world such as ours, it's not hard to see that I can easily increase others' happiness by less than mine would diminish in the process.'

'Ethics shouldn't taint all our actions—only those within the moral sphere. If I spend time reading a book rather than giving blood, that's just irrelevant for morality. Asking me to behave fairly well and not hurt people is about all you have a right to demand. Also, you're more likely to get people to be moral if it's something they can hope to achieve. Saying someone ought to do something implies at the very least that they *can* do it.'

'And how does it help Ben when you say that all his options involve a wrong action? What's he supposed to do?'

'I thought we'd gone over that already,' sighed Ian, neatly folding up the yogurt lid and tucking it into the empty pot.

'We have, but you haven't given me a satisfactory answer.'

'In that case,' said Lila, standing up, 'instead of going round in circles, we shall go somewhere else. Come on, Ben.' She walked away from the picnic to a nearby ridge.

'Oh, right.' He put down his half-finished yogurt (that mild-cheese taste again) and ran off after Lila, waving goodbye to Ian and Jeremy. They were arguing, although whether it was about morality or the relative merits of peach and strawberry yogurt was hard to tell.

'Let's go the quick way down,' said Lila. She lay on her side and rolled, spinning, down the hill.

Ben rolled after her and ended up, panting and laughing, in a heap at the door to the corridor. Ben edged a bit closer to Lila, but she pushed her hair out of her eyes, took a deep breath and stood up. Her cheeks were flushed, he noticed, as she offered him her arm.

Ben wanted to discuss with her what he had heard, but he'd got hiccups from rolling down the hill. Before he could get rid of them she shoved him unceremoniously towards the hole through to the utility room.

CHAPTER FIFTY-ONE

Ben crawled out the other side, and went into the kitchen to drink a glass of water upside down. He'd always thought being moral was either just writing your thank-you letters, or something for really evil people to worry about. Since he wasn't the type to mug old ladies, morals hadn't been much of an issue.

He filled another glass of water. It seemed morality might matter even if you were just minding your own business. As Ian had pointed out, if you took Jeremy's theory to its limit then you were more or less immoral all the time by not helping others. That was terrible. Wasn't it better to have a system that just said you can be good if you avoid doing these things? Some clear rules, but not too demanding? For a real dilemma, though, the rules didn't help at all. Whatever you did was wrong. There would definitely be times when you'd want to break the rules. It seemed that both Jeremy's and Ian's moral systems made you into a bad person, since it was pretty much impossible to follow either one properly. Not very helpful.

'Ben. There you are,' said his mum. 'Dad's in the car already. We'll be late for Granny. What are you doing?'

Ben was still holding his breath. He gestured frantically, until he exhaled. 'Hiccups.'

'Oh, OK. But please get changed. You know how Granny hates it when you wear your hooded top. Have you still got your pyjamas on underneath? Why are you covered in grass?'

He'd gone for proper advice and they had only confused him. Now he couldn't even think that there was a right thing to do, let alone work out what it was. Enough! He'd stick with the real world. He wished it wasn't lunch with Granny.

CHAPTER FIFTY-TWO

'There you are!'

Ludwig Wittgenstein started. He shuffled his papers rapidly.

'What are you reading?' asked Socrates.

'Just some propositional logic. Very sterile. You wouldn't get it.'

'Try me. I thought I saw a splash of red.'

'Red?'

'Not reading *Hello!* magazine by any chance? It is missing from the library. Iris Murdoch was looking for it.'

'Oh that. I was just ruminating on how a picture can represent a state of affairs.'

'Is that so? And how are David Beckham's affairs represented?'

'David who?' Wittgenstein replied unconvincingly. 'I was just leaving anyway.'

'I don't suppose you've been keeping track of Ben's progress?' asked Socrates.

'Is he still coming then?'

'Yes.'

Disappointment showed on Wittgenstein's face.

'Can you think of any reason why he wouldn't be?' Socrates asked pointedly.

'Oh no. But do you think it's all right to leave the airing cupboard open like that? Where any man and his dog could wander in? What about illegal immigrants?'

'You're handy with tools, aren't you?' asked Socrates. 'Wouldn't shy away from a big welding job.'

'Oh, is she going out with him now?' Wittgenstein looked at the magazine.

Socrates glanced down. 'Is she? I thought she was with that other one. Don't change the subject.'

'Well, I'm off. Late for something.'

'Will you be needing *Hello!*?'

Wittgenstein hesitated. 'Absolutely not.'

Why is she wearing a dress that looks like a lampshade? thought Socrates.

Perhaps I should visit Ben for a man-to-man chat, thought Wittgenstein.

CHAPTER FIFTY-THREE

By 8 p.m., Ben was already fast asleep on the sofa. His mum worried that he was working too hard at Cod Almighty: had he taken on too much this summer? Ben certainly had—but not in the way she thought. Ben had been up for several extra hours—and survived lunch with Granny. No one else could have noticed, but Ben's long summer days often lasted at least twenty-seven hours.

Ben was so far gone that he didn't even feel the pressure on his arm as his sisters wrote graffiti on it in blue permanent marker.

I . . . am . . . the . . . biggest . . . prat . . . in, wrote Matty in deliberate capitals.

'You've run out of space, you idiot,' Katie whispered.

'It'll fit on his hand if I write it smaller,' said Matty.

CHAPTER FIFTY-FOUR

'What's that blue stuff on your arm?' Tony said.

'Nothing.'

'Show me.'

Ben pulled up his sleeve and showed him the barely-faded writing.

'Hygiene, Ben. I'd appreciate it if you would confess your inadequacies in a more sanitary way,' Tony said, putting his cup of coffee down on the counter. 'I'm just popping out to get a paper. You can take care of everything, can't you?' And he left before Ben could answer.

Ben had been taking care of everything most of the time since he'd started work here. Despite the grand concepts, Tony was a fairly hands-off manager.

Grown-ups had always given the impression that you got more freedom as you got older. When you're fifteen you can . . . When you're eighteen you can . . . When you leave home you can . . . But that was just to keep him tame. What with work and traffic lights and rules about how many vegetables to eat, adults were even less free than children. The people in the World of Ideas seemed free—they didn't have to do anything they didn't want to. Did he really have to wait till he was dead to do what he wanted? Just when there was hardly anything you could do, and everything tasted of cheese.

Ben whistled the tune to his favourite computer game while he finished wiping the counter.

The shop-door bell rang.

'That's wrong.'

Wittgenstein was leaning on the counter. Ben jumped back in surprise.

'It goes like this,' he said, and whistled the tune in a powerful virtuoso tone.

'You're brilliant at whistling.'

'I know. Beethoven. You've gone up in my estimation.'

'It . . . er . . . thank you.' Honesty was an overrated virtue.

'So tell me,' Wittgenstein said, unsmilingly. 'What can we say about what it means to enjoy a piece of music?'

'Err. Well . . .' Ben enjoyed whistling but how could he say more than that? He enjoyed it because he enjoyed it.

'Wherein lies the value of a Beethoven sonata? Hmm? The sequence of notes? The feeling he had while composing it? The state of mind produced by listening to it?'

'Right. The last one, I suppose. The state of mind that comes when you hear it.'

'No!' Wittgenstein shouted. 'I reject your answer, because you're trying to give an explanation. It's not expressible in words. Can I have some chips?'

'But you insisted I answer you. I didn't want to.'

'You always do what people tell you? I hope so.' He looked into Ben's eyes. 'Giiive meee some chiiips.'

Ben scooped a few of the less fresh chips off the hotplate into a white paper bag and put them down on the counter.

'Whereof one cannot speak, thereof one must be silent,' Wittgenstein said, and placed a chip in his mouth.

Ben dutifully shut up. He busied himself getting sauce sachets out of the large boxes and piling them on the counter. Wittgenstein was savouring his banquet, chip by forbidden chip, chewing each one carefully and keeping it in his mouth for as long as possible.

'It's like asking why a joke is funny,' Wittgenstein said suddenly. 'The same joke— one person laughs and the other doesn't. The state of the world (that is, the joke) is the same, and yet everything is different.'

Ben felt very much like the one who didn't get the joke.

'Philosophy is about policing the border between sense and nonsense. Are you up to the task?'

'I . . . er . . .' It wasn't fair. That wasn't a job he'd applied for. He wondered which side of the boundary Wittgenstein was on.

'Fancy finding you here,' said a voice from behind the counter.

'Lila!' He was even more pleased to see her than usual.

'Ludwig Wittgenstein, I think you'd better get back home. No, leave the chips where they are.'

'A case of the fish calling the eel slippery,' he said. But he went round the counter and back, via the cold store, to the World of Ideas, eating a last handful of chips as he went. It is better to be feared than loved, he reminded himself.

'Come on, Ben, let's go.' Lila went towards the cold store, expecting Ben to follow her. She turned round. 'What is it?'

'I can't leave the shop,' he said.

'Yes you can. You know nothing happens while you're gone. What is it really?'

'I'm not a philosopher. I'm a . . . normal person.'

'Thanks.'

'I meant—'

'Don't let Ludwig Wittgenstein put you off. That's what he's trying to do.'

'Why?'

'He doesn't approve of the kind of philosophy we've been teaching you.'

Ben wondered why Ludwig Wittgenstein would care what kind of philosophy he learnt. And it occurred to him to wonder, for the first time in a while, why they were bothering to teach him anything at all.

'At least come one more time,' Lila said,

230

smiling at him. 'I've got a treat for you today. Really, a proper treat, not a philosophical one. Please come.'

He could put up with a few more philosophical doubts if that was the price of Lila's treat. I'll live life rather than worry about it, he promised himself.

CHAPTER FIFTY-FIVE

I am the biggest prat in—the whole world? Lila read.

'Are you?' said Ben. 'I thought it was me.'

'People always pitied me for being an only child, and I could never understand why.'

They set off through the walled garden. Lila opened a small wooden door in the far wall.

'Through here is Socrates' private estate. He's having a wine-tasting. We've got various vineyards here.'

People were gathered under the shade of the trees. There were two long wooden tables laid out with bottles and glasses. They helped themselves.

'This is good,' said Ben. 'Is it?'

'I like this one best,' said Lila.

'Me too. Excellent.'

'Would you say that Socrates is old?' Lila asked.

'Sure. He's really old.'

'I don't just mean the fact that he was born nearly 2,500 years ago—as you would see it.'

'He's still really old. Like sixty or something.'

'Seventy, actually.'

'My granny's eighty-two, which is about as old as anyone can possibly be. She might say Socrates was young. Actually, she's probably the only one who would believe that I've met him. She claims to have met everyone.'

'Anyway, it's just an example. Let's suppose you do want to call him old.'

'OK. Suppose away.' He touched Lila's glass with his.

'So, if Socrates is old, would you agree that he was old yesterday?'

'Obviously.'

'So someone one day younger than Socrates is still old?'

'Ye-es.' This was disconcertingly easy so far.

'What about last week: was Socrates old then?'

'Of course. One week doesn't make a difference.' Ben helped himself to another glass of red. The taste was growing on him.

'So the person one week younger than Socrates is still old? And presumably the person one week younger than *him* is also old, since a week can't make a difference to whether you are old or not, as you said?'

'Right.'

'And we can carry on, taking a week away

each time. And we agree that a week less doesn't change the fact that he is old. But then we reach the conclusion that *you* are also old. Take away enough weeks and we arrive at your age.'

'Don't be silly, I'm not old. Well, I'm fifteen and a half so I'm not *young*, but Socrates is ancient. You can't just keep taking weeks away like that, one at a time, and then say that everyone is old.'

'Why not? Where should I stop? You agree that one week in age can't make the difference between being old and being young? You can't say a person is not old at sixty but old at sixty-plus-one-week.'

'No, but surely you agree that some people are old and some are young, and that there's a difference?'

'Of course I do, but that wasn't the result we got.'

The words 'old' and 'young' had always made sense when he used them, but suddenly there were no boundaries. There had to be some point where a person *became* old, or he would never *be* old. But it wasn't that one day you went to bed young and woke up old. Maybe there wasn't a 'point' where you became old after all? But then how did you get to be old? He poured some more wine for inspiration.

'And I'm not just tricking you because old and young are special concepts. Let's sit down

233

for a moment.' They chose the shade of a venerable tree. 'Look at these.' Lila pulled lots of coloured pieces of paper out of her pocket. 'What colour is this?'

'Red.'

'And this one?'

'Orange.'

'You sure?'

'Of course I'm sure. It's not a difficult question.'

'Let's put the orange one away for now,' she said, writing *orange* on the back. 'So, you agreed that this one was red. What about this next one?'

'I can't really tell the difference. The colour's practically the same as the first one.'

'So it must be red. Now compare the second colour with this third one. Are they the same?'

'They look pretty much the same to me.'

'So it must also be red.'

Lila showed him piece after piece of coloured paper. 'And what about this final one?' she asked.

'As before.' Ben was getting tired. The day was warm and the wine was drunk. 'It's hard to tell the difference from the previous colour.'

'So it's red?'

'I suppose so.'

'Look at it properly, though. What colour is it?'

'Actually, I'd say it was orange.'

'That's what you said before.' She turned

the piece of paper over. He saw *orange* as she had written it a few minutes ago. 'So now we have moved away from red to orange. But when? Each time you agreed that the colour was in the same category as the one before.'

'I don't know.' Ben was annoyed. Had he been tricked? He could call an orange 'orange' and a strawberry 'red' without any difficulty outside the World of Ideas. He knew what was what when there were no philosophers around.

'It's called a paradox. You have concluded that what is orange must be red. But we know that it can't be, because orange and red are different colours.'

'So, what's the solution?'

'What's the problem?'

'Very funny. If you did the colour experiment backwards, you'd get the opposite result. End up calling red "orange", wouldn't you?'

'Yes,' Lila said encouragingly.

'OK. So the problem arises because we can't notice the small changes in the colour—or in the age for that matter—but the two end points are definitely different.'

'You could never make this mistake with a triangle. It couldn't change into a square without you noticing. But colour and age are less definite concepts. We know there is a difference between red and orange, but we can't say for certain where the boundary is. It's not defined by "having three sides" but it's a matter of judgement. How many grains of sand do you have to add to a handful before it becomes a "heap"?'

'That's easy, 324,946. Can I have some more wine?'

'I don't think so. Perhaps the middle colour can be either red or orange. Even if we would prefer the world to provide more definite answers, it just doesn't.'

CHAPTER FIFTY-SIX

The wine-tasting registered as soon as Ben staggered into the gloomy utility room. There was something unfamiliar about the familiar landscape. He stood for one minute, or twenty, trying to work out what was different. He held on to the ironing board and it fell over with a crash.

'Hello?' Ben's mum called from the kitchen.

'Ow.' The washing machine moved and blocked Ben's way.

His mum came into the room. 'Ben! What are you doing here?'

Ben felt incredibly tired. 'I might just lie and go down.'

'Aren't you supposed to be at work?'

Work. Of course he was. 'Just going.'

Ben crawled behind the washing machine and into the World of Ideas.

'Lila!'

'What is it?'

'I'm supposed to be at work. I forgot.'

'Oh bugger. Sorry.'

Lila opened a door. Ben found himself back in the cold store.

A customer was waiting.

'Finally I can get some service round here.'

'Shorry.'

'I thought you were trying cryogenics in there, I've been waiting so long.'

Thank goodness Tony wasn't back from the paper shop yet.

CHAPTER FIFTY-SEVEN

Socrates had had a tip-off from Lila. He stormed into the workshop and was hit by a blast of hot air and fumes.

'*Turn off that blow torch!*'

Wittgenstein looked up and shut off the gas.

'And take off that helmet when I talk to you.'

Wittgenstein shook his helmet from side to side.

'I know you went to see him,' said Socrates. 'You went to the fish-and-chip shop.'

There was a muffled reply.

'You even ate chips!'

The helmet came off. 'The chips are a red

237

herring.'

'You ate fish too?'

'What? No! The point is not what I ate.'

'The point is that you went there. We can't have just anyone popping over for day trips whenever they feel like it. It was OK for me to visit Ben, because I'm in a position of responsibility.'

'You visited him too?'

'Err, well, in the interests of research. They've got these shoes on wheels.'

'Shoes on wheels?' asked Wittgenstein, puzzled. 'Did anyone see you?'

'Everyone has eaten chips except for me! And I am President.'

'Enjoy it while it lasts.'

'I'm clearly not enjoying it enough. I can't believe you ate chips!'

CHAPTER FIFTY-EIGHT

Ben needed time to think about everything that had happened. He was pleased that they had shown him a new way to look at the world, but if only he could switch it off from time to time. No one else seemed to see the world that way.

Ben remembered Lila's face in Cod Almighty when she was trying to persuade him to go back with her. If there was even a chance that she was happy to see him then, well, he had to see her. She was probably lonely amongst all those old dead fogies.

Philosophy was hard work, it's true, but what had that man in the Symposium said about higher pleasures? Greater pleasures were more fulfilling because they were harder to reach. Something like that. Would he rather have a boring girl who was easy to pull or a stunner who was hard to get? More a physical than a metaphysical example, it's true. For all his new philosophy, Ben was still a teenage boy. Who had he wanted to spend time with this summer—Lila or Clare?

He was still looking for answers.

CHAPTER FIFTY-NINE

'Hey Ben,' said Lila. 'Nice to see you.'

Nice to see you! 'I was at work earlier and that guy came in,' Ben said. 'You know, the customer who left the wallet last Friday, the wallet Joe took.'

'I remember.'

'Well, obviously he asked if I'd seen it and I pretended not to know anything.'

'I see,' said Lila.

Ben couldn't tell if she thought he was a bad person or not.

'I know that Ian would disapprove. Stealing

239

is supposed to be wrong. But I don't want to lose Joe as a friend just because of this. I mean, maybe Jeremy would even argue that Joe did the right thing. If the customer's richer than Joe, then isn't there more happiness overall with things this way round?' Ben paused, not sure that this argument would convince anyone outside the World of Ideas.

'Since you're still wondering about these sorts of questions, we can think some more about ethics today, if you like.'

'Speaking of ethics, kind of, why did Ian and Jeremy care so much about whether it was strawberry or peach yogurt, when it all tastes of cheese?' Ben asked.

'It's a point of principle. It makes them feel alive. We miss flavours. We miss lots of things. You wouldn't understand.'

'What's it like being dead?'

'Like being alive, but with the mute button on.'

'Whistle, what are you doing here?' Three-quarters of dog were sticking out into the entrance hall. Ben pulled the rest of him through and fell on his back. Whistle landed on top of Ben, shook himself out and went over to sniff Lila. 'He must have followed me in. Mum sometimes shuts him in the utility room. I'd better get him back home before someone else arrives.'

But Whistle had other ideas. He wasn't going to give up a whole new world of smells

240

so easily. The far door had been left ajar and the dog scampered towards it.

'Whistle! Come back here now.' The dog disappeared through the door. 'I said come back!'

'Well, it didn't work,' Lila said unhelpfully.

Ben ran towards the door. 'Come on. Before we lose him completely.'

'He's gone to the market,' Lila said.

They chased after the dog, who crashed into a flower stall, spilling water. Ben trampled over the blooms as he ran past.

'Oi! Get off my carnations, you vandal.'

Whistle tripped up a man carrying a huge pallet of tomatoes. Ben slipped in the slush. Whistle ran through a pile of fallen leaves, which stuck to his tomato-covered fur. He veered down a side street that led out of the marketplace.

'Stop that dog!' shouted Lila.

A man threw open his arms and ran towards Whistle, who jumped up playfully, knocking him to the ground. Whistle licked his face.

'Good dog.' He pushed Whistle's head away, got up and brushed himself off. 'Sit. Sit. SIT. Dogs' minds are very inferior to ours, you know.' Whistle stopped wagging his tail. 'It's not entirely their fault. Sophisticated thought is simply not possible without language.'

'Why is that?' asked Ben, stroking Whistle's ears and picking leaves off his back.

'Well, this dog may believe that you are

about to take him for a walk, but can he believe that you will also do it tomorrow?'

'Err . . . Why is that so much harder?'

'To plan for the future and to remember the past—these require concepts like "tomorrow" and "yesterday". You need to represent times other than the present moment, so that you can talk about episodes (and things) that are not here and now. If the chair is not in the same room as you, you cannot point at it; instead you need some way to signal "that ugly pink chair next door". This all requires a language of sorts.'

'I didn't think that "I'll go to the park tomorrow" was such a complicated idea.'

'If you want to go to the park now, you just go there. Imagine trying to plan the trip without being able to indicate "tomorrow". Language is also necessary in order to have ideas about ideas.'

'Why do I want to have ideas about ideas?' He held Whistle tightly by the collar and patted his side.

'You have them all the time. I feel scared is a basic thought. But what about: I wish I didn't feel scared? You need to turn feeling scared into an object that you can have opinions about. This requires language. So, to get back to what we can do and dogs can't'—he looked pityingly at Whistle—'any silly dog can have the idea: I want a biscuit, but never a thought about this idea, for example: I don't want to

242

want a biscuit. You definitely need language to be able to represent the two layers of ideas.'

'No dog would be stupid enough to think: I don't want to want a biscuit.' Whistle nudged Ben's leg.

'Whistle? Was that you?'

The dog growled. 'All this chauvinism about language is so old hat.'

'You can talk!'

'It's no big deal.' Whistle scratched his ear. 'Language is overrated. There are plenty of interesting thoughts that can be had without language. You can visualise the route to the park, recognise someone by their smell or imagine a piece of music in your head.'

Ben didn't know whether to be more shocked that Whistle could speak or that he was so good at philosophy. This was the dog who walked into the glass door in the kitchen every time it was shut.

'Oh come on!' retorted the philosopher. 'That's fine as far as it goes. But if you want someone else to play your music, you need some way to communicate it.'

'I could sing it.' Whistle gave out a vaguely tuneful bark.

'You don't have the concept of a cat.'

'The concept of a cat indeed. Why would I want to?'

'Hang on.' Ben was getting left behind. 'I do know about cats, but what are you on about with your "concepts of cats"?' How annoying if

243

his dog knew more philosophy than him.

'Has it given you paws for thought?' asked Lila.

'Think of it as labelling types of things in the world. You learn about "bread" and later when you come across another loaf, you know that it's also bread, even if it looks quite different because it's brown and not white, square and not stick-shaped. Imagine if every time you found something new in the world you had to figure out whether to eat it, ignore it or run away from it. If you don't have language to classify things as biscuits, cats and cars then your relationship with the world is very basic.'

'I've had enough of this,' said Whistle. 'You humans need to think that language is very important because otherwise you wouldn't feel special. But, let's face it, you have no idea what we dogs really think about cats. Ben, we're going home.' He trotted round in a circle. 'Which way is it?'

'Follow me,' Lila offered.

'Wait,' called the philosopher after them, desperately. 'Tell me what you really think about cats! I want to know.'

Lila took them the long route back, to bypass the market and its angry stallholders.

'Can you always speak?' asked Ben.

Whistle put his head on one side, mysteriously.

'And you're covered in mud and tomatoes.' He might be a philosophising dog, but he was

244

still just a dog. 'Time for a bath.'

'I hate baths. And, while we're talking, I hate being told to "sit". People don't tell *you* to sit down all the time.'

'They do quite a lot, actually. Now, if we lift you up, you can squeeze through to the other side.' Lila and Ben struggled with Whistle's hind legs. 'And don't get tomato on the sofa.'

CHAPTER SIXTY

'Babysitting' wasn't a very accurate term, really. It would have helped if he could have actually sat on his sisters to maintain control. Sadly that wasn't possible since there were two of them and only one of him.

'I can't believe this still won't wash off,' Ben said. After four days it was like a large bruise on his arm, with the words 'biggest prat' just legible.

'LOSER,' said Katie, making an L with her hand.

'MINGER,' said Matty, as she made an M with her thumbs and forefingers.

'WHATEVER,' replied Ben, doing a W. He went into his room, but Matty followed him, hanging on to his sleeve.

'Beeeennn.' Matty stepped on his feet. 'Will you play Monopoly with me?'

'Of course not.'

'Pleeeeeeeease.'

'No.' He tried to push her away.

'Why not?'

'Because we played it yesterday.'

'That was *ages ago*.'

'Can't you play with Katie?'

'She says I cheat.'

'You do. You should learn that dishonest behaviour is not rewarded.' Listen to him, he was talking like Ian. Ben thought about Joe and the wallet and felt a bit of a fraud.

CHAPTER SIXTY-ONE

Ben tied Whistle up in the kitchen. The dog whimpered pathetically.

'Sorry, Whis, but the World of Ideas is my special place. Don't tell anyone where I've gone, will you?'

Whistle growled, his ears flattened back.

*   *   *

'Did you get all the tomato out of his fur?' Lila asked as they walked down the corridor.

'Most of it.'

'At the picnic we looked at practical questions: what would be the right thing to do, and why? But you can also ask about whether, when different groups answer this question in

246

different ways, one of them must be wrong. And there is always the problem of why you should bother to do the right thing, even if you do know what it is.'

They passed two men arguing vigorously in what sounded like Russian. Lila indicated a door: *Morality: Fact or Fiction?*

It was dark inside. At first Ben thought it was a big room with the lights dimmed but he quickly realised that they were outdoors and it was night-time. Ben followed Lila down a muddy, grassy path. In the distance were flashing lights. He heard bits of music, clanks and shouting.

'It's a fairground!'

'We're not here just for the waltzers.'

'Surely we're not going to talk about philosophy all the time? No rides at all?'

'We'll see.'

They walked past a coconut shy.

'Roll up, roll up, great prizes!' They were a strange mixture—enormous pink fluffy elephants, bottles of cheap wine, and huge fat books.

'Hang on.' That big beard was familiar. 'Aren't you—?'

'Karl Marx, yes.'

'Do you live here too?'

'Not usually. I'm travelling with the fairground. Want a go on the coconuts?'

'Maybe. Isn't it a bit capitalist?'

'Oh no. I glue the coconuts down to subvert

247

the bourgeois system.'

'Really?'

'However, I often give out prizes to those who miss. From each according to his ability, to each according to his needs. Stuffed giraffe?' Marx offered a cuddly toy almost as tall as Ben. Its head waved menacingly.

'No thanks.' Ben was not convinced that his needs were best met by a giant toy giraffe. How would he get it home?

CHAPTER SIXTY-TWO

At the dodgems, there were at least twenty philosophers bumping around in the brightly coloured cars, shouting friendly abuse at each other. Jack Cavendish and Oliver Whitby were sharing a car. They caught Ian Faulkner by surprise with a sideways lunge and laughed like naughty schoolboys. Ian whizzed away as fast as he could go: which was not very fast.

A man with prominent cheekbones and a severe expression approached him. He was wearing khaki trousers and a cricket jumper. 'I'm Samuel Hawthorne. Sam. Good to meet you.'

'Hello,' said the man behind him, who was much rounder, with black eyebrows like caterpillars. 'Albert Chalk.' He was wearing a slightly worn grey suit with a white T-shirt.

248

Beneath his large ankles was a pair of old white trainers.

'Ben,' Ben said, unnecessarily.

'Remind me what we're supposed to be talking about,' said Albert, gazing at the dodgems. 'Good charge!'

'Today,' Sam said seriously, 'we are discussing the status of ethical truths. Do you know what that means, Ben?'

'Not really.' Not at all.

'It's probably best just to tell you what we think and then you'll get the hang of it,' suggested Sam. 'I'll begin, since Albert's only half listening. Ethical truths—by which I mean things like "Murder is wrong"—are, quite simply, facts about the universe. In the same way that the law of gravity is a fact about the universe. Certain things just are wrong, no matter who does them, where or when. However the world had turned out, the rules of morality would have been the same.'

'I am listening, actually,' said Albert. 'Not that I like what I'm hearing. How can moral codes be this sort of fact? They don't exist in a vacuum. Things are moral or immoral insofar as they affect humans in certain ways. It's about doing what is right by other people. How could it be wrong to steal if there were no people to mind if you took their stuff?'

'Morality is fundamental,' said Sam. 'It's pre-humanity.'

'It's a bit like maths,' Lila said. 'People

disagree about whether maths is discovered or invented. Did people make up maths to deal with the world, or was it out there to be revealed when you explored?'

'The law of gravity would function even if no humans had ever existed, but morality is a human invention,' said Albert, raising his bushy eyebrows. 'Something that society creates to function well.'

'A human invention, you say?' asked Sam, removing his jumper and tying it round his shoulders. 'But, to a degree, each society—at different times and in different places—comes up with different moral codes. If you won't accept that values are fixed, permanent facts about the world, then you have to say that every set of moral codes generated by a society is right. So slavery was right, female circumcision is right, and so on.'

'I certainly don't want to say that.'

'But how can you not, if you say that the rules of morality are merely generated by humans to make society function well? How can you say that some rules people come up with are right and some are wrong? Surely all must be equally right, if they have been agreed upon by a group?'

'You want there to be an absolute moral standard so that you can say that certain moral codes are misguided?'

'Yes. That's about it.'

'And where does this standard come from?

A burning bush?'

'For example, God could give authority to a set of moral commands, yes.'

'Is something good because God says it is good, or does God command whatever is good because it is good?'

'God reveals what is good.'

'Whatever. But what makes it good?'

'That God requires it.'

'So if He requires something "bad"—mass murder, say—then this becomes "good" because of God's instructions?'

'God would never do that.'

'Of course not. But say He did.'

'God is good, therefore He commands what is good.'

'He commands it *because* it is good?'

'Absolutely.'

'But then there must be something else that makes it good already, other than God choosing it.'

'Ah,' said Sam, touching his pale cheek.

'So you don't really need God at all.'

'I suppose you want to tell some trendy evolutionary story about altruism.'

'That would explain why we have certain moral feelings—why we ever help people, why we resent it when we are cheated and so on.'

'So we should just act on our instincts then? Rape is natural, oppression is natural—'

'No! Well, yes, they might be *natural* but that doesn't mean that they are *right*. Disease is natural, poisonous berries are natural, but natural isn't always good and unnatural isn't always bad. All of our characteristics can be attributed to evolution, but that doesn't mean we have to be slaves to our instincts. Just as we can have sex without reproduction—though that's the evolutionary reason for it—so we can rationally work out what is right and wrong and surpass our primal urges, whatever they may be.'

'You make it sound so easy.'

Lila handed out candyfloss. 'If everyone in the world preferred candyfloss to toffee apples, would it be a *fact about the world* that candyfloss is nicer, or just a widely held opinion?'

'It's just a matter of taste though, isn't it?' Ben said, stuffing a ball of pink sugar into his mouth and letting the woolly sweetness dissolve on his tongue. 'Someone could easily have preferred toffee apples. Although, if no one ever does prefer toffee apples, and no one ever will, then why not just say that candyfloss is nicer?' He tore off another piece and stuffed it in his mouth. 'But I don't see how this affects the question here.'

'What the question shows,' said Sam, candyfloss stuck to his hair, 'is that food is a matter of taste and that morality clearly is not. Asking if someone would be "wrong" to prefer candyfloss in a world where everyone liked toffee apples is a ridiculous question.'

You would be wrong to prefer toffee apples, Ben thought, since candyfloss was much better. But he supposed that it wasn't wrong in the sense that you were *evil* if you preferred toffee apples. Boiled sprouts, maybe.

'It does make sense, however,' Sam continued, 'to ask whether it is wrong to kill. People can prefer whichever food they want. But there is only one right way to be moral. Here, I don't want this.' He handed the rest of his candyfloss back to Lila.

'Oh no,' Albert said, greedily accepting a second pink sugar bush from Lila, 'if everyone always prefers candyfloss, then candyfloss is better. Human judgement is the key. Everyone prefers candyfloss to cod liver oil and we accept that it is a *fact* that candyfloss tastes nicer. It is wrong to kill and steal because everyone prefers not to be murdered or robbed. This is the standard.'

'Candyfloss is a silly example,' said Sam. 'Think about beauty instead. A beautiful world has more value than an ugly one, even if no one is there to experience it.'

'My arse it does!'

'Your arse has no place in a discussion of aesthetics.'

Albert wobbled his bum, and said, 'How is beauty to be judged separately from human experience? What value does a Picasso have if no one appreciates it? What does it mean to say that something is beautiful except that someone will find it so?'

'Beauty is a fixed value. Humans may differ in what they think is beautiful, but some people are simply wrong in their judgement. Just as there are absolute moral truths and some people don't appreciate them. Do you want to say that something is good as long as anyone finds it so?'

'Of course not. Some people are psychopaths.'

'And some have very bad taste in decoration. Morality is not in the eye of the beholder.'

'Let me get this clear,' said Ben. He turned to Albert. 'You think that humans are the judges of everything. If all people agree something is delicious or beautiful or good, then it is?'

'Yes,' Albert said, tearing the last bit of candyfloss off the stick. 'Man is the measure of all things.'

'But'—Ben looked at Sam—'you think that there are absolute standards in morals and art, but that candyfloss is just a matter of taste?'

Sam nodded.

'But look,' Albert said, handing the sticky stick to Lila, 'relaxing an absolute standard doesn't mean that anything goes. You can believe that morality ought to be entirely driven by human needs without thinking that all human desires are automatically good, and that any moral rule a society comes up with is right. And you don't need everyone to like a sculpture for there to be beauty there.'

Sam shook his head. 'If some people love the work of art and some despise it, how are we to decide whether it is beautiful? We just have various points of view? How can you say that a particular society has got its moral rules *wrong* if you don't have an absolute standard?'

'But an equally big problem applies when you say there is an absolute standard. How do you know which moral codes are right when there are several candidates for the standard?'

'I think mine is right.'

'Yes, you do. So does everyone. You need a better reason than that, or it's just prejudice. You think there is an absolute standard of beauty too, but coincidentally it's exactly the same as your aesthetic judgement.'

'How about judging by what produces the greatest happiness for the greatest number?' suggested Ben, remembering Jeremy Cox's idea at the picnic. 'Couldn't that be a way to decide which moral codes are good?'

'Maybe slavery would have passed this test,' said Sam. 'Since the slave owners gained, it is possible that happiness was maximised under this system. If you consider that society might be better off having an infrastructure built by cheap labour, then there's even more reason to think so.'

'I doubt it,' Albert said uncertainly, 'since the slaves suffered far more than the owners gained. Whichever system makes people's lives go best, whatever that might be. What I know for sure is that nothing is good or bad except that someone finds it so.'

'So if all humans enjoyed being tortured, it wouldn't be wrong?' said Sam.

Albert considered this. 'Just as, if everyone prefers toffee apples, then they are nicer? I suppose so. But then it wouldn't be *torture*, would it?'

'That's true,' agreed Ben. 'If we all liked it, it could hardly be called torture.' That was a confusing thought.

Sam looked rather alarmed.

'Morality must be focused around what is good or bad for humans,' Albert repeated. 'I mean, it's about doing right for people, so it cannot be a fact about the world, unrelated to human needs and desires.'

'Humans cannot be central,' said Sam, 'because humans cannot be trusted. People are not instinctively or naturally moral. They need external sanctions to get them to behave.'

'What do you mean by external sanctions?' asked Ben.

'These are various elements in society and the legal system that encourage us to behave morally,' explained Sam. 'Legal sanctions involve fines and being sent to prison. The more social, soft, sanctions include being made to feel ashamed of what you did, other people resenting you, being admired if you behave morally, and so on. We need such things to enforce moral behaviour: we can't do it by ourselves.'

'Sam thinks that everyone is only moral if it's in their interest,' explained Albert. 'In fact, heaven and hell are the ultimate persuasion to be moral.'

'So people who do the moral thing for religious reasons are the most selfish of all?' Ben said.

'Hardly,' said Sam. 'Anyway, imagine you had a cloak that made you invisible—you would behave badly if you were certain that no one would know about it.'

'I might not,' said Ben hurriedly. He wondered if that was true. What would he do? Would he steal something small? A new computer game? A new computer?

'Similarly,' Sam continued, 'you wouldn't do good deeds if you didn't get the credit for it— we do it for praise. Self-interest really is the motivating force.'

Ben was still thinking about the possibilities if he were invisible. Maybe he could sneak into Lila's bedroom. Was that immoral? He wouldn't know how to find it, anyway.

'I disagree,' said Albert. 'Most people have natural limits that stop them behaving very badly and put evil acts beyond their reach.'

Ben pulled himself back into the conversation. 'What sort of limits?' he asked.

'Well, it's unlikely that you would murder

someone even if you could get away with it. Most people have a moral sense,' said Albert.

'I doubt it,' scoffed Sam.

'Empathy is the key, the ability to imagine what it is like to be someone else. It's an almost supernatural force against the necessity of self-interest. That's why we feel bad when we cheat someone. Most of us don't actually enjoy it. And why we can't torture or kill. We simply couldn't live with ourselves if we had done these things. It has nothing to do with whether we get to hell.'

'Aha!' Sam jumped up and down. 'So you behave in a way that means you can sleep at night. That's self-interest after all. And would you do any good deeds if no one ever praised you for it?'

'I'd like to think so,' Albert said uncertainly.

'A blood donor seems selfless, but perhaps they do it to feel good about themselves. Isn't that just self-interest after all?'

'If we end up doing the right thing,' said Ben, 'why does it matter why we do it?'

'If good intentions and *empathy* were sufficient to keep us in check, then we wouldn't need a moral code,' said Sam, 'but we do.'

'But no one would follow the moral rules if they didn't have empathy—if they didn't care about what happened to other people,' said Albert.

'They wouldn't, some don't, and that is

258

where external sanctions come in. People do what is expected in order to fit in, to avoid prison,' said Sam. 'And we know that people conform to external sanctions because they continue to follow them even when the rules are perverted: when the immoral thing is praised by society.'

'How?' Ben said. Wasn't society supposed to enforce morals?

'It does happen, of course it does. You can easily think of situations where brutality is rewarded.'

'Ah, but,' said Albert, 'sometimes the immoral thing is praised by society and yet people still behave morally. People fight back against a corrupt regime. This is where the moral sense kicks in.'

'But usually it doesn't—these people are remarkable because they are the exception. When genocide is socially acceptable then many join in. Humans are capable of shocking things. Our capacity for cruelty is immense. Think about how many people you know, Ben. All the people who overlapped with you at school—maybe 1,000. Your whole family—forty? Friends and their families—a few hundred? People in shops you have been to, customers in your fish shop, the drivers of buses you have been on, and so on—another few thousand or so, perhaps. So how can you *contemplate* 20,000 deaths? One estimate suggests that 800,000 people were murdered in

Rwanda in only a hundred days; that's just over three months. You can't even imagine what that means.'

Ben thought about everyone he had ever met being killed at once, and then some more people. Was he a moral failure because he couldn't imagine this?

'But any *goodness* in the world also originates with humans,' persisted Albert. 'Good deeds can only be done by people after all. People are instinctively good to those within their moral circle. There are countless examples of evil killers also looking after their sick mum in hospital. People think the contrast is disturbing, and it is. The trick is not to get them to be more moral—but to expand this circle of concern. To be just as moral, but to more people.'

'Indeed,' agreed Sam. 'The circle is amazingly narrow for most people, although they won't admit it. Concern for others plunges away with any kind of distance: geography, race, age, religion, class.'

'So how do we widen the circle?' asked Ben.

'How indeed?'

'Philosophy classes for all,' suggested Albert.

'That's your plan?'

'Got a better one? Can we go on the upside-downy thing over there?'

'Yes. But we're going on the spinny thing first.'

Sam and Albert ran off towards the waltzers.

'Can we have a go?' asked Ben.

Lila looked at her watch. 'OK. But I'm sitting on the outside.'

CHAPTER SIXTY-THREE

Ben dipped a piece of fish in batter. Could you do the right thing for the wrong reason? If you helped someone just to impress others, did that mean that you weren't being good? Was someone who hated helping others actually more moral when they did it than a naturally generous person? After all, it was hard for the first person but the second one got pleasure out of it. Ben decided society would be on to a bad thing if it called selfless people immoral.

He heard a clatter behind him. More letters had fallen off the menu board. He climbed on to a chair to try and repair the 'ADDOC'. He licked his finger and rubbed it on the back of the H and K to make them sticky again. There was always someone who ordered '.l. ice and chips' or 'cod and chip' (just the one!). One day he'd give them exactly what they ordered. Some boomerangs do get lost, after all.

What about the people who did the wrong thing for 'good' motives? You could try to help someone but end up making things worse.

Drown them when trying to save them. People are judged on what they do, not why they do it. But that was simply practical because we only see their actions, not their motives. Another letter fell off the menu board, but Ben was much more worried about whether he should start the project of widening people's moral circles. Perhaps tomorrow.

CHAPTER SIXTY-FOUR

The two groups sat separated by a no-man's-land of shiny floor. Someone was mopping the neutral territory between the tables. The foreign camps, wary, eyed each other up. A lone ambassador, returning from the counter, approached the male faction.

'Hi, Ben.'

'Clare.'

The others held their breath—pure spectator sport. Ben looked down.

'Just wanted to say hi.'

'Yeah. Hi.'

'See ya.' She retreated.

Ben's company sputtered into laughter.

' *"See ya!"* '

'Bothered,' said Ben.

'She's weird, that Sarah.'

'Clare,' said Ben.

'She's fat,' said Mike, who was much fatter.

262

Joe was still laughing so much, he spat his chicken nugget on to the table.

'Come on. She's not that bad,' Ben said, pushing the nuggets of nugget away with a napkin. In his heart he wanted to defend her more chivalrously, but that would have been social suicide.

'Ben's got a girlfriend.'

'I have actually.' Ben paused. 'But she's much older. She's twenty-four and gorgeous.'

He looked round at the gawping faces. Why had he said that?

CHAPTER SIXTY-FIVE

'So how do we work out who has won the bet?' asked Socrates. 'What would prove it one way or the other?'

'Well, if he stopped coming, that would be pretty definitive,' suggested Wittgenstein, who hadn't quite given up on making this happen.

'Not necessarily. He might just be taking a break.'

'Very convenient.'

'So does that mean that if Ben continues to visit I've won? If he comes, he must enjoy being here.'

'People often do things that make them miserable.'

'Not everyone is so perverse. If he keeps

returning then he must love philosophy.'

'Ah! Even if he does love it, that's not relevant. It has to make his life better, or I win.'

'Hmm.' Socrates was hoping that Wittgenstein had forgotten that part. But it was foolish to hope for an indifferent view of words from a man obsessed with the philosophy of language.

'Does love always make your life better?' said Wittgenstein, not without bitterness.

Socrates was up against the harsh truth of the terms of the bet. Loving philosophy and it improving your life were not necessarily the same. He'd argued for one—and bet his future on the other. He loved philosophy and he'd put his money where his big mouth was. But it was hard to argue that it had made his life better. It had made him a public joke in Athens and hooked him a death sentence.

'So how do we judge it, then?' he asked, rallying a little.

'It's a subjective thing, so it should hinge on his own judgement. Let's ask him.'

'Just like that? Ask him what?'

'Is his life better with philosophy in it than it was before.'

'That's a bad question.'

'You're just worried there'll be a bad answer.'

'By the way, what do you make of Kant's transcendental idealism?' asked Socrates. 'I'm

264

still trying to get my head around it.'

'I don't read other philosophers. But I'm quite sure it's pointless.'

CHAPTER SIXTY-SIX

Ben hated getting dressed. It was a waste of time deciding on something new to wear every day. Matty, on the other hand, loved it. Every night, before she went to sleep, she would lay out her outfit for the next day, in the shape of a person on the floor. She'd meticulously arrange her coloured tights in the shape of legs, carefully placing her skirt over the top and her underwear below. T-shirts would be spread out under jumpers, with arms in a jaunty pose. Ben would leave getting dressed to the last minute, keeping his pyjamas on until he actually had to leave the house. Afterwards, too, if he could get away with it. He had, briefly, wondered if he should smarten up to impress Lila but decided against it. Lila might be great, but no woman was worth the trauma of clothes shopping.

Ben scrabbled round the pile of clothes classified as dirty but not offensively so in search of an acceptable pair of trousers. He found some jeans that just about passed the deep-sniff test. He reached out for his favourite jumper in the 'grey area' pile in the wardrobe. His arms seemed to resist him, not to follow his wishes. He found himself pulling a jumper off the hanger in the wardrobe and putting it on, one he'd never worn, knitted by the next-door neighbour and defiantly disgusting. Where did she *find* wool in those colours? Surely some knitting patterns were illegal? Perhaps Mrs Foley had underground sources.

He scooped up the first-choice jumper and the rest of his dirty clothes and carried them downstairs to the washing machine.

'You've brought your washing down,' said his mum in amazement.

Ben bristled. He didn't mind being helpful, but there was no need for her to point it out.

'And you're wearing the jumper that Maureen knitted! Where's the camera?'

Ben ducked out of the room and went into the kitchen to get some breakfast. He felt like having orange juice but, on opening the fridge, he had the weird feeling again. As if something else were controlling his actions. He found himself pouring and drinking a glass of milk. He never drank milk!

When the phone rang, he grabbed it.

'Ben? It's Lila.'

'I can't believe you're phoning! My mum could have answered!'

'I wanted to know if you'd noticed anything strange this morning.'

'So it was you again. I'm wearing the most

266

awful jumper ever.'

'Oh really? I thought it was time we had a chat about free will. How much do you really choose what you do? Most people never even think about it: they just assume that they decide freely. But it's not that simple.'

'Nothing is simple any more.'

'I gave you a shake-up to start you thinking. Of course, as you will see, those who deny we have free will don't pretend that someone else is literally controlling our actions, as happened to you this morning. They claim, though, that everything is entirely "caused" and determined, and so we couldn't have done anything different from what we did.'

'I see.' This time he almost did.

'Of course you do. Come over when you can.'

CHAPTER SIXTY-SEVEN

'Like your jumper!' Lila was in the entrance hall.

How could he have been so stupid? He really meant to change but he'd forgotten in the rush to hear more about free will. And anyway all his other clothes had been taken hostage by the washing machine.

Lila smirked. 'Shall we start?'

Ben followed her down the corridor. She

stopped at a door marked *Born Free?*. Ben found himself in a sunlit picturesque landscape where everything was in proportion.

'It's always brilliant weather here.'

'Of course—what would you choose? Although, now you mention it, some of our philosophers can be perverse. I think I've kept you out of the way of most of them so far.'

Lila led him down to a fast-flowing, shallow river, where a man with a short white beard and a woman with lots of eye make-up were sitting.

The man was bald, about Socrates' age, whether that was old or young. He shook Ben's hand. 'Hello, young man, I'm Saul Wolfson.'

'Nice to meet you.'

'Lila darling! How are you?' the woman said, smiling thinly. 'I always wonder why we never see more of each other—form an alliance against the awful old fogies.' She squeezed Saul's arm and looked at him under her eyelashes.

'I often wonder that myself,' said Lila, accepting a perfunctory kiss on each cheek. The woman was about Lila's age, maybe a few years older. She was attractive too, wearing long boots and a tight skirt which rode above the knee.

'Hello you. This must be the famous Ben. No wonder you've been keeping him to yourself, Lila.'

'I've hardly been—'

'What magical green eyes. They reveal a special soul,' said the woman, engaging him in her finest eye-meet. 'Are you a Leo?'

'I, er . . .'

'Wonderful to meet you, whatever you are.' She kissed Ben on each cheek. Her perfume was dark and spicy. 'I'm Chloe Sharp, but you'—she touched his chest, recoiling slightly from the garish knitted zigzag—'can call me Clo.'

'Shall we start, then, Chloe?' said Lila.

'Yes, please,' said Saul.

'Let's play Pooh sticks,' said Lila, pointing at a little humpback bridge.

Ben was pleasantly surprised.

'I'm definitely going to win,' Chloe said, grabbing a stick. 'Get a move on, Saul.'

Lila called '1 . . . 2 . . . 3 . . . Go!'

Ben wondered if he was allowed to point out that Chloe had thrown her stick on '3' not 'Go'.

Ben's stick came out first. He was far too grown-up to be excited, but it felt good to get one up on the philosophers—at Pooh sticks, if nothing else. Chloe and Saul's sticks came out more or less together, but there was no sign of Lila's.

'Mine's got stuck,' she said. 'It's not fair. Let's try again.'

'Who said life was fair, sweetheart?' said Chloe.

They each selected another stick, threw it in, and ran across the bridge to wait.

Saul said, 'You know, from the moment the sticks leave our hands, it is entirely determined which of the four will emerge first. Given the weight and shape of the sticks, the flow of the current, the way we throw them and so on, there is only one outcome. If you knew enough about the precise state of the world and the laws of physics, this could even be predicted.'

'That's mine! Mine was first,' cried Chloe, pointing, smiling in spite of herself. 'Is yours stuck again, Lila?'

'And all human actions are just as determined as the path of the sticks,' Saul added.

Chloe's smile faded. 'I can't bear it when you say that.'

'But surely,' Ben said, 'human behaviour is not really the same sort of thing as a twig in the river? I mean, I know I was being controlled this morning, as a demonstration but—'

'Yes indeed,' said Saul. 'That's a fine jumper.'

That was a bit rich coming from someone wearing a pink shirt and purple trousers. '*As a demonstration*,' Ben said firmly, despite his embarrassment. 'But normally I decide what to do and then I do it.'

'Of course you decide. We all do,' said Chloe. 'Thoughts are simply not like billiard

270

balls, where one bumps into the other and causes a movement according to set laws. If you hit the cue ball exactly the same way, you always get the same shot. But people don't behave like that.'

'The thing is, old chap,' said Saul, 'Chloe and I disagree on this matter. But I imagine you'll see sense in good time. To start with, think about the process of deciding. Obviously most actions have *causes*, otherwise they'd be totally irrational. I'll give you an example: you pick up some bread. Your movement to get the bread is caused by several things: the thought that you are hungry, the belief that eating the bread will satisfy this hunger, and seeing the bread close by. Thus, your action is caused by various mental factors (thoughts, beliefs and desires) and things in the external world (such as the bread being in the kitchen in the first place).'

'That makes sense,' said Ben, imagining himself reaching for a piece of bread, 'but I don't see how it makes all of my actions inevitable, like you claimed.'

'For that, we need to flesh out the story some more,' said Saul. 'First, we all agree that the physical world is subject to laws of cause and effect. When you drop your stick into the river, its path as it falls and floats is determined by the various "laws of nature". Second, our thoughts, beliefs, desires are intimately dependent on physical events. They are either states of the brain or at least closely connected with such states.'

'Well, I learnt about that before.' Ben thought of Oliver Whitby driving his point home with a swoosh of his fencing foil. 'But how does it fit in with this?'

'Like this: if all the physical world is governed by laws of cause and effect, and our thoughts and actions are just part of the physical world, they must also be governed by laws of cause and effect. The state of the world now and the laws of nature dictate absolutely the state of the world in the next moment, including our thoughts and decisions.' Saul pushed the tips of his fingers together.

'I suppose so.' Ben wasn't sure he liked where Saul was going, but he couldn't see anything wrong with the argument.

'I'll give you another example,' said Saul. 'You see a cat, because certain lightwaves hit your eyes.'

Ben felt something brush his ankles. A ginger cat was rubbing its shoulder against his leg.

'This visual information causes you to have the belief that you are seeing a cat. So a thing in the physical world—a cat—has caused a mental thing, a belief. The belief about the cat then causes a physical movement—stroking the cat. Thus the physical and mental interact in a strict causal way.'

Ben stroked the cat, which purred

272

contentedly. He picked it up and the purring increased. The cat picked contentedly at Ben's jumper with his claws.

'He'll make a hole in your top,' said Chloe.

'Let's hope so,' said Lila.

It was complicated but it made sense that one thing caused another, even if some of them were cats, some were thoughts and some were cat-stroking actions.

'Whether you want to stroke the cat when you see it,' added Saul, 'depends on whether you are the sort of person who likes cats. But how you are as a person depends on two things: what sort of person you were recently, and other recent external events (such as being bitten by a wild cat). You cannot control the external events. And the sort of person you were yesterday in turn depends on who you were just before that and on other past events in the world. This regression goes back to before you were born, certainly before it can be said that you were in a position to be responsible for your character. Everything in the world—including everyone in it—is subject to physical laws and hence determined.'

'So, if physical objects are subject to causal laws, as everyone accepts, then so are mental events, and so are your actions,' Ben said. 'My actions too! You're saying that everything I do is caused by something that has gone before? I am the sort of person I am because of all these factors beyond my control?' The cat slipped

273

out of Ben's arms and jumped on to the wall of the bridge. Lila moved to tickle it behind the ear.

'That's exactly the problem, Ben. According to him'—Chloe shot a dark look at Saul, who had no trouble ignoring it—'everything we do, everything *we think we decide to do*, is determined. Given the state of the world and our minds, anyone's actions could in theory be predicted. At any given moment, there is no way we could ever do anything except what we in fact do. Except that it's not true. It can't be.'

'And this is the problem of free will?' asked Ben.

'Yes,' said Chloe. 'If this theory is right then we never really choose what to do. How can it be a choice when we are only ever going to do one thing, which we are caused to do by other forces? Whether you stroke the cat or kick it, you couldn't possibly have done anything else at that moment.'

'That's exactly it,' said Saul.

Chloe shook her head. 'That's exactly not it. I don't act out a script that's already written, I write it myself as I go along. I just cannot—will not—accept that I don't make my own decisions. I absolutely know that I can change my mind at any point—'

'And frequently do,' muttered Lila, playing with the cat.

'And that things are not fixed.'

'How can you "absolutely know" this?' said

Saul. 'On what evidence? "Absolutely know" is a pretty strong claim. The only way to test that we have this kind of free will is to want something other than what we want, or choose something other than what we choose. Which is impossible—therefore it's beyond proof.'

'I just know. I spontaneously make a decision and the world changes. I feel that this choice comes from me.'

'Just as you can predict an eclipse that will happen in 200 years, how you will spend your seventieth birthday is already decided.'

'That's the most ridiculous thing I have ever heard. I could decide to move to Hawaii tomorrow, or I could kill myself next week. Either could happen.'

Ben had to admit that Chloe sounded more sensible, but then she hadn't given him any reasons for her view, like Saul had.

'It is not the same as a bloody eclipse, or the path of a comet. I, me, *myself*—she stood on tiptoes—'am not subject to any causal laws.'

'OK, Chloe.' Saul pushed his fingers together. 'You say that if our actions are totally caused then we can't have free will, yes?'

'Yes.'

'So what is it that you want to be true when you say we have free will?'

Chloe was confident. 'I want to say that I cause my actions. That they are due to me in myself and not a result of certain states being caused in my brain according to fixed laws.'

'Perhaps you want to invoke quantum theory to suggest that anything is possible, even if the obvious things are still overwhelmingly likely. In other words, you claim that events do not necessarily follow on from other events.'

'Why not?' said Chloe, freely invoking whatever it took.

'But if your decision to . . . I don't know . . . eat some Turkish Delight. If it is a genuinely random event, a quantum spark in your brain, how does this make you any more responsible than if your decision were part of a causal chain?' Saul fiddled with the glasses on a chain round his neck, while he waited for Chloe's answer.

'I er . . .' Chloe looked a bit uncomfortable. There was obviously nothing random about her eating Turkish delight.

'You think that God rolling the dice, as Einstein would say, gives you your freedom? If you are deciding freely, you want it to be on the basis of your beliefs and wishes, not because of some chance molecular impulse. If a decision is a random event then nothing controls this decision, certainly not *you*. Chance is as much an enemy of choice as necessity.'

'OK, maybe quantum theory isn't the solution.' Chloe's forehead wrinkled with the effort of thinking. She realised her mistake and relaxed her eyebrows. 'Look, the stick doesn't decide to fall, but I decide to buy a car. I may not decide to see the car—this does depend on physics—but choosing to buy it is something I do. It's a different sort of animal.'

'You are not conscious that your decision is caused in the way I claimed?'

'Of course not.'

'But that doesn't mean that it isn't caused. The decision to buy a car is as caused, although it feels different, as the surge of adrenalin that hits you at the moment of a near miss on the motorway. All this causation could be going on behind the scenes, as it were, and we are simply not aware of it. Just as lots of complex processes involving muscles and nerves and tendons are involved when we stand up. From our internal perspective, we see it as standing up, not in terms of the individual muscle movements. Equally a decision feels like it comes from nowhere, but it's really just a certain perspective on brain mechanics.' Saul leant his back against the wall of the old stone bridge.

Chloe shook her head. 'It seems so wrong. It is so wrong.'

'So you would say that you originate your actions?'

'Definitely.' She sighed. 'That's exactly what I'm saying.' Chloe appealed to Lila, who shrugged.

'How?' asked Saul.

'How? I decide what to do,' said Chloe.

'Ye-es? "I decide" is not much of an explanation. Are you really aware of deciding, as such? Yesterday you were unsure about whether to buy a car, today you know you want to: what exactly has happened in between? How can you describe the process?'

'I, that is, my "self", I suppose, review my thoughts and the options out there in the world and decide what to do. This is what I feel myself doing, although the process is perhaps not always so conscious.'

'So now you've got a little person in the head making decisions? And how does she decide? Basically, Ben, although everyone assumes that somehow there is a "self"—an "agent"—that decides what to do, it's almost impossible to describe what this might mean.'

Ben remembered David Sherborne's attack on this idea, on the beach.

'What sort of thing could the self be? A "prime mover" like God? Certainly it doesn't help to explain anything.'

'Why not?' said Chloe.

'Presumably this real you—let's call it an "agent" for now—can cause things to happen, yes? Or else the decisions would never get implemented.'

Chloe nodded. 'But what the agent does is not caused, because you think that would take away free will. Am I right?'

'Yes,' Chloe said impatiently. 'Where is this leading?'

'Nearly there. Leaving aside the problem of what weird Godlike things can cause stuff in the outside world but have no cause themselves, I have a more serious point. The agent's decisions must be caused by *something*, or you would be insane. As I explained before, decisions have reasons. And every reason, that is, a belief, is a brain state that is part of the physical world.'

'No! There must be some trick.'

'You want your soul to propel you like wind on sails? But some mysterious wind that is not caused by air currents and the earth rotating, as normal, but sent by Aeolus.'

'What's that?' Ben whispered to Lila.

'The Greek god of the winds.'

'You do decide,' said Saul. 'But this is just something that happens, not something that you do, in the transcendental sense. Nevertheless, it is still *your* decision, based on *your* reasons, not forced on you.'

'It's like saying that a watch is free to tell the time.' Chloe was adamant. 'That's not enough free will for me.'

'But why not?' asked Saul calmly.

'Because then it doesn't matter what I do. There's no point trying, since whatever is going to happen will happen anyway. And that's a pathetic way to live.'

'There's no need to be depressed.' Saul set off along the bridge back to the riverbank. The cat jumped out of Lila's arms and followed him.

Surely Saul Wolfson couldn't just leave it there! No need to be depressed? What kind of freak didn't get depressed at the idea of no free will?

'But wait,' Ben said, catching him up, 'you're saying that everything that will happen is determined. So what's the point in trying to change things? Why bother practising football when the match result will be the same, whatever you do?'

'Being fatalistic is self-fulfilling. If you believe that you cannot change anything by your actions, then you will stop trying and that will definitely make it true that you are powerless.'

'But isn't it already true?'

'Imagine that you did give up making decisions for a week. Of course this would make a difference to your life. Our actions do really have consequences.'

'But it is already decided what these actions will be,' Chloe said, running up behind them.

'Yes,' said Saul. 'But you can go two ways from here. Either one thinks: the future is fixed—I should do nothing, which is your instinct. Or one can say: the future is fixed, no one knows how—I should get on with my life and work hard and be happy, which is much healthier.'

'But you're also saying that there is only one path in life, which will necessarily be as good as it is possible to be,' said Chloe, exasperated.

'And as bad,' said Lila.

Ben was also struggling to understand how this helped. There had to be more to solving the free-will problem. It seemed like a sort of trick to make it all right for our lives to be set on one path. And that couldn't be all right, could it?

Chloe seemed to be reading Ben's thoughts. She linked arms with him. 'If you are right, Saul, it's all so undignified! But I don't believe it. The past may be fixed, it has happened; the future is open. At any moment there are all sorts of possibilities.'

'The future's not really open. After all, there can only ever be one.'

Chloe threw her arms up, letting go of Ben.

He couldn't help thinking that the problem of free will (or lack of it) hadn't really gone away. He sat on the bank and ran his hands through the shallow water. He picked up a pebble from the riverbed. He tried to imagine that deep down he was as helpless as the pebble as it sank, but he couldn't manage it.

'It's like buying a lottery ticket when they've already decided who'll win,' he said.

'In a sense it is,' said Saul, sitting down beside him. 'But your chance of winning is as great whether the numbers are decided before you buy the ticket or they fall out of the machine afterwards. Your buying a ticket doesn't change anything—the numbers will

281

come out as physics dictates, either way.' Saul picked a dandelion and blew away the feathery bits in three goes. 'I am not worried about this so-called lack of free will. I think there's a different kind of freedom—one that's good enough to live with. Indeed it's all we have to live with, since Chloe's version of free will is impossible.'

Chloe lowered herself on to the grass, tucking her skirt underneath her. 'I think your solution is a wimpy attempt to avoid the problem that your theory makes us Not Free.'

Lila flopped on to the grass next to Ben.

'At least I face up to the truth.' Saul was unrepentant. 'Give me a chance to explain why I'm not bothered.'

'Because you have no imagination?' suggested Chloe.

Saul remained dignified, with some struggle. 'Acting freely just means acting voluntarily, that is, without compulsion or addiction. Acting in accordance with your wishes and beliefs. It's perfectly compatible with a world determined by laws. Indeed it requires that your action is caused by your own desires. Being free to act does not mean being able to do otherwise than what we do at a given point in exactly the same circumstances. This is irrelevant.'

'It's not irrelevant, it's crucial,' said Chloe. 'This is exactly what freedom of action means to me. It's not about being free to protest against the government, it's about being free to *choose to protest.*'

'You would realise that the freedom to protest is more important if you lost it. But, anyway, the freedom to choose differently is not available to you. Why do you need it? The experience of choosing is not a fiction—you really do make a decision.'

'It's not a real decision if the decision could not have been different!' Chloe shouted. 'And of course I need this sort of choice to be available to me, to everybody. Can't you see why?'

She looked to Ben for support.

'Why?' he asked. He could see that it mattered but he didn't want to say the wrong thing, especially when she was so fierce.

'If I hold someone responsible for a terrible thing, if I blame them and resent their behaviour—maybe even punish them—then I expect that there is a real sense in which they could have acted otherwise. It's not fair to punish someone for doing a bad thing if they couldn't have done anything else. We imprison *people* and not their acts. This is only right if the *person* had a choice.'

'But, Chloe,' Saul said, 'when someone commits a crime and we ask whether they could have done otherwise, we mean things like: did they really foresee the consequences of their action? Are they mentally competent? Were they forced into it? Is it in their

283

character to behave badly? We do not mean: Is it a possibility in our world that a given action is not entirely caused at the moment it happens?'

Saul made sense, then Ben found himself being convinced by Chloe just a moment later. Maybe they were both right? But how could that be, since they disagreed so strongly?

'A belief in true free will is a vital illusion,' said Saul. 'But it is an illusion nonetheless.'

'I still want there to be more,' Chloe said. 'I think things like institutionalised punishment and being grateful for generosity just collapse under your scheme. They don't work if "free" doesn't mean we genuinely originate our actions.'

'Punishment is useful because it changes the external causes of people's actions. It affects the way they decide in the future.'

'Does it?'

'Yes! A decision never to punish people would change the world in big ways!'

It was like watching a tennis match. Ben waited for one of them to hit the ball into the net so that he could catch his breath and work out which argument he preferred. Presumably there was such a thing as 'unforced errors' in philosophy, just like tennis? Or would it, in an argument like this, count as a 'forced error'?

'But we are punishing them for the past, not as an instrument to change the future,' said Chloe. 'We say that a mentally ill person has diminished responsibility because they are not fully in control of their actions. It's like extending this concept to all of us. That's dangerous.'

'If someone commits a crime because they are jealous, we still hold them responsible. But strong jealousy is not an emotion we can control.'

They were staring fiercely at each other now. It was obvious that neither of them was going to change their mind. There was a lot at stake.

Ben glanced at Lila, who seemed to be enjoying the stand-off. To ease the tension, he said, 'I think that, even if true free will doesn't exist, we can never stop believing that it does. In our hearts we will always feel responsible for what we do.'

'Well, yes,' they said together.

'Let's go, Ben,' Lila said.

'Bye, darling.' Chloe kissed him on both cheeks.

'Farewell.' Saul shook his hand.

It was like focusing very close up and then straining your eyes to concentrate on something in the distance, Ben thought, as Lila led them through the meadow. In one sense Saul had a point: it was very hard to argue for complete free will, hard even to express what it meant. Maybe we could live with his reduced day-to-day freedom and still have meaningful hopes for the future and talk about responsibility. But as soon as Ben's mind refocused he couldn't help but think that having true free will, the kind that Chloe Sharp wanted, was desperately important. Weren't people just robots without it?

'What do you think, Lila? You must have heard all this a few times.'

'Well, as you know, you have to form your own opinion.'

'I've formed loads of opinions recently!'

'So you have.' Lila smiled broadly. She rubbed the lipstick marks off Ben's face. 'In my view, determinism is pretty hard to escape.'

'That's the idea that all our actions are caused?'

'That's it. In terms of the implications for whether we're really free, it's hard to know.'

The answer annoyed him: Lila wasn't going to tell him what she thought.

'But how about this? It's a really interesting question as to where, or whether, we place the responsibility for people's actions. Chloe thinks that if we don't have an ultimate freedom of choice then we can never be truly responsible, although Saul disagrees. Now, imagine that I win a race. If I have trained a lot then somehow I deserve it, I can claim the achievement. If I have taken drugs to improve my performance, I am deemed to have cheated, even if I trained just as hard. And yet, being born with the natural talent to run fast is a matter of luck; it is not at all part of my control. We are allowed to take credit for certain things for which we are not responsible. But changing our innate abilities through chemical means is disallowed.'

'But—'

'See you soon.' Lila gave him a hug.

*   *   *

Lila smiled as Ben's feet disappeared. It had all started out as an experiment, and he was just here because of the bet, but she'd grown genuinely fond of him. He was different from most of the people she spent time with nowadays. Chloe was right about the old fogeys, if not about the solution. Ben's visits were also a welcome change from running around after Socrates. Of course, for Ben, it wasn't about the bet at all. Maybe she should have told him what was going on, but it was too late now. Anyway, there was no reason why he ever had to find out. Much better if he didn't.

CHAPTER SIXTY-EIGHT

Ben dreamt he was back at the river where they had played Pooh sticks. The river spoke to him: 'I can do anything. I can be enormous stormy waves, I can be clouds in the sky, I can boil to make coffee, I can gush down the rapids, I can erode a cliff. Today I choose a tranquil life in this river. But I could do anything else because I am *water*!' Was Ben's perception of free choice just as deluded as the water? Was he, in fact, stuck as a shallow stream until the laws of nature dictated that he evaporate into a storm cloud?

Then he was in his bedroom. He was happy there, playing on his computer—he had no desire to leave. He became aware that someone was guarding his door and he was locked in. Previously he had chosen to stay in the room, but now, he realised, he couldn't have left even if he'd wanted to.

He woke up, disconcerted. This was the problem with the freedom offered by Saul's view. Ben had been acting totally voluntarily, but in fact he couldn't have done anything else. Saul had said that the future is as fixed as the past because there can only ever be one path. In no sense could he ever stay in bed and get up and have a shower. The important thing was that, if his life were determined, then it didn't make any difference what he did. Right there and then, Ben decided to give up on life. It seemed only fair: his future life had given up on him.

After twenty-two minutes in bed doing nothing, Ben wondered what he was missing out on. Obviously he wasn't missing out on anything: this was the only way life could be.

An hour later, his mum popped her head round the door.

'What's wrong, Ben? Are you ill? Why aren't you at work?'

'There's no point.'

'Well, I've got Tony Swan on the phone. He says if you're not there in twenty minutes, or you've got a *bloody good excuse*, then you're fired.'

'It is a bloody good excuse. It makes no difference whether I go in or not. Nothing matters if the future is determined.'

'Really? He did say he wouldn't sack you if you got there by twelve.'

It seemed that decisions did make a difference. He could stay at home and get sacked, or go to work and keep the job. But did that mean that he had real choices?

'What shall I tell Tony?'

'Tell him I'm leaving in ten minutes.'

Ben tried to get his head around the problem. He couldn't think of any good arguments against his life being determined, except that it was hard to believe it and if you did believe it then life was impossible. Perhaps he did shape his life but he had no choice about how. Did that make sense? Ben was glad to be going to work: it would be a relief to have something that took his mind off it all.

CHAPTER SIXTY-NINE

Ben and Joe were in the newsagent. Snickers bar or Crunchie? Crunchie. Actually, Snickers. Or maybe Whole Nut. No. It was a Snickers moment. According to Saul, given the sort of person Ben was, the mood he was in (which meant his current brain state) and the selection available in the shop, Ben would only ever have bought a Snickers bar. The element of choice was an illusion. It didn't feel like that, but it could well be true. Ben couldn't decide if it didn't matter, or if it was the worst thing in the world.

Joe was at the counter buying a lottery ticket. '4, 13, 25, 29, 44 and . . . What shall I have for the last one?'

'It might be,' said Ben, 'that you don't really have any choice. Given the state of the world right now, and your brain chemistry, there is only one set of numbers you could have selected.'

'Don't be an idiot. Of course I'm choosing them.'

'But maybe you are not *free* to make a different choice.'

'47!' Joe handed over the ticket. 'What are you on about?'

Ben looked to the woman serving for support.

'36p, please,' she said.

'Can I meet your mystery girlfriend?' said Joe.

'No.'

'Have any of the others met her yet?'

'No.'

'You ashamed of her?'

'I'm ashamed of you. She's amazing.'

'That's because you made her up. How would you ever get a real live girlfriend?'

'I didn't make her up. She's definitely . . . real.'

'Does she have a name?'

Ben could feel himself reddening. 'Lila.'

CHAPTER SEVENTY

Lila was playing badminton with Nietzsche, who was an extremely competitive opponent. 'Another game to me,' he said smugly.

Lila stopped for a drink of water and caught sight of her pager, flashing with a new message. 'Oh no. I have to go.' She grabbed the racquet and her towel and ran out.

'You forfeit the game!' Nietzsche shouted.

*   *   *

Ben stood up and stretched his legs. He looked around for Lila. The entrance hall was eerily deserted. He waited, feeling self-conscious. If it could be said that he was conscious of a 'self'. After a minute or so, he was bored. After a few more minutes, he was really, really bored. 'Lila!' he called, but there was no answer.

He looked through the long windows at the garden. The lilac was flowering. That was one of the few plants he knew, because it was lilac-coloured. He remembered his mum accosting a bush one summer: 'Lilac! You're out!' Why was it that gardens were so incredibly boring until you reached a certain age, when suddenly they were all you could talk about?

The main door that led to the corridor was open but he was worried that he'd get lost down there. Then he noticed a small door in the corner of the room. It was probably locked, but worth a try. The handle was a bit stiff but the door opened.

He sat in a wheely chair just inside the door, spinning one way and the other, lifting up his knees to spin faster. He pushed the chair on to the smooth wooden floor of the empty hall. Sitting in the chair, he drew himself up to one wall with little steps and then pushed off backwards all the way across the room. And then back again. And then a few more times. He stopped: Lila might arrive at any minute. Could he justify it as a philosophical experiment? An investigation into the nature of motion? Human free will over chair?

Probably not.

Ben tucked the chair back in the dark little room. Flickering lights caught his eye. TV! Not just one, but loads of TV screens. Philosophers might do the high and mighty talk but they watched reality TV like everyone else. And it was just as boring here as at home.

Ben's face went hot, his hands cold. That looked like him. That was him. Yesterday in the chip shop, talking to that customer who wanted Atkins-friendly fish. In the shop with Joe last week. His empty bedroom; but nothing was happening there—because he was here.

They were watching him: why?

He felt dizzy as he wandered down the familiar corridor. He passed a door marked *Think You Know Something?* and one marked *Fair's Fair*. He lingered next to *Verify or Die*. Why not? A gust of icy wind blew through the door. Ben peered into the snowy landscape. Three penguins waddled past. He wanted to follow them—penguins always made him laugh—but it was too cold. Reluctantly he closed the door and moved to the next one: *The Truth Is Out There*.

He was in the warmth of an olive grove. The knobbly trees stretched as far as the eye could see, marking out parallel lines in the sunshine. He followed a winding path until he reached a small stone house. 'Hello?' He wandered round the other side of the house and flopped

293

into the hammock tied between the trees. He rocked himself in the warm air, until he felt sick from swinging. A little better, too, though still upset by the sight of the TV screens.

CHAPTER SEVENTY-ONE

'Surely you've had enough of this stupid game by now? It's outrageous.'

Ben stirred, and tried to get up, but he knew enough about hammocks to know you couldn't get out of them in a hurry, or quietly.

'Oh don't be such a spoilsport. Will you explain the bit about synthetic a priori knowledge again?'

Ben recognised the voice. He pulled the cloth up around himself. Not much of a disguise, admittedly, but he felt more secure.

'Don't change the subject, Socrates.'

'Surely you, of all people, Immanuel, can see the danger of Ludwig Wittgenstein being in charge.'

Immanuel: the grumpy man Ben saw in the café.

'You shouldn't have made the bet in the first place. I don't approve of gambling.'

Ben stuck an ear out to hear better.

'It's a fascinating experiment. And Ben's been a great success.'

Ben jolted upright, flipping himself out of

the hammock with a thud.

'You're using him for sport. You know that you should always treat people as ends in themselves, not as means to an end.'

'Ben's getting something out of it too,' Socrates said.

'But you've involved him in a bigger purpose whose goal he doesn't share. Doesn't even know about. And that is wrong: people ought to have dignity, not a price.'

'Don't be miserable, Kant.'

Ben rubbed his elbow where he had landed. He couldn't hear them now. He tried to follow them, crouching down below the trees, but olive groves didn't offer much protection.

What did he mean about the bet? Surely they weren't betting on *him*? Ridiculous idea. But that's what the man had said: Ben was being used for a sport he didn't understand. He slumped against the tree trunk. That was why he'd been approached and invited here, not because he was special. They didn't care about him. It was all because of some stupid bet. He resolved to be treated as an end, not a means, as soon as he knew what that was.

CHAPTER SEVENTY-TWO

Lila ran into the entrance hall. Damn. No sign of Ben. Her heart sank when she saw that the door of the monitor room was open. The room itself was empty; he must have gone down the corridor. It was all her fault: she should have been there to meet him. She opened a door. 'Ben!' Then another. She couldn't possibly explore them all. She'd have to go back to the entrance hall and wait, think about organising a search party.

'Ben! I've been looking for you everywhere. Where were you?'

'In the olive grove,' he muttered.

'What?'

'In the olive grove,' he shouted, hoping she'd let him go home.

'Are you OK?'

'I overheard Socrates talking about some bet. And I saw the TVs.'

'Yes.'

'What's going on?'

'I'm sorry you found out this way.'

'I think you're sorry I found out at all. But now, please, just tell me the truth.'

Lila opened her mouth, then shut it again.

Ben sniffed deeply. 'Forget philosophy for a while. Let's *assume* that there is a straightforward truth, and that you are going to tell me what it is.'

'As you've heard. Socrates and Wittgenstein had a bet.'

'About me?'

'Socrates thinks that everyone should do philosophy. No one should get away without

296

being made to question and justify everything they believe. About what is right, about how the world is, about who we are.'

'The unexamined life is not worth living—I know all that,' Ben said impatiently, feeling his own life had been examined too much.

'That's just it. But Wittgenstein thinks that this sort of philosophy is all incoherent babble, that nothing concrete or meaningful can be said. And more importantly, he thinks most people aren't up to the rigours of proper thinking. That people like you have nothing to gain from it. Socrates was determined to prove him wrong: that philosophy could make your life better. But for that we needed a case study.'

'*Case study?*'

'Bad choice of words.' Lila paused. 'But don't you see? What you think is incredibly important. The fact that you tried to share philosophy with people at home—'

'You saw that?' He shook his head. 'You've been spying on me.'

'Not as such. Well, sort of. We wanted to keep track of your progress, know when you were coming to visit. I'm sorry we tricked you, but it wouldn't have worked if you had known what was at stake.'

'You've been playing games with me. Like I'm some toy.' Yes, that was what Immanuel Kant had meant. Because of them, he'd made a fool of himself in front of his friends; and it

297

turned out that even here, where he thought he was special, they were making a fool of him too.

'It's not like that,' said Lila. 'You were vital. It was all about you. Don't you see? The future of the World of Ideas depends on you. If Wittgenstein wins the bet, Socrates will have to give up control. We'll all be sent away. At least those of us Wittgenstein doesn't approve of—which is more or less everyone.'

Ben started to feel better. He almost managed a smile. 'All that depends on me?'

'You were chosen because you're special. You were the one I wanted to meet.' She smiled at him. 'And I was right. I'm happy you came here. Aren't you? Not even a bit?'

'A bit.'

'You've really impressed us.'

Ben smiled properly now. He remembered ice skating and swimming with Lila; getting drunk and playing Pooh sticks; Oliver and Jack fencing; and all the other things he'd learnt and seen. 'Actually, it's been amazing.'

The main door opened and Socrates and Wittgenstein ran in.

'Ask him then,' Wittgenstein said, hitting Socrates on the arm.

'All right, I'm getting there.' Socrates took a deep breath. 'What we want to know is . . . has philosophy made your life better? At all . . . in any small way?' Wittgenstein hit him harder on the arm.

Ben milked his moment for a few seconds. He caught Lila's eye. She was giving him a powerful yes-look while trying not to move her head.

'Yes,' Ben said. 'I'm definitely glad I came here.' He smiled at Lila. 'My life is better now than before.'

'Yes!' shouted Socrates.

'After all,' continued Ben, 'the unexamined life is not worth living, right?'

Wittgenstein howled. 'Brainwashed!' Of course, Lila had been taking him round—she worked for Socrates. He shouldn't have let Socrates' people have such access. It's just that he couldn't bear to do the job himself. And he didn't have any 'people' as such.

'Ha ha he he hee,' said Socrates, skipping.

'OK fine. Fine,' said Wittgenstein. 'You win this time. You've proved that philosophy can make one person's life better, but you have not proved anything in general.' He walked out, leaving Socrates to his gloating, for now.

'Ben, thank you so much,' said Socrates. 'Although we say goodbye now, I'll always think highly of you.'

'Goodbye? Is that it then? You've won the bet and you don't need me any more?'

Socrates looked at Lila, who looked at the floor.

'Do I have to go home? Can't I stay here a bit longer?'

'You don't belong here; this is not your

place,' Lila said sadly. 'Not yet, anyway. But when you do come, whenever that is, I'll still be here—same as ever.'

'But if I die when I'm seventy-five, you'll seem like a child and I'll be really old. Not that we couldn't still be friends, of course.' Lila hugged him. Was she always going to lose the people she cared about?

Ben squeezed in return. She smelt of fresh, ripe melon. 'Can I maybe still visit from time to time?'

Lila and Ben looked at Socrates. Lila could see he was torn. She knew it wasn't good to have too many links between the World of Ideas and the outside.

'From time to time,' he said. 'But remember to live in the world as you find it. It's also true that the unlived life is not worth examining.' He embraced Ben. 'Goodbye.'

'One more thing before you go,' said Lila. She handed the camera to Socrates and put her arm around Ben. 'You just press that red button. It's all set up.'

'I don't know why you assume I can't use simple technology,' said Socrates. 'My friends *invented* geometry.' The camera flashed.

Lila kissed Ben on the cheek. 'Bye then.'

'Bye then.' He plucked up the courage—this might be his last chance—and returned Lila's kiss. On the cheek.

Ben arrived back home, his cheek blazing from Lila's goodbye kiss, his lips blazing from his own. He didn't mind so much about the bet, he decided. What an honour to be the only ordinary visitor to the World of Ideas, and to have won the bet for Socrates. If only he could tell everyone about it, but who'd believe him?

Ben's euphoria ebbed away. Without his visits to the World of Ideas, he realised, he wouldn't be able to share philosophy with anyone.

CHAPTER SEVENTY-THREE

'Ah, sweet taste of victory,' Socrates said, sipping a vintage champagne from his own vineyard. 'Champagne?'

Wittgenstein wanted to refuse, but Socrates' champagne really was very good, and he needed a drink. He took a large gulp. 'Technically, Socrates, this isn't really champagne. The grapes need to be grown in the precisely defined Champagne region.'

'Call it tuna fish if you like: it tastes good.'

'Ugh no. I'd enjoy it much less as "tuna fish".' He drank some more.

'So, Ludwig, will you admit that I'm right?'

'Hardly. You won this one only. There's a beetle in this box. It doesn't mean there must be a beetle in every box.'

'Meaning?'

'One case does not prove the rule. One white swan does not prove all swans are white. One black swan, however, proves they are not.'

'So I have to teach everyone in the world philosophy and make them happy before you'll believe me?'

'And if I can find someone whose life is not made better by philosophy, then I prove my point.'

'Those rules seem a bit harsh.'

'Let's try again, anyway.' Wittgenstein couldn't deny that the experiment had worked with Ben, but surely he was the exception? There couldn't be many people like that in the world. And next time he'd have to find a more creative way to obstruct Socrates' plans. Lucky he hadn't given any money to Machiavelli, the useless charlatan.

'I'm game,' said Socrates.

They walked towards the monitor room, carrying their glasses and the half-empty bottle of champagne.

'Let's spread the word to everyone. Think of yourself as a fly buzzing round the head of humanity.'

'It's a dungheap of humanity,' said Wittgenstein bitterly.

'If you prefer.' Socrates emptied his glass and refilled it.

Wittgenstein fiddled with the TV controls. 'How do you work this thing? Lila! Where are you? Come here and help—'

But Lila had a different errand.

CHAPTER SEVENTY-FOUR

Lila looked at the photo of her and Ben. Despite Socrates' confidence, there was a lot of empty floor in the picture. She tucked a copy into the book she was reading and put another into an envelope. Checking that no one was watching, she slipped out of the World of Ideas.

*   *   *

It was nearly the end of the holidays. Ben wouldn't miss Cod Almighty, but he would miss the World of Ideas. His eye caught a cream-coloured, expensive-looking envelope on the counter, his name written on the front in black ink. He didn't recognise the writing. There was no letter inside—just a photo. On the back was written *A copy for you. We'll meet again. Love, Lila.*

Lila had her arm around him. She was smiling her lovely smile. He could show this to Joe and the others: they'd have to believe it then. Or perhaps he'd keep it private.

Two girls walked in, about his age, the most annoying type. Ben tucked the photo back inside the envelope and hid it under the counter.

'I'm starving,' said the dark-haired one. She looked a bit like Lila.

When he handed her the fish and chips she unwrapped the paper straightaway and stuffed a chip into her mouth.

'Hey,' she said, waving a chip at her friend. 'What if this chip tastes completely different to you than it does to me?'

'Don't talk bollocks, Becky,' she said, concentrating on the ketchup bottle.

'No, really—it could, and you'd never know.'

'"Salty" could be different on the inside for everybody—we just learn to use the word in the same way,' Ben said.

'Exactly,' Becky said, and smiled. She had lovely eyes, not that he'd admit he'd noticed.

'Am I surrounded by weirdos?' Becky's friend took her chips and walked out.

Becky stood there at the counter. 'See you around,' she said, and was gone.

'Fill my heart with song, and let me . . . hmm for evermore. You are all I long for, all I . . . hmm hmm and adore . . .' Ben sang as he wiped up. 'Fly me to the moon, and . . .' He whistled the rest.

Chivers Large Print Direct

If you have enjoyed this Large Print book and would like to build up your own collection of Large Print books and have them delivered direct to your door, please contact **Chivers Large Print Direct**.

Chivers Large Print Direct offers you a full service:

✧ **Created to support your local library**

✧ **Delivery direct to your door**

✧ **Easy-to-read type and attractively bound**

✧ **The very best authors**

✧ **Special low prices**

For further details either call Customer Services on 01225 443400 or write to us at

Chivers Large Print Direct
FREEPOST (BA 1686/1)
Bath
BA1 3QZ